DARKLANDS

DARKLANDS

An Ulrik Torp Thriller

———

Niels Krause-Kjær

Translated from Danish
by David Young

Published in 2023 by Podium Publishing, ULC
www.podiumaudio.com

Podium

DARKLANDS

CHAPTER 1

No one took any notice of Daphne Preca when she walked into the pub. She wondered, as she always did, what it was that made the place so cosy.

It could be the two brothers who owned it and had faithfully run the bar for more than twenty-five years. It could be the guests: the mix of the older generation, local islanders, and a few stranded tourists. It could be the small, banal signs on the back wall of the bar: *Men without shirts are not welcome. Women without shirts get free drinks.* It could be the narrow terrace that stretched along the building, where you could sit on uncomfortable benches drinking your beer and watching life go by in the harbour below—the local fishermen, the ferries that sailed a shuttle service to the main island, the tourists who tried to make up their minds between the four to five eateries at the harbour and ended up choosing the island's signature dish—rabbit in garlic—often to their great disappointment. Perhaps it was the unfinished business from the time the country was under British rule that gave the place the final touch of something timeless and embracing. Whatever the reason, she was always in a good mood when she entered the Gleneagles Bar at the port town of Ghajnsielem on Gozo. If Malta was peripheral Europe, then this small island was peripheral Malta.

She was born here. She felt at home here.

It was at the end of the afternoon, at the end of August, the end of the tourist season, the end of a local bank holiday, and the end of the hottest part of summer, nearly thirty degrees and blue skies. It was bearable. Even so, Daphne Preca could feel her white blouse sticking to her back. It had been a long, productive day. Now she just needed the last—and most important—meeting before taking the ferry back to the main island and the flat in Valletta where she now lived.

She looked around. It was a little before five and he hadn't arrived yet. She ordered two small draught beers and sat outside on the terrace, following the activities in the harbour and mulling over the day's interviews on the other side of the island.

They had clearly been afraid to talk to her, afraid that other people would see them together. One interview had taken place in one of the island's many large churches and had been conducted in a whisper, as if the former auditor would go to hell if He heard it. Who He was had never become entirely clear. It could be the Italian Mafia; it could be Russian oligarchs; it could be Maltese judges. It could also be the country's Prime Minister or people close to him.

She had been researching the Prime Minister and his connections for almost a year as a freelance journalist. The Prime Minister was young, energetic, and an economic liberal, even though he was the leader of the revitalised Labour Party. She had even voted for him the first time around. The economy was booming, unemployment was falling, and the Prime Minister was, in every way, just what they liked in the European capitals, not least in Brussels. After several years of misrule in Malta, the European Union's smallest state was under control, in the view of the mainland: no threats of veto, no individualistic points of view. In return, there soon wouldn't be a stretch of asphalt in the country that wasn't paid for in whole or in part by Brussels.

It was of lesser importance that corruption at all levels of the small island kingdom was well known and widespread—the ten richest people in the country, according to *Forbes*'s latest list, were all politicians.

Agreement in the EU was what was most important.

Through the exposé of the Mossack Fonseca law firm in Panama, Daphne had mapped out how overseas companies sold Maltese passports to the highest bidder—Malta, together with Cyprus, had become the gateway to EU citizenship, especially for wealthy Russians with dubious backgrounds. At the same time, she was close to obtaining conclusive evidence of massive transfers of money from the government of Azerbaijan to Malta via Panama. This apparently included millions exchanged between the daughter of the President of Azerbaijan and the pretty wife of the Maltese Prime Minister.

That was the reason for her meeting here.

She considered herself a journalistic one-man army, but that was how it had been for most of her fifty-two years. And right now, she was about to talk to a former banker who claimed to have papers detailing some of the transfers between the former Soviet republic and the Prime Minister's wife.

She took a sip of her beer. Where had he got to? Daphne checked her mobile; she tried the number he had given her and on which they had communicated. His phone must be switched off.

She sat like this for another hour, moving on to the flat, lukewarm beer that had been for her guest. She left five euros—it was an ample tip, also for the next time she might come by—nodded to one of the brothers behind the bar, and went down to her car in the square below. She could see that the next ferry had just come in.

Damn it. She needed those papers.

It turned out later that the bomb was made of about 500 grams of Semtex—the same size as the one used in the Lockerbie bombing in 1988, in which 243 people had lost their lives. The blast from the car bomb could be heard over half the island and was significantly louder than the powerful fireworks that the islanders would get so excited about at every special occasion.

The bomb did exactly what it was supposed to do. It silenced Daphne Preca.

CHAPTER 2

Against his better judgement, Ulrik Torp had two important appointments that day. That was more than he had had in total during the past five years, he reasoned.

"It's been a long time, Torp. You ought to take better care of your teeth."

Torp tried to nod, but didn't dare with all the metal that was stuck in his mouth. The dentist was used to monologues.

"It's like with children and cars. The three M's, Torp. Maintenance, maintenance, maintenance."

He was almost talking to himself, while continuing to rummage in Ulrik's teeth and oral cavities. It wasn't a pretty sight after eight years. In the beginning, it had been forgetfulness and procrastination. The last five years was because of money. It was late summer and pleasant for a September day, as Karen had remarked when he had left home earlier. He had been complaining for a long time about a small toothache, or maybe it was nothing. Karen pressed him, and eventually, he had given in. He could glimpse a treetop through the window behind the dentist's head. The leaves were fluttering in the light breeze. Under the ceiling, just above the dentist's chair, hung a colourful drawing of some children around a lake. Six children—two girls and four boys. One of them had a small fishing rod.

"Now we'll remove the plaque and do a clean-up, I'll fix the little hole that has been bothering you, and after that we'll make an appointment for next week to change the filling in your back molar. Then we'll be up and running again, Torp."

He took out a small drill and let it whine a while before pressing it to the tooth. Ulrik's ears sang for a brief moment. The dentist continued talking indefatigably, about his holidays in Spain, house prices in Frederiksberg, and the large number of refugees. Did he talk like this at home, too? Did people who like to never be interrupted choose dentistry for that very reason? Ulrik nodded in agreement whenever possible.

"Initial signs of periodontal disease, but we can probably take that in our stride. Do you floss? It doesn't look like it."

Ulrik shook his head very carefully.

The dentist began to prick him a little more in the right side of his mouth, down by the lower jaw.

"Hmm," he murmured.

He sucked the area dry and pricked it once more.

"Does this hurt?"

Ulrik shook his head a little at first, then nodded. "A iddle," he said between cotton swabs, the suction, and the instrument the dentist had just chosen to stick in his mouth.

"Hmmm. You have a little lump, or whatever it is, down here." He took out the cotton swabs and the instrument and let his patient rinse. "Have you had it for a long time?"

Ulrik hadn't thought much about it, but yes, six months, maybe a year.

"Has it got any bigger?"

The atmosphere had changed. The self-absorbed and chatty dentist now looked at the patient he hadn't had in the chair for many years with concern. Ulrik thought for a long time, involuntarily putting his hand to his right cheek.

"A little, yes."

"It's probably nothing, Torp. But we just need to get a biopsy taken from it so we can be absolutely sure. I'll refer you so that you can have a sample taken. It will probably be at Rigshospitalet."

"What is it?" Ulrik had sat straight up in the dentist's chair, even though the backrest was still down.

"It's probably nothing. We just have to be absolutely sure."

"But what could it be? What needs to be investigated?"

The dentist hesitated. "Listen, you don't need to get unnecessarily worried, Torp. But it could, and I stress could, be a tumour. And a tumour can in rare cases be malignant."

Ulrik Torp felt the room getting smaller. The air disappeared; his mouth dried out. Why did no one dare say the word *cancer*?

"And if it is, then it's important that we find out in time."

"And that's that? Find out in time?"

The dentist's gaze wavered. "It's impossible to say. Now I'm going to refer you, Torp. Then we'll see."

The dentist didn't say it, but Ulrik could sense in his tone and look that eight years of absence wasn't the best start.

At the counter, he agreed on a time to replace the filling, even though it felt insignificant. Yes, he could pay right away. Ulrik entered his PIN code and anxiously accepted the amount, 1,213 kroner.

That was the first appointment of the day. Had he had any important appointments at all since he left the *Daily News*? The day he'd lost his unemployment benefit a few years later had been important in a way, but it hadn't been an appointment.

Ulrik stood on the pavement feeling slightly dazed a couple of minutes later. Twice before he had stood like this, with a strange sense of watching the world go by as if nothing had happened, even though in reality everything had taken a sharp turn. The traffic lights changed from red to green, cars drove by, people walked past. Everything was as before, but it wasn't. Couldn't the world see that?

The first time he had had this experience was on the morning after Karen had given birth to Sofie. The birth had been long and arduous, but at seven o'clock their daughter had finally arrived. A few hours later, Karen had asked the new dad to go into town and buy a nail clipper for the baby. Later, he had wondered if it was just so that she could get some peace. And then he had stood there, in the parking lot in front of the hospital, in search of a nail clipper in a world that seemed strangely unaffected by the miracle that had just occurred.

The second time was when his father had died some years back. That time it had been the parking lot in front of the nursing home that had become the stage for his reflections. In a reminder of the indomitability of the world, everyone had been carrying on as if nothing had happened. A postman in blue from PostNord had come by on his electric bike—did they really only deliver letters once a week now? Two overweight teens had strolled by on the pavement with their mouths full of pizza, presumably bought at the 7-Eleven up on the corner. Didn't they know that there was a dead man on the other side of the wall?

And then there was now, on the pavement in front of his old dentist with the promise of a biopsy to see if a lump—a tumour—in his cheek was malignant. Tumour. Could such a thing ever be benign? Ulrik watched people hurrying past, getting on buses, and chatting with each other. People didn't give a shit. Of course they didn't.

Ulrik got on his bike.

Hi, Ulrik. We would like to have a meeting with you about some options that may also affect your benefit payment. It is quite urgent. Could you come to the job centre tomorrow at 1:00 p.m.? Warm regards, Ane.

Ulrik Torp reread yesterday's email on his mobile.

"Warm regards." He wasn't sure how warmly they regarded him at the job centre. He could see from the automatic signature that Ane's surname was Vildmose and her title was job consultant. I guess they all are, he thought. He was fifteen minutes early, mostly because he had decided to cycle directly from the dentist instead of going home first and making a sandwich. That would have to wait. He hitched up his trousers, which had become a few sizes too large, went in, and sat down without registering his arrival. Ulrik looked around and tried to divide the twelve other people waiting into the three groups everyone knew they consisted of. One third were unwilling to do anything; one third couldn't do anything; and the last third could do something, as long as everyone involved made an effort. By now, he was in doubt as to which group he himself belonged to.

Opposite him sat a girl of twenty, perhaps twenty-two, extremely overweight, maybe pregnant, it was hard to determine. Definitely a couldn't. Next to her a guy in his early thirties with tattoos up both his arms and some of his neck. He was bald and his right leg was bobbing nervously up and down. He was looking uninterestedly at his smartphone. He probably could, but no doubt had better things to do than take a job, guessed Torp. To the right, an older man. Torp was a little startled when he assessed him to be around the same age as himself. Older? Nice clothes; maybe he had once been a travelling salesman in crisps or sweets to smaller retailers—the kind of service that algorithms and supermarkets now managed themselves. He was very willing. But what could he do? To the left sat an immigrant, or a refugee. Ulrik knew very well that in principle there was a difference, but he couldn't make the effort to differentiate anymore. A young man, not turned thirty. Arab, maybe Iraqi.

Ulrik looked around at all twelve. Six couldn't, four wouldn't, two could, perhaps, was his reckoning. He was hungry and cursed himself for not having quickly gone back to the flat. He looked at his phone again and checked the *Daily News* app.

A political crisis was about to get completely out of control.

The Nationalists, the new party that was likely to enter Parliament after the next election, had long been demanding a referendum on EU membership as the only condition for supporting the centre-right Prime Minister, the Liberals' Palle Enevoldsen.

No one had so far paid any particular attention to it. The government's major supporting party, the People's Party, was actually against the EU, wanted a referendum, but would rather be in government after the next election. *"After all, we can't vote for anything in the chamber that no one has proposed yet,"* was the party leader's way of fending off questions each time with his wolfish smile.

But now the New Radicals were making a mess of the arithmetic, and it had triggered a chain reaction that few really wanted, *"a traffic accident in slow motion,"* as a commentator had remarked. The New Radicals supported the opposition, were themselves supporters of the EU, but were even greater supporters of referendums. A random interview on television with the party's unorthodox leader had triggered the events.

"Since you're such a big supporter of referendums, why shouldn't Danes be allowed to vote on EU membership?"

"But they may very well be allowed to, as far as we're concerned."

"So why not make that proposal in the parliamentary chamber?"

"But it could well be that we'll do that."

Just like that.

No more than that.

The clip had been shown over and over again.

And then the devil had taken over the snake pit at Christiansborg. The leader of the People's Party had to declare that if the New Radicals made such a proposal, then his party would vote in favour. So would the left and one of the small centre-right parties. All of that wouldn't matter—almost—provided that it didn't spread to one of the old governing parties. But, suddenly, it had triggered a clash in the Labour Party. A minority—or was it a majority?—in the parliamentary party was supporting the wish for a referendum, if for nothing else than to overthrow the government and trigger a general election.

It was, Ulrik thought, like the story that when a butterfly flutters its wings in Asia, storms follow in Europe—almost literally, in fact. In several EU countries, strong forces were speaking in favour of following "the Danish example."

But first, the New Radicals had to actually come up with the proposal.

After that, the power struggle in the Labour Party would have to be decided.

It would all be settled next week, wrote the *Daily News*'s political analyst, Jørgen Høegh.

Torp scrolled down the page. It was on such occasions as this that he most missed his past as a political journalist.

A new government in Italy was being formed after the assassination of the popular Prime Minister before the summer holidays. A vague cocktail of Euro resistance, sympathy with Russia, a total halt to immigrants, and universal basic income had brought him to power six months earlier. There was no one else in the relatively new party who could take over—the party was, as predicted, crumbling without its founder and charismatic leader. So now the former conservative Prime Minister had become Prime Minister again—albeit with the support of the populist former ruling party. Well, well, thought Torp. The car bomb that had killed a journalist in Malta the other day had probably been placed by the Italian Mafia, according to an expert.

"Ulrik Torp?"

He looked up. She was in her late thirties, blonde hair, fashionable glasses, and a twinkle in her eye. He nodded and got to his feet.

"Hi, Ulrik. I'm Ane," she said, offering her hand.

He shook the outstretched hand, hitched up his trousers, and followed her to her desk. Ane's skirt was way, way too tight.

She took turns looking at him and her computer screen while she talked.

"You have—I can see—been a bit protected as a job seeker, Ulrik," she began.

And that was right. Job seeker was an extreme term in this context. After tailoring his experience at the *Daily News* for his CV—one of quite a few versions—he had steadily applied for jobs on the internet as the system required in order to receive his unemployment benefit. Communications worker in Gentofte Municipality. Journalist in the International Service System's communications department. Part-time editor of a new magazine published by the Red Cross. Maternity leave cover as sub-editor at the *Express*. It came up to well over a hundred applications in the two years he had been entitled to unemployment benefit. He had been invited to a single interview in a large company, but could immediately sense at the meeting that they were surprised at his age. That information was in his standard application, dammit!

Like all unemployed journalists, he had initially called himself a freelance journalist, with obligatory cheap business cards in his inside pocket. *Torp Communication—competence and experience.* He had had 1,000 printed, since the last 500 were half price, and had probably handed out twenty before he gave up. He had written a little and sold some of it for ridiculously low sums, which had immediately been set off against his unemployment benefit. And then on to social security benefit. Due to Karen's part-time job as a schoolteacher, he could get a little from the public sector—less than 3,000 kroner a month—even though he was largely supported by his wife, as the staff member at the municipal benefits centre dispassionately put it. Ulrik had several times carefully aired the question with Karen about doing without it, so he could completely get rid of the benefits centre, job centre, job consultants, social workers, schedules, attendance, control, and legal incapacitation. Nothing good had come of those conversations with Karen, so he had stopped having them. On the other hand, the job centre had done the same—they hardly bothered him anymore. He wasn't costing the welfare state much money and had long ago been classified in the "unwilling" group by the job consultants. Some of them had considered him a "can't."

"We must get something done about that," continued Ane. "Maybe it's also about time that we expanded the job search to other professions. After all, there is a lot of demand for unskilled labour at present. But first to what is currently available, Ulrik."

She turned her professional attention towards her new client.

"We have received an inquiry about work activation that is almost tailored for you. It won't pay more than the 2,814 kroner a month you already get now, but it is for four weeks and a great opportunity to get a little foothold in your profession and the labour market again."

Ulrik looked at her without saying anything. He observed her well-groomed nails and sensed the energy in her body, the energy that comes from still believing in one's work. She must be brand new. Why in the world had his file ended up on her desk?

"The *Daily News* is looking for a company intern. I can see from your file that you know that newspaper."

Ulrik felt the emptiness in his stomach, brought a hand up to his right cheek, and for a brief moment thought about the referral for a biopsy—would he get a message directly from the hospital or from the dentist? It would no doubt be the hospital. In fact, he had been able to feel the lump—the tumour—for a year, he thought. The first time he had noticed it was last summer, when they were painting the living room. Ulrik pressed his tongue against the lump in his lower jaw. It had definitely got bigger. Did it hurt, too? The dentist had asked this several times. Of course something hurt if you pressed it hard enough.

"Isn't that right, Ulrik? You were at the *Daily News* as a political journalist for many years, I can see."

It made him twitch. It was about time they fucking stopped. Was there no lower limit to the shabbiness and depth of the crisis at the newspapers? Now they were hiring sacked employees on work activation. Ane continued her sales pitch.

"The *Daily News* writes that, in connection with the general election, which is expected to be called next week, journalists who can write will be needed. That's right up your alley, Ulrik."

Torp envisioned his old workplace. Everything was probably the same as five years ago, except for a hundred fewer employees, what with part of the editing having been outsourced to an agency with poorer employment conditions, all layout except the front page outsourced to India, and the almost halved newspaper sales. Other than that, it would be the same. The eternal editorial meetings. The postmortems, which were so terribly predictable: We did well. Especially with the ideas that came from the bosses, which most ideas eventually did because the staff were just shovelling words onto the Web like nutters from morning to night.

"And what if I can't?"

Ane misunderstood his doubts.

"Of course you can, Ulrik. Even though it's been five years since you worked as a journalist, you've been one all your adult life."

She tilted her head professionally.

"Ulrik. Now, I'm going to tell you something. One can well lose some confidence from being fired and unemployed. Indeed one can. And we think you have. But it's just something you're imagining. It's about getting started again. I can see lots of resources in you. I really can."

All this reminded Ulrik of why he had on several occasions cautiously suggested to Karen that they could manage on 2,814 kroner less per month.

Ane played her trump card.

"You're tough, Ulrik. I can feel it. This will do you good."

"And what if I can't?"

"You can. I know you can. But otherwise, I'll just have to talk it through with the local benefits centre." She smiled.

That's how she was. Ane with the energetic eyes, all the clichés, and the overly tight skirt. A stickler for rules who with a click on the keyboard would take his—or rather Karen's—measly 2,814 kroner if he didn't toe the line. He thought about the dental bill he had just paid.

"Today is Tuesday. The *Daily News* would like you to start next Monday. They remember you, Ulrik. I'll arrange the paperwork, and then we're done. Congratulations, Ulrik. Give it all you've got. Show them the best version of yourself."

Ulrik Torp forced himself not to ask her which idiot course she had learned to say that shit in. He stood up and shook hands while pondering how many times she had called him Ulrik, even though they had never met each other before. Ten times? He hadn't said "Ane" a single time. That much he knew.

Every time Ulrik put the key in the front door of their two-room flat in Frederiksberg, bitterness penetrated his whole body with a feeling of paralysis in all of his joints, even after two years. Karen was a little sad at times, but no more than that.

"Stop that, Ulrik," she would content herself with saying when it became too obvious.

She was better at swallowing and accepting. She rarely took it personally. He did. Even if it wasn't necessarily meant personally. Why had it become like this? When had he taken the wrong turn? Had he even taken a wrong turn? Was it other people's fault? Not according to the new political logic—now everything was personal. It was easier in the 1970s when it was all society's fault. Ulrik thought of the many articles he had written as a journalist at the *Daily News*, about experts' reports, recommendations, expansion of the workforce, incentive structures, labour market reforms, the policies that were necessary, considerations of international competition, the EU, and globalisation. That's just how it is, as a minister put it. But did it have to be that way? He had written it all in the certainty that it would never have anything to do with him personally, because adaptations, limitations, and leftovers belonged to a world without him and those he associated with.

And then the flat. The final materialisation of his humiliation. He entered the narrow hallway. Karen was already home. She was sitting in the living room in their leather Wegner wing chair—one of the last testimonies to a time that had once been. It looked wrong in the small living room with too much furniture pressed together. They said brief hellos before he scuttled out into the narrow kitchen to make a sandwich. Even conversation kitchens were for other people.

"How did it go at the dentist?" Karen looked up from her designer chair, obviously a little surprised that he hadn't been in the flat when she came home from work at the small private school.

He hesitated. "The toothache is gone; a little periodontal disease which can be taken in stride. I have to have a filling replaced next week."

"Sounds like you got off cheap after so many years." There was a touch of reproach in her voice. Just a touch. They had saved a lot of money by dropping the dentist.

"The job centre wants me to go on work activation at the *Daily News* from Monday. Four weeks."

"Is that good?" She looked at him with concern.

"Yeah, well . . . maybe," he lied, and took a big bite of his liver paste sandwich so that he didn't have to say any more.

She took a long pause. He let her take it.

"Has anything else happened?"

Shouldn't they be talking more about the *Daily News*? What he was going to do? Whether he was looking forward to seeing his old colleagues? Was it a chance to come back? Ulrik knew she wanted to spare him. He, on the other hand, didn't know if he was happy or irritated over her consideration.

"Such as what?" He stroked his right cheek. Was it tomorrow he would be notified about the referral?

"Indeed," said Karen, turning back to the book that her friends in the book club were to discuss later this month. Albert Camus's *The Stranger*. They were doing the classics. He had read it himself many years ago, without fully understanding what it meant.

Her "indeed" irritated Ulrik. She used it many times every day. It sounded both old-fashioned and arrogant. As if she had more important things to attend to, which she probably did.

"I'll just go and fetch some milk," he said and left.

CHAPTER 3

The *Daily News* façade was exactly that. A façade. The new editor-in-chief had had the newspaper redesigned with new, allegedly modern fonts, which consequently also had to be visible on the outside of the building. Tight and simple. The revolving door had been replaced by a security sluice, where the inner, bulletproof glass door could only be opened when the glass door to the street had slid back into place. The rebuilt reception now consisted of steel and glass.

The only thing Ulrik Torp could immediately recognise was the elderly lady in reception.

"Torp!" Charlotte smiled when she saw him. "What on earth . . ."

Torp took a quick look at the piece of paper he had been given by Ane at the job centre.

"Charlotte! I have an appointment with your HR manager. Yvonne."

She initially ignored his appointment.

"Torp. It's been a long time. Which round was it? The third—where the whole sub-editors' section also bit the dust?"

Torp shook his head. Then it must have been the round just before, they agreed.

"How are you? Are you on your way back?"

"Apparently, there's going to be some extra work for the next month if a general election is called. I'm going to provide a little help. It's Yvonne I have to see—the HR manager."

Torp wanted to move on, although to his own surprise he was genuinely happy over the reunion with the receptionist who had been answering the phones for more than twenty-five years. Now it was mostly the terror-proof sluice she was looking after. The paper's landline phone didn't ring very often.

Torp initially preferred to avoid the editorial staff on the first and second floors, so, wearing a guest sticker on his chest, he took the elevator directly up to the third floor and the HR manager. He remembered her vaguely from back then; same office, now with a manager's title.

"Torp. What a scoop to get you back. I actually had no idea that you were . . . you know." She hesitated. "That you were . . . available, I mean."

Torp ignored both the introduction and her half-saving of the situation. "Available" was a fine compromise for him in the newspeak borderland between *Torp Communication—competence and experience* and social security benefit. If they agreed not to waste more desperate sentences on it, they could both maintain the façade.

Torp and Yvonne exchanged the formal information for the job centre's and the *Daily News*'s bureaucracy; he was given an ID card "with four weeks' expiration," a laptop, and a cheap Chinese mobile phone—and he was suddenly an employee at the *Daily News* again.

"You can go down to the editorial office yourself and say hello," said Yvonne. "You should contact the chief news editor, Arne Lund. You know him, after all. He knows you're coming."

Torp removed his guest sticker from his chest and replaced it with the *Daily News* ID card bearing an old picture of him from the newspaper's archive. He remembered immediately what it was like to walk around the building with the card dangling from his jacket or belt, like a club membership card he only afterwards understood didn't provide automatic access.

* * *

Torp took the stairs down and cursed the hours that awaited him. A lot of greetings—hellos and amazing-that-you-are-heres and how-unreasonable-that-you-were-fireds—to seventeen varieties of how-are-you-doing, even though most of his old colleagues knew very well how. Copenhagen and its pool of journalists were far too small to hide such a solid, comforting story, as is always the case when things are worse for others than for oneself. Arne Lund's office was so far the one that looked most familiar. In fact, nothing had changed, Torp noted. The desk covered with folders and newspapers. The bookcase behind him crammed with books in a mess of a system that even Arne Lund scarcely had any control over. The Cavling statuette for journalism on top of the shelf in solitary majesty as a testimony to Lund's time before he became chief news editor many years ago. Torp knew that he couldn't have been fired five years earlier without a nod from Arne. There were many who got the sack. Karen and several of his colleagues at the time had tried to convince him not to take it personally, that there was a dif- ference between a sacking and a dismissal. Fuck them. You can bloody well bet your life it was something personal. Twenty-three had to go. Nearly 200 remained. How could it not be personal? Even so, he felt no anger or bitterness towards the chief news editor. Nearly 100 had been fired—or made redundant, he didn't give a damn what word was used—since then in other rounds due to circumstances over which he had no influence. The blame could only to a limited extent be placed on the old or new editor-in-chief, the managing director, or the chair- man of the board, for that matter. Google, Facebook, advertising shifts, the internet, new reading habits, globalisation, time. There were many reasons for the fact that newspapers—which at one time almost ran themselves financially—were now in an existential crisis, regardless of whether they were published on paper or online.

"Torp! Good to see you."

Arne Lund looked up and greeted Torp with the same expression one would give an old classmate chanced upon in the street. It spoke volumes about their history.

"You too."

"I want you to know that this wasn't my idea. This is something that HR and our benefits department cooked up together."

He noticed the question mark on Torp's face.

"Yes, we've got a benefits department. It has to find money in the public coffers so that we avoid footing the bill ourselves."

Torp still said nothing.

"It's my impression that it generates a profit," Lund added, trying with a smile to suggest that it was a little joke. "I take this as an acknowledgement that your 'Torp Communication' never really got off the ground."

Arne was the same as Torp remembered him: liberatingly straightforward.

"That kind of thing never does," he continued. "Most unemployed journalists put a 'communication' after their name and think of it almost as a brand."

Arne said this last bit mostly to himself, while lightly shaking his head. If early retirement had still been a possibility, he would have had the age but not the mind for it. Bald and slightly unshaven, just like five years ago, and wearing a worn, grey cardigan—the same one?—over a crumpled, light blue shirt. There was a thermos and two cups on the desk. Yvonne had told the truth. They had been expecting him.

"No. It never really got off the ground," said Torp.

It was probably the most honest way he had formulated his own situation since his dismissal. Arne poured coffee.

"I'm good at this, but for me, the *Daily News* is a refuge from the real world. I couldn't survive out there on the prairie either. I mean it," said Lund, pushing a cup of coffee over towards Torp. "Enough of that. You're going to be here for the next four weeks. I guarantee you a general election will be called tomorrow. The New Radicals have no credible reverse gear to the demand for a referendum on EU membership. Their parliamentary group will meet tomorrow afternoon to formally decide to throw the proposal into the chamber. The People's Party is going to go along with it, and so, probably, is the Labour Party. When that happens, the Prime Minister will have to respond. I have my doubts about whether they really mean it. But neither the Liberals nor the Labour Party can get out of this one now. Good Lord, what a bunch of clowns!"

Lund shook his head.

Torp joined in. "It's the classic situation," he said. "The worst thing that can happen to a party is that there is suddenly a majority for the party programme. It wasn't meant to happen like that."

They both laughed at the in-joke.

The People's Party was now caught up in its own rhetoric and its fear of losing votes to the new party, the Nationalists. The Labour Party wanted to overthrow the government, and the New Radicals were . . . well, neo-radicals. They lived in a fantasy world. Lund and Torp had almost always seen Danish politics through the same lens.

"So there's a lot to be written about politics from now on, and until the election is over, I presume?" Torp straightened up.

Lund nodded. "You bet your life. It will be a crucial election. Can the old parties hold the fort, or do we say hello to ga-ga land?"

Torp laughed again. *Ga-ga land*. That was an expression they had often used when talking politics. He had completely forgotten both that and the good times at the *Daily News*. The editorial meetings, the evenings before the deadline and print started. The cliquish chats, the professional pride when a story resonated and made sense. He became quite eager.

"Is there going to be a daily election supplement, like we usually do?"

"That hasn't been decided yet. Paper costs money, but we'll go up at least a few pages every day—just so that we avoid totally forgetting the rest of the world."

Torp smiled again. The rest of the world had the habit of being pushed to the sidelines once the election campaign began.

"And this is where you come into the picture, Torp," continued Lund. "Some journalists from the reportage group will be assigned to the political editorial staff. That's already happening, starting today. Our intention is then for you to step into the reportage group and cover some of the gaps that come up."

Torp was just about to take a sip of his coffee when Lund said that last sentence. He stopped mid-movement and spilt a bit, without the desk owner noticing anything.

"With your experience, you can slide in right away. It's going to be pure hack work for you, Torp. Pure hack work."

"Of course . . . that's fine. Hack work. I can easily do that."

Torp had taken himself by surprise. How was it possible for so much crap to come out of one's mouth? Had he been called in to rewrite Ritzau bulletins, write about traffic accidents, and flip through press releases?

But what was he supposed to say? That after five years out, now on a work activation programme contrived by the newspaper's benefits department with help from Ane in the job centre and for 2,814 measly bloody kroner for four weeks of work, he only wanted to write about Danish politics? That even a fifty-five-year-old social security benefit recipient and cancer patient has a limit? Technically speaking, he wasn't a cancer patient yet. He hadn't even had a biopsy taken of the lump in his cheek. The tumour.

Rigshospitalet had advised that, due to a technical error, he hadn't been called in for an ultrasound scan and biopsy. He would get a new text message over the next few days about an appointment. The lady was profuse in her apologies.

"Where will I actually be sitting?" asked Torp resignedly.

"Only me and a few others have their own office and desk. Almost everyone today has a small locker for their laptops and papers but sits at a vacant desk. Many complain about it, but it actually works very well," said Lund, getting up.

"It's almost eleven o'clock. There's a joint editorial meeting now. Let's go there together, then you can also say hello to the others."

Torp recognised several faces around the table. The editorial meeting was held in the same meeting room which, after the many layoffs, was now almost large enough. Two more rounds of savings—a year or two—and that's that, he thought. There were about a dozen people sitting around the table. Just as many were standing along the walls. There was clearly an extra turnout due to the expected general election. Arne Lund wasn't sitting at the head of the table, but that was where he effectively found himself now. The young editor-in-chief, who had begun immediately after Torp's dismissal, was standing close to the door—apparently with the intention of being able to slip out unnoticed at some point. Asbjørn Henriksen was his name. Forty-two years old, tanned, wearing a light blue, slim-fit suit and white shirt with a hint of pink. He had briefly been a studio host on television and had a reputation for being a little more loyal to the system than is good for an editor-in-chief with a responsibility for impartiality according to press ethics. Torp knew very little about him, apart from the fact that he was the son of a highly respected former top official, Niels Henriksen, who had headed first the Ministry of Justice and then the Ministry of Foreign Affairs for several generations. Was he still alive? He probably was.

"Hi there," said Asbjørn Henriksen from a distance with a smile and a friendly look, when Lund began the meeting by introducing an old acquaintance, Ulrik Torp, "who will be here for the next four weeks to keep the level up in reportage during the election campaign."

Hi there?

Torp contented himself with a nod. He had deliberately not sat down, although there had been a few empty chairs when they had entered the room.

He recognised several of his old colleagues around the table. Jørgen Høegh, the newspaper's political analyst, also called "the Hawk," a nickname he had been given many years ago because he was the exact opposite. He seldom caught anything, was not very proactive, flew low—very low—and no one, neither within the newspaper nor outside, understood why he was allowed, year after year, to fill column after column with generalities, clichés, and the parroting of the top politician—most often centre-left just like the readers—with whom he had most recently had lunch.

Torp nodded to Grandma-Bente, Bente Clausen, who had been at the *Daily News* forever—really, forever. He knew that she was no longer an employee; she was just allowed to come and go at the newspaper and write for a modest freelance rate. This happened sometimes with individual staff members. The newspaper industry had, in fact, in its better days, introduced its own early retirement pay scheme, and it was still surviving in a modified version. It had to be Arne Lund who had arranged it. There was jewellery dangling around the neck of Grandma-Bente, as it had done since 1968. She was affectionately called the leader of the amber-mafia. A magnet had the same effect on a compass as she had on political analysis—all corners of the world disappeared—but she meant well.

"I don't understand why the New Radicals have the same opinion as the Nationalists. I know many of the New Radicals," she exclaimed, while the head of the political editorial staff at Christiansborg, Malene Astrup, tried to explain the highly explosive political situation and the odd, temporary partnership between the two parties.

Malene Astrup had been an intern at the Christiansborg editorial office when Torp had been fired five years earlier. Now there were three journalists and one intern doing politics—half as many. Astrup was often used as an analyst on television and did a good job. No one used the Hawk.

Next to Asbjørn Henriksen stood a young woman whom Torp hadn't seen before and whom he found it difficult to take his eyes off of. She wasn't especially pretty, but she had a sweetness and immediacy about her that automatically attracted attention; around thirty, he guessed. Part of an apparently small tattoo could be faintly seen high on her left shoulder. *Katrine Taber-Nielsen*, it said on her ID card.

Torp was pleasantly surprised at how few greetings he had to exchange after the meeting. Several came by, patted him on the shoulder, and said hi, but hurried off. The phenomenon, thought Torp, is known from disasters, accidents, and violent relationships—the survivors often feel guilty, justified or not, at having come through it. But it could also just be because they were busy. He could see it was mostly the latter.

Katrine Taber-Nielsen came over to him.

"Hi."

"Hi."

"So you're Ulrik Torp."

She looked him straight in the eye with her bright blue gaze. It wavered between nice and intimidating. It was nice. She continued without the confirmation that neither of them needed.

"I remember my father sometimes talked about you. You exposed that business about illegal financial support for political parties."

Torp nodded, affected by a vanity he had forgotten. The story had been about to land him the Cavling Prize that year. Both the Labour Party and the Liberals had received financial transfers from businesses and private individuals in an interwoven system of business clubs, service payments, union money, and party workers who were in fact employed by, and therefore on the payroll of, various trade associations, companies, and unions. It had been going on for many years and wasn't really an exposé in itself. Most people were well aware of it. What was new was the scope, the systematisation, and the documentation. Torp had almost been thrown out of reputable society several years earlier for actively choosing sides in an internal party struggle, but he had regained the respect of the *Daily News* and his colleagues when it later became clear to most people that he had done the only right thing, though the action he had taken was hardly something that was taught at the School of Journalism.

The exposé of the illegal party support had two consequences. Firstly, the massive trafficking of cash flows and ghost workers from companies, industry organisations, and unions ceased. Almost. Secondly, a year later, a majority in Parliament, led by the Labour Party and the Liberals, decided to double financial support from the public purse for the political parties at Christiansborg.

The story and the—almost—Cavling Prize led to a brief period for Ulrik Torp when he flourished, both professionally and personally. After a number of years spent in various shades of grey, he believed in his profession and himself again. It was worth it. He was making a difference. But slowly, slowly, he had slipped into a melancholy that no one, least of all himself, had understood.

Karen thought it was a midlife crisis, which she was no doubt at least partially right about. But it was also something else. It was frustration over an erosion he saw all around him.

"Is it something you know, something you've just heard, or an opinion?" he would ask his son-in-law, to Karen's disapproval, when he was excelling in Wikipedia knowledge at the dinner table. He saw people confirmed in their ignorance on Facebook and watched gifted politicians who no longer dared to come up with three complicated sentences for fear of being shamed as elitist. And at the same time, he felt that he himself was being dragged down, too. How the intellectual ceiling was becoming lower. That he had been among those chosen in the savings round five years ago shouldn't have come as a surprise.

"You can sit here. Opposite me. Gorm usually sits at that desk, but he is one of those who have moved to Christiansborg for the coming weeks."

Katrine Taber-Nielsen spread her arms as if she were presenting him with a trophy. Torp switched on his newly issued laptop, entered the code, and was immediately on the *Daily News*'s internal network. Half an hour later, with a sandwich from the canteen at his side, he was about to write his first story. The reportage manager—a young guy with overlong neck hair—had asked him to check out a Facebook fight between an estate agent and a reality show celebrity whom Torp had never heard of. "A deal that hasn't turned into anything because of something or other," as Neckhair explained it.

"Is that a story?"

"Of course it's a story. And we should preferably have it online before the *Express* does. Call those two if necessary, but if they don't answer, nick the quotes from Facebook. It's ready to go."

Neither of the two answered their mobiles. Katrine, who was working on a story about the good late-summer weather, assured him that it was of absolutely no consequence. The quotes on Facebook were something they had written themselves, so he didn't even have to reveal to the readers that the *Daily News* hadn't had any contact with them at all.

Fight over property deal, wrote Torp as a headline, taking a bite of his salmon sandwich. *An estate agent from North Zealand has ended up in a dispute with a seller because . . .*

"No, no, no," laughed Katrine, who was unobtrusively reading over his shoulder. "This isn't for the business pages in the *Financial Times*. This is for the *Daily News* and the Net."

Torp looked up. She rolled over a chair next to him, took over his keyboard, and hung her fingers just above the keys for ten to fifteen seconds while thinking. Then it came:

Nasty Nina: Celebrity estate agent cheated me, the headline now read.

"You cannot be serious," objected Torp.

"I've never been more serious in my life." She smiled. "Why do you think I studied for three years at Harvard and Cambridge?"

"Seriously?"

She nodded. "Absolutely. About Harvard, Cambridge, and the headline. If we don't get electronic subscribers, we'll die. And if we don't get people onto our website, then we won't get any electronic subscribers. It's that simple."

"Is the estate agent a celebrity estate agent?"

"He will be now."

"And Nasty Nina?"

"Nasty Nina. Exactly," assured Katrine, rolling the office chair and herself away and sitting down again at her own desk opposite Torp. "And with that headline, the article almost writes itself, doesn't it?"

She smiled and dived into the late-summer weather that would continue for the rest of the week.

"Right up my alley," he mumbled to himself and started the story of Nasty Nina and the celebrity estate agent. She was right. It wrote itself.

Torp managed to write two more stories before he finished at 4:30 p.m.

"Do we actually finish, as in finish work, at four-thirty?"

Katrine replied with an "of course" he didn't understand. Maybe the Christiansborg editorial office was different, or else things had changed the past five years. He had managed to complete a readable story about a tenancy on the Strøget shopping street that had become more expensive but still couldn't compete with either Stockholm or Oslo, and a report about wild boars and wolves still crossing the border from Germany, even though the politicians had set up even higher fences and laid out even more effective floating barrages in Flensburg Fjord. One politician thought it was time for two fences with a strip of fallow land in between. Some of the other spokespeople wanted time to think about that. The wild boar/wolf story was on the verge of becoming a Christiansborg story, but the expected announcement of a general election the next day meant that it wasn't interesting enough for the political editorial staff.

Torp found himself standing on the pavement outside the *Daily News* at 4:35 p.m. Many of his other temporary colleagues were hurrying away. Katrine squeezed his arm, smiled, and said goodbye before she cycled off. Torp hitched up his trousers. He had made a decision. He would buy a new pair that fit and to hell with the price.

CHAPTER 4

On this late Monday afternoon, everyone on Slotsholmen, the Copenhagen island where the Christiansborg Parliament and many other government ministries are located, was expecting a general election to be called very soon. It would provide some relaxed September days for the civil service. No questions from MPs to ministers. No minister to draft a bill for or who suddenly had to go into joint consultation in order to write a rebuttal notice. No planning of ministerial visits to the provinces or abroad. A few meetings in Brussels during the election campaign, certainly, but only to keep the store running. A central administration so gloriously free of politics, politicians, and popular sentiment for three weeks was promised. It meant desks that could be more or less cleared, and that getting off work early and maybe even some regular days off ahead of the tsunami in the form of a new minister, and maybe a new government, were waiting on the other side. Would it be a new one, inexperienced, or, even worse, opinionated? Or would it be one of the competent ones, of which there were, fortunately, quite a few? Experience on Slotsholmen showed that it could be anything. Not so long ago, there was an understanding among leading politicians that a handful of ministries—such as Finance, Justice, the Interior, Foreign Affairs, and a few others, all depending on the cut of the portfolio—should always have reliable, strong ministers. Then Transport, Culture, Ecclesiastical Affairs, Environment, and the like could get some of the others. Here an inexperienced minister would not cause so much damage, and one of the strong ministries—usually the Ministry of Finance—could always take over in individual cases if it came to it. This was no longer the case. New parties in new governing coalitions made the puzzle difficult for any incumbent Prime Minister. Ministerial appointments were, in effect, outsourced to the leaders of the parties in the coalition. Suddenly, consideration for internal power struggles in a completely new or dysfunctional party or desires for special profiling towards, for example, pensioners could result in ministerial appointments that astonished the public and were a challenge for the civil servants.

This wasn't the case in the Ministry of the Interior, where Jeppe Mikkelsen sat as a senior administrator this Monday afternoon unable to make a decision. The current Minister of the Interior was tough and very demanding; he had been in politics for many years and had held several different ministerial posts over that time. He was a political craftsman like few others. It wasn't with his goodwill that the world had changed drastically, but it was with his good abilities that the changes were being managed fairly and competently. At university, Jeppe Mikkelsen's professor had spent one lecture talking about the advantages and disadvantages of very strong ministers. The advantages were obvious. The disadvantages were absolute power and fear in the system. The Tamil case from the 1980s—the biggest scandal in Danish politics and the administration of the state since World War II—was an example of the latter; a strong, feared Minister of Justice who forced his department to administer illegally in anticipation of political forgiveness and perhaps even reward. This was where the civil servants' notes came into the picture, warned the professor. He then went on to list the civil servants who had taken detailed notes during the Tamil case, and those who hadn't. He had also explained to the students about the duty to inform one's superior—all the way up to the head of department, the minister, and, if necessary, the Prime Minister, if something was really wrong.

Mikkelsen sat alone in his office. It was at the end of the most remote corridor with the photocopier room on one side and the toilets on the other. The office could just about accommodate his desk and a narrow bookcase and was commensurate with his seniority. Most of his colleagues had gone home in anticipation of a little peace in the coming weeks. Some had become busy because the Ministry of the Interior was formally responsible for the conduct of the election. He had promised to be home by 6:00 p.m. Dorthe had invited her friend and her friend's husband to a mid-week dinner. Dorthe and her friend were both on maternity leave and had quickly clicked with each other in the mums' group. The man, who was an engineer, wasn't Mikkelsen's type, but that was okay. They had babies in common.

He read his note through for the fifth time. It was short—less than a letter-size sheet—and it was formulated in precise, concentrated, official language. He had considered whether he should settle for an oral transmission, so that there wouldn't be any risk if a journalist should demand access to documents, but he had dropped the idea with his professor's words of warning in the back of his mind: *Always in writing. It only exists in writing.* But he wasn't sure. Not totally sure. Fuck it. Instead, he had written it at home the night before while Dorthe was asleep. It should be in writing, but not in the Ministry's system, waiting to be accessed by some meddlesome journalist. Just imagine if he was wrong on this. He folded the paper and made the long walk along the narrow corridors and stairs up to the department head.

"Hemmingsen has gone for today," he was told in the front office. The words of his old professor came back to him: "The head of department, the minister, and, if necessary, the Prime Minister."

Mikkelsen could see that the door to the Minister's office opposite was closed. Most often that was a sign that the Minister was in there. It was getting on for 6:00 p.m. It wasn't unusual, and certainly not if a general election was to be called the next day. He was probably talking to his constituency about posters and advertisements. In less than a day's time, he would in reality just be a parliamentary candidate. Mikkelsen's throat constricted. Was there any point? Was he sure? Did he dare?

"Could I have five minutes with the Minister?"

The Minister's personal secretary looked up at a man he didn't think he had ever seen before. With his slender body, blushing face, and scruffy, once-white sneakers on his feet, he looked like a boy of twenty. He had to be a little older.

"What's your name?"

Mikkelsen managed to say his name in a way that sounded natural.

"How long have you been here in the Ministry?"

"Five months."

"I could assemble a football team of civil servants who have been here for five years without having had a personal meeting with the Minister."

"It's important."

"Then you can tell me."

The secretary's patience was thin. He also wanted to go home, but couldn't go before his boss.

"I'd rather not. I mean, I can only talk to the head of department or the Minister."

This time, Jeppe Mikkelsen didn't succeed in getting the sentences out in a natural way. His mouth was dry and he stuttered.

"You can't be in your right mind. Speak to your office manager or department head if it's so important. Believe me, the Minister has other things on his mind right now."

The personal secretary turned to his computer screen. The secretary who had first told him that the head of department had gone for the day suppressed a smile.

Mikkelsen stood with his neatly folded A4 sheet in his hand. Then he turned around and left the front office. He could hear the secretary giggling on his way out.

The young administrator picked up his windbreaker in the office. The sound of a single door slamming caused him to turn his head in fright while putting the A4 sheet in the inside pocket of his blazer. He texted Dorthe that he was a little late but she shouldn't worry, took his bicycle clips and helmet from the bookshelf, and hurried out of the Ministry. It would have to be tomorrow.

* * *

Jeppe Mikkelsen was found by a dog walker early Tuesday morning in bushes in Ørstedsparken in inner Copenhagen. It looked like a full-blown execution. The bicycle clips were in place as they should be; the helmet lay next to the body. Police found the bike less than a hundred metres away on Israels Plads, just off the ramp down to the car park. Forensics were later able to report that he had been shot in the temple at a maximum distance of fifty centimetres with a nine-millimetre Neuhausen. The gun was found the same morning in a rubbish bin in the park, emptied of cartridges, cleaned of fingerprints, and without a legible number. The Neuhausen was a popular and widely circulated pistol, produced after World War II and used for decades in the Danish defence forces as a personal weapon for officers and military police. Its prevalence and stability made it popular among sports shooters as well. Even though production had stopped in the late 1970s, there were so many on the market both in Denmark and abroad that the find was of little use as evidence.

The victim's wife had reported him missing early the evening before, but no one had seriously looked for him at night. There were so many husbands who only came sneaking home the next day, as the police explained to his wife.

There was no immediate motive, and the police were keeping all options open. That meant that they didn't have the faintest idea.

During the same hours that Jeppe Mikkelsen's body was found and removed from Ørstedsparken, Daphne Preca was being buried 3,000 kilometres away in her hometown on the island of Gozo in Malta. The attendance at the small church on the outskirts of the village of Qala was massive. Although Daphne Preca had worked by herself most of her journalistic life—she was a divorced loner and had become unpopular with most of the people she wrote about—in less than a week since her violent death, she had become the symbol of a struggle against injustice and lawlessness in the small, corrupt island kingdom. Many people from the village had, of course, turned up. The Preca family had been a part of life in the small community for generations. In addition, a number of journalists, as well as politicians past and present, participated. The killing had gained international attention, which meant that people who would have preferred not to attend also felt the need to make an appearance. The authorities suspected branches of the Italian Mafia of being behind the car bomb. It wasn't the first car bomb in the EU country and would hardly be the last; several of the earlier ones were demonstrably Mafia-inspired.

Daphne Preca's adult son stood at the front of the family graveyard in the small cemetery, which was full of large, ornate marble tombstones with dates going back hundreds of years. His grandparents and great-grandparents were all lying here. He would also lie here himself at some point. He had never had a close relationship with his mother but had always had a certainty that what she was doing was important, courageous, and dangerous. He was proud of her, even more so on a day like today.

From the small, fenced cemetery, there was a magnificent view over the Mediterranean and the main island. To the left, to the north-east, less than 100 kilometres away, lay Sicily and the entrance to Europe. To the right, to the south, less than 300 kilometres away, were Libya and North Africa, plagued by corruption, overpopulation, mass unemployment, Islamic extremism, and anarchy. Sometimes you could be so unlucky as to see overloaded boats coming from that direction, with refugees trying to get ashore in search of the small foothold that was on its way to making the foundations crumble under European politicians.

Today, the sun was shining and the sea was calm and inviting.

If Daphne Preca's son had looked behind him while the priest was sprinkling earth on the coffin, he would have seen two men standing in the parking lot outside the church and the cemetery in quiet, devout conversation with each other.

"We'll meet in Vienna in a month. Then we'll find out," explained the eldest of them with his head slightly bent so as not to be dazzled by the sun. The other one nodded and looked at his watch. The next ferry to the main island would sail in thirty minutes. He looked up. The priest hadn't yet finished spreading the earth. They wouldn't be able to make it in time.

Torp had turned up for work with the *Daily News* reportage group at 9:00 a.m. The day was overshadowed by politics. There was no longer any doubt that, at their parliamentary group meeting that afternoon, the New Radicals would officially decide to table a proposal for a referendum on EU membership. That would trigger the chain reaction—first the People's Party, then the Labour Party, after which the Prime Minister would have to respond.

"Would a referendum on membership of the EU really be so terrible?" Grandma-Bente asked.

She looked at Torp, who was standing by the same desk as the day before, opposite Katrine Taber-Nielsen. For the fourth time that day, he wanted to hitch up his trousers just to enjoy the feeling that they were a good fit. Katrine had noticed the new trousers. Grandma-Bente was used, from the old days, to being able to ask Torp about politics and valued his opinion.

"I mean, it's democratic to ask the population. Who could have anything against that?"

Torp took an empty cola can from the desk beside him and placed it between himself and Grandma-Bente. "Can you see this can?"

Grandma-Bente most certainly could.

"If we hold a referendum on this can, then it will probably turn out fifty-fifty. Some hate Coca-Cola and think it should be Pepsi. Some want their fizzy drinks in bottles. Some will see it as a symbol of cultural struggle and Americanism. Some as consumerism and an onslaught on the planet's resources. Some will get angry about having to vote for a stupid can at all. Some will think that those who are imposing the referendum should just have a kick up the backside. Others love it all without any reservations. Others just like cola."

Torp was warming up.

"Referendums divide people. They don't gather them together. The result is completely random. Politicians decide what is to be asked, but not what the answer is based on. It's impossible to answer deeply complicated questions with a yes or a no. It's an unreasonable request to a population to ask a question where one answer will have consequences that no one has any possibility of foreseeing. Do you want more arguments against referendums?"

"Do you think people are too stupid to be asked?" She apparently hadn't addressed a single one of Torp's objections.

"If you want a straight answer: yes," replied Torp. He didn't really mean it. Or did he?

"But you can't say that," exclaimed Grandma-Bente.

Katrine chuckled in the background.

"I've just said it." Torp tried to disarm the words with a smile and a shrug.

"What about the general election that's coming? Can't we figure that out either?"

"Sometimes. But not always." Torp laughed.

Now Grandma-Bente laughed, too.

They were interrupted by Arne Lund, who regularly came into the editorial section from his office.

"The Prime Minister is going to hold a press conference in ten minutes. Ten o'clock. He's going to call the election now!"

"But the New Radicals haven't held their meeting yet," objected Grandma-Bente.

"He's doing it 'because of the general deadlocked situation at Borgen.' He's trying to avoid a general election based on the EU."

"Is that a good idea?" asked one of the reporters.

"It's worth a try, at least," said Arne Lund, while switching on the editorial section's large television screen.

"The big question," said the Hawk, "is whether the Nationalists and the New Radicals get over the threshold or not."

That wasn't the big question, thought Torp. That was the obvious question. If both parties fell below the votes' threshold, the matter was decided, regardless of which party came to power after the election—Labour or the Liberals. Then there would be no referendum on the EU.

That was how it was. Both the Nationalists and the New Radicals were bobbing around the 2 per cent threshold.

Arne Lund turned up the volume. The country's Prime Minister stepped up on the podium.

First came a long screed about how much his government had accomplished in two years. It wasn't actually very much, but if you split things up into small pieces, scraped the barrel, and tarted it up with elegant formulations, it could sound plausible to the believers and the ignorant. He was good at that, the Prime Minister.

Then followed a not so long screed about him having to deal with the worst and most cantankerous opposition in Danish history. He didn't mention either the Nationalists or the New Radicals at all, and certainly not the People's Party, the party that had actually made him Prime Minister but had since forgotten all about him.

Then it came:

"I have therefore come to the conclusion that it will be best to clear the air. To get parliamentary Denmark restarted by consulting the voters, so that we can really get going on the new working year, when the parliamentary year begins on the first Tuesday in October. I have therefore recommended to Her Majesty the Queen that a general election be called, to be held on Thursday, the twenty-sixth of September."

Today was the tenth of September. Sixteen days. That would be a historically short election campaign, thought Torp. He was torn out of his political thoughts by the reportage chief, the lad with the slightly overlong neck hair.

"While the expanded political editorial staff is going crazy on the general election, we others will be keeping track of the rest of the country. We'll have a quick mini-editorial meeting in ten minutes." And turning to Torp, he continued, "Good stories, Ulrik. I especially liked that one about Nasty Nina. It got lots of hits online."

Ulrik. No one at the *Daily News*—or in the whole journalism branch— called him Ulrik. Everyone called him Torp and had done so since the School of Journalism.

"And, Ulrik," continued Neckhair. "Remember the by-line on your articles. Full name and email address on all articles. Readers need to know who we are, and they need to be able to reach us, right?"

Torp had actually added his name to the other two articles. Only Nasty Nina had had to manage without it.

The supply of news always seemed to fit with the scale of a newspaper. When there were big stories around, it was as if the stream of other stories dried out all by itself. Torp had often thought about the phenomenon but had never found an answer. That's just the way it was, even on this Tuesday morning with sixteen days of election campaign ahead. The supply of other news immediately dwindled, but not because less was happening. There was just less of it visible in all the food chains. Even so, a reportage group of just three—Katrine Taber-Nielsen, Ulrik Torp, and an intern—was too little, the young reportage manager proclaimed. There would be a couple more arriving during the week, and Grandma-Bente would be joining in, editor-in-chief Arne Lund had promised.

Katrine had an idea that a local story about some pollution limit readings, which had been exceeded at a couple of water wells in North Zealand, might be a national story. She wanted to check if the drinking water was similarly threatened elsewhere in the country.

The intern—Emma was her name—wanted to go to Roskilde. New problems with an overhead line had yet again been causing problems for the Danish Rail commuters. The head of reportage nodded. That was a great idea from an intern.

"Take a photographer with you and do a report containing some angry commuters. Ulrik?"

Everyone looked at Torp. He shook his head.

He didn't have any ideas.

"A twenty-eight-year-old Danish man was found shot dead this morning in Ørstedsparken. According to the police, it looks like premeditated murder, but it doesn't, at first sight, seem to be gang-related. Will you take that, Ulrik?"

"Ulrik" would be happy to take that. He promised a version for the Net almost immediately and then a few columns for the printed newspaper.

Back at his daily desk, Torp dialled a mobile number he hadn't used for a long time, but he knew that his source at Police Headquarters for the last fifteen years was still in his post.

"Anton."

"Torp."

"Torp, goddammit. Long time no hear. Have you become a journalist again?" This last was said with a mixture of sincere solicitude and curiosity in his voice.

"A little; I'm sitting at the *Daily News*. What do we know about the man who was found in Ørstedsparken this morning?"

"Shouldn't you be writing about the election?"

"It's a long story. At the moment, I'm covering Ørstedsparken. What do you know?"

"Not much. There's a touch of the missing clerk about it."

"Missing clerk?"

"Yes, he's been found now, but his wife reported him missing last night and was completely out of her mind. Usually, they've been out drinking or have found a woman or some other innocent reason. But this time it was serious."

"Clerk?"

"Civil servant on Slotsholmen. Just graduated from university. Toddler. Wife on maternity leave. Flat in Nørrebro. It's really sad."

"Motive?"

"No idea. He seems very ordinary. There's nothing on him immediately."

"Was he gay? Is Ørstedsparken still used as a meeting place?"

"Not really. That's mostly a cock-and-bull story these days. Besides, it's not normal for gays to shoot each other with a nine-millimetre Neuhausen."

"Was he gay?"

"No, damn it. Or . . . we don't actually have any idea about that, but there's nothing to suggest it."

"When was he killed?"

"About six to ten o'clock p.m."

"Someone must have heard the shot. Just one?"

"We're checking that now. There are cordons and forensics down there, and doorbells are being rung on Israels Plads. But he's only been hit with a single shot. Right in the melon."

"Roger. More?"

"Roger. No more."

As if the pause button had just been released, they ended the conversation as they had always done when they had really been collaborating. They both laughed and hung up at the same time.

Torp took the opportunity to become a roving reporter and walked the short distance down to Ørstedsparken. The political parties were already hanging up posters. A few candidates were handing out pamphlets. Torp received a *Denmark Out of the EU* from the Nationalists and a *Them or Us*. It was a bit unclear whether *them* were the bureaucrats in the EU or Muslims—maybe both.

He rounded the corner from Nørreport and saw the forensics and the cordons at the entrance to Ørstedsparken. There were a number of spectators standing up against the red-and-white plastic ribbons. He could see a couple of journalists from the *Express* on the other side of the roadblock talking to a police officer.

"Press card!" the officer shouted. He looked at Torp as, having apologised to some of the public, he tried to hop over the cordon, which was just high enough to make it difficult to do so elegantly. Torp had no idea what he had done with his press card. He had never in his life used it for anything other than getting into places like Legoland and Givskud Lion Park for free, when the children were small and they didn't have much money. Could you still use the card for that kind of thing? Probably not. He produced his ID card from the *Daily News*. That was enough.

Back at the editorial office, he watched the election campaign on television while trying to pull together the story around the murder of a twenty-eight-year-old man in Ørstedsparken. The Liberals, led by the Prime Minister, were to hold a press conference to present their election manifesto. Normally, a leading government party would wait until the day after the election announcement. After all, the first wave of news would be around the announcement itself. But maybe Torp was just getting old. There had been innumerable postings on the Web and uninterrupted live TV in the six hours since the election had been declared. The first wave had washed ashore long ago. Moreover, there were only sixteen days. It was a matter of throwing everything in quickly.

A familiar face on the television attracted his attention. It was Ulla Hasting, a former minister for both the Labour Party and the Liberals at ten-year intervals. Before that, she had been a member of a myriad of parties and movements since she had broken through the media wall as a Redstocking in the early 1970s. By her side stood her spouse throughout the years, Poul Hasting, who had followed the same political development.

"What the hell are those two doing on television?" exclaimed a subeditor, turning up the sound.

". . . therefore we are urging everyone not to vote in this general election," came Ulla Hasting's characteristic falsetto voice. Poul Hasting—the "commissar," as he had been called by both friends and foes alike when he had taught Marxist economics at the University of Copenhagen in the seventies and eighties—stood stiffly next to her, nodding.

"You shouldn't return a blank voting slip. You should simply abstain from voting," she stated in the news item, which was clearly the television station treading water before the Liberals' press conference. The text rolled across the chyron at the bottom of the screen: *We are waiting for the Liberals' press conference and election manifesto.*

"Who the hell are they?" asked a young journalist of no one in particular.

"The darlings of the far left in the seventies," explained Torp. "Poul Hasting defended the German terrorist group Rote Armee Fraktion back then. He even wrote a both mysterious and complicated political statement of support," he continued.

"They're not on the far left nowadays," said the young journalist, pointing at the TV screen and the nice, elderly married couple, who were kindly allowing themselves to be interviewed.

"No, not at all," exclaimed Torp. "They've been all the way around," he said, thinking that it was perhaps very natural that they had now apparently disappeared completely off the compass. He had interviewed them several times. Ulla Hasting had been an effective minister, but neither of them was a team player and had never been.

"What a pair of idiots," the young journalist concluded.

No one contradicted him.

In the middle of one of Ulla Hasting's sentences, "we can't trust . . . ," the news channel cut back to the studio, where the host proclaimed that the Liberals' press conference was about to begin. Cut to a ship in the middle of the Sound, where the party for some reason had arranged its presentation. It wasn't clear why Prime Minister Palle Enevoldsen had to pitch and roll on a wooden schooner at sea to report on fewer refugees, less EU, more welfare, and better cancer treatment. The intoned refrain from the Prime Minister was supplemented by the party's deputy chairman, who was also Finance Minister, and the party's political spokesman. Tomorrow, the Labour Party would say roughly the same thing.

Torp paused at the mention of cancer treatment and briefly followed the press conference more closely. If he hadn't heard anything from Rigshospitalet before Friday, he would call them. At all events, he would call the dentist and postpone the replacement of the old filling. That and the incipient periodontal disease really had to wait.

He looked at Katrine Taber-Nielsen and the intern, Emma, who had come back from her Danish Rail commuter report in Roskilde. They were writing like crazy. Then he remembered that they finished work at 4:30 p.m. Torp looked at his watch. It showed 4:12. He turned to the computer screen and got his slightly rusty fingers typing.

It was actually quite nice.

CHAPTER 5

They were sitting in the local train on their way to Klampenborg, looking like the old married couple they probably were.

Ulrik in his new branded trousers with his hand on his right cheek and his tongue checking the lump. Karen in her own thoughts with her eyes fixed on the stations they passed through. They were silent, without them feeling it was embarrassing or strange. They were in a period when they didn't talk very much. That was how it had been for some years, and Karen didn't put any pressure on. She had gradually had to acknowledge how much her husband's well-being and personality were linked to his work as a journalist, and to believe that, in its own good time, she and the family would come to take up more space than was the case now. She watched how he fought in vain with his *Torp Communication—competence and experience* and, for each day, week, and month that passed became a little less Torp, a little more Ulrik.

Was this the man she had fallen in love with? Did he have a wimp gene that hadn't had the opportunity to unfold itself until now?

"Look at those villas." Ulrik pointed out the window. They were approaching Klampenborg. "And it's the worst ones that are closest to the track," he continued. Once he had said it with enthusiasm in his voice.

"Indeed," she replied.

They got off at Klampenborg and walked the rest of the way to their daughter and son-in-law's villa. The work activation at the *Daily News* had in fact revived him in less than forty-eight hours.

"I can't stand it," exclaimed Ulrik when they had reached about halfway.

"Isn't it nice to have a few weeks at the *Daily News?*" objected Karen.

Ulrik shook his head in irritation. "Jonathan. And then that air horn of a brother. Why are they coming, too?"

"We're doing it for Sofie's sake. And he isn't all that terrible."

Ulrik let the silence hang between them while he thought about their daughter. Sofie had always been able to fend for herself, apart from the flat her parents had bought for her when, for the third time in seven months, she had moved into a new, expensive, and damp room in Nørrebro with drug addicts for neighbours. She had met Jonathan during her last year of studying at the teacher training college, and neither Ulrik nor Karen had ever understood why she put up with the little needling jibes that came from him—the poorly concealed humiliations, the condescension, and the lack of respect. *Sofie just can't find her way anywhere, can you, darling? Sofie says she reads a lot of books, but they certainly aren't cookbooks, ha ha.* She still saw one single female friend, but always without Jonathan. Could self-confidence be peeled away layer by layer? What had happened to his proud, strong, and independent daughter?

And then his fucking gas grill and his fatuous red wine.

He stroked his right cheek with his hand. In the course of a few days, it had become his little tic, which Karen had noticed without commenting on. He still hadn't heard from the hospital. They had promised to send a text message during the week about the examination that would probably show that there was nothing wrong. Which meant that there was no need to mention it to Karen. In any case, he reasoned, it would be strange if he suddenly told her about it now. Why hadn't he said something last week?

They had reached the villa's pea shingle driveway, walked past the plaster lions and the large wrought iron gate that was open because of the expected arrivals, went up the wide granite steps, and rang the bell.

Out in the garden, the son-in-law was swinging steaks over his voluminous gas grill.

"Father-in-law! Take a glass." Jonathan turned to face them.

They both got a hug. He had introduced hugs into the family. Now they all had to do it. Ulrik had a huge glass of wine placed in his hand.

"South African. Meerlust Rubicon. You'll really enjoy it."

Ulrik took a taste, let the air through it so that the wine was oxygenated in the mouth, and let it be understood that it was something very special, which it actually was.

"It was one of the vineyards we visited down there. I ordered some cases to be sent home; they came the other day with the shippers. A damn sight more efficient than PostNord delivering a letter from Jutland."

Addressing himself to Ulrik alone, Jonathan continued in a subdued voice.

"We just need to have a chat, the two of us, about the flat. No panic. But my accountant has a little better grip of things than the accountant you used when Sofie was living there. We'll figure something out."

Ulrik nodded. What else was he supposed to do? They had bought the flat for Sofie several years ago at another time to support her studies with a stable, cheap place to live. When she had finished and got a job, she had taken it over at 15 per cent under the official valuation, which was what was now done in finer, and not so fine, circles to avoid paying tax on the gain in price, while at the same time giving a leg up to the next generation. Now Jonathan was managing the flat, which Ulrik and Karen had moved into shortly after he had lost his unemployment benefit.

"So it'll still be a kind of parental purchase flat," as the son-in-law had expressed it with a laugh that had stopped abruptly when no one else laughed with him. "No, honestly, Ulrik, I'm just glad I'm able to help."

Maybe he meant it, Ulrik had thought.

The doorbell rang.

"I thought your brother would be busy campaigning," Ulrik said.

"Ah, he's just a candidate to fill the list here in North Zealand. Their leader, Annegrethe Hulsig, is standing up here, so it's her they're all fighting for. But he's very much into it." Jonathan looked up. "Sofie!"

Sofie got up from the garden chair where she was sitting with her mother and went out to receive the guests.

Ulrik hitched up his trousers, which were still sitting as they should. He thought of the story of the young man who had been found killed that morning in Ørstedsparken, and who perhaps wasn't as clean and immaculate as one would immediately think, and whom the *Express* had made a big deal of. *Young father murdered in cold blood*, read the headline in their online version. It was sort of implicit in the text that a young father is innocent. But Anton at Police Headquarters had later told Torp that the murdered man, Jeppe Mikkelsen, had a brother who was involved in drug trafficking and had a short prison sentence as baggage. It didn't necessarily mean anything, but there could be a connection. It was at least something the police were looking into. Torp was the only one who had this story in the version that was in the printed newspaper on Wednesday. Neckhair was very satisfied, Torp had been given to understand from Katrine Taber-Nielsen.

The son-in-law's brother came out on the terrace with his young wife, on whom it was apparent that not everything was natural. Everyone got a hug and a Meerlust Rubicon. Ulrik looked at his watch.

"So now we damn well have an election campaign," the brother exclaimed when everyone had tasted and commented on the Meerlust.

"Indeed," Ulrik heard himself say.

"It's now or never if we're going to get out of that bloody community," the brother continued, as if he was already handing out pamphlets in the square.

Jonathan twiddled some knobs on his new gas grill.

"We could also do like that Hasting couple says—not vote at all," laughed his wife.

The brother turned his head. "You're bloody well voting for Daddy here," he exclaimed.

She laughed a flustered "of course" back at him.

"Have you seen? It also has a timer." Jonathan gave the lid a slight tug downwards so that it lowered itself in a gliding motion like the hatchback of a car. "Ten minutes, then the vegetables and meat are done."

The brother continued his political campaign unchallenged during the meal, which—Ulrik had to let his son-in-law know—tasted excellent.

"Now it's time to end all this business with refugees, liquorice pipes, wolves, crooked cucumbers, forced maternity leave for men, and Romanian strawberry pickers on unemployment benefit."

Ulrik had promised Karen that he would hold back, so he said nothing.

Jonathan agreed: "EU—Enforcer Unwelcome. Then Danes can again be allowed to decide what happens in their own country."

"A hundred thousand bureaucrats sitting in Brussels deciding how this meat can be produced and what your new gas grill has to look like. It's completely insane," the brother added.

"Twenty-three thousand."

Everyone looked at Ulrik, who reached for his wine glass.

"What?"

"There are twenty-three thousand officials working under the auspices of the European Commission in Brussels," Ulrik said. "That's about ten thousand fewer than there are public employees in Aarhus."

Ulrik took a big sip of his Meerlust Rubicon and continued indifferently cutting a piece of meat on his plate. It was an unusually tender fillet steak.

"It probably depends on how you count," objected the brother, looking around the table for like-minded people.

"I think you could be right about that. I count one, two, three, four, five, and so on. The numerical system," said Ulrik with his mouth full of meat. Karen looked at him disapprovingly.

There was a brief moment of silence around the table.

"In any case, they decide too much. It's the elite's project. Not the people's," the brother made clear, as if that settled the conversation. Sofie sensed the danger.

"What about your election campaign? Are you ready, Svend?"

Svend brightened up. "We're as ready as anyone can be. I'm not going to get elected, of course, but I'm just helping out a bit on the square in Hillerød, a pamphlet here and there and a few debates."

"Why are you standing if you're not going to get be elected?" asked Karen in a friendly tone.

"It's a little bit a feeling of national duty," came the answer, dressed in a touch of pathos. "National duty," he repeated, now seriously in a more personal way than before. "I sincerely feel that Denmark's self-determination is threatened. I imagine it's a help when I, as a local IT manager and active in the local community, stand up and say what needs to be said."

"That's true. There are many people who listen to Svend," said Susse, his young wife.

The candidate's younger brother broke in. "The Nationalists are a small, new party. You won't even get a thousand votes in Hillerød, brother." Jonathan despised politicians. "They're all equally corrupt and incompetent. Nah, if a talented businessman came along, then I'd jump on."

They had come along at the last election—a whole new party filled with business people who knew exactly how to run a small shop like the Danish one. Now the party was supporting the government, without making any difference, but he either didn't care or hadn't noticed.

"Do you want to bet?" Svend asked. The parliamentary candidate brightened up. They had been betting on everything possible since they were little, and they loved it. "A case of good red wine?"

"Excellent," laughed Jonathan. "Under a thousand votes, you owe me a case. It had better be a bloody good one, and I hate Merlot."

"What do you mean about it being the elite's project?"

Ulrik heard his own words and immediately regretted them. It had actually been quite pleasant for a brief moment.

"What?"

"You said the EU was the elite's project. Not the people's. What do you mean by that?" Ulrik defied Karen's desperate look. There was no way back now.

Parliamentary candidate Svend looked disoriented for a moment. Then he regained his composure. "You should know," he replied.

"Am I the elite?"

"You and the media people, writers, artists, TV hosts, and the whole bloody industry."

"Am I the elite?" Ulrik straightened up and pointed to his own chest, but didn't raise his voice. Even the son-in-law suddenly seemed uncomfortable.

Sofie got up. "Is there anyone who'd like to help clear the table? Then I'll bring out the ice cream."

Everyone except Ulrik stood up as if on reflex.

They didn't say a word to each other on the way to the train. Ulrik knew full well he had broken the agreement with Karen—*when they talk politics, you just hum.* It had been completely impossible, though. He should never have made that deal. It had been worse, however, when Jonathan later in the evening had pulled his father-in-law aside.

"There was just that business with the flat." He hesitated. "My accountant says we need to raise the rent. It's simply far, far too cheap compared to the market, and I'm not much in favour of the tax authorities taking a closer look at me because of a small detail."

"Low," said Ulrik.

"Low what?"

"A rent can be low. Not cheap. Skimmed milk can be cheap, but the price is low."

Ulrik was using the only weapon he had: pedantry, the condescending kind. The son-in-law had previously hinted that the rent should be increased, partly due to an almost new kitchen. It couldn't at all be compared with the overly cheap—there it was again—rent that Sofie had paid before they had met, the son-in-law had explained several times.

"It can only have gone so well with the tax authorities because you're such a little fish," he said.

Ulrik had nodded without saying anything.

"So I thought," he said in an even lower voice, skipping the skimmed milk, "that in the New Year, we increase the rent by two thousand a month. The accountant thinks that will just about do the trick."

Ulrik nodded again.

"If this is a problem for you," continued Jonathan, "then we'll have to find a way for me to give something back in cash. The most important thing is the amount transferred from your account to my account each month. It has to look right."

"We shouldn't have anything back. We can increase the rent right away," said Ulrik. It sounded aggressive, he could hear that.

"No, damn it, Ulrik. January first. Not before. The money doesn't matter to me. It's the accountant."

He sounded like the landlord in *An Evil Man*, thought Torp. *It's not the money. It's the principle!* Didn't the evil man end up throwing the money in the fireplace? He probably did. Why was his son-in-law now top dog? Why was he downtrodden? It was as if time was crumbling between Ulrik's fingers. Once it had been on his side—time, that is. Legislation, tax rules, house prices, wages, and morals. It all somehow fit in with his life, without him thinking about it further. Almost Cavling Prize. Almost chief news editor, he fancied. Almost. Almost. And then suddenly too late. Now society was apparently arranged in favour of Jonathan, who was blithely raking it in for himself. Ulrik had the impression that his son-in-law was good at his job, but no more than that. Even so, companies and consulting firms were queuing up with job offers for an IT expert in his mid-thirties with management experience and a salary that made no sense in Ulrik's universe. The villa was exploding in value. The small flat in Frederiksberg, which Sofie had taken over so cheaply, was doing the same. That his son-in-law in addition only knew about wine, mortgage conversion, and the football club FCK didn't matter, apparently. How could that be enough for Sofie? Ulrik felt old and bitter.

"It's no problem," he lied. "You shall have what you shall have. Cheap or low. January first." They went back to the others.

* * *

"You turned up the timer on the gas grill." Karen broke the silence as they sat on the local train towards Copenhagen. "When you went to the toilet. Right after Jonathan announced that there would be a delicious late snack of butcher's sausages in fifteen minutes. They were completely black."

"They were more than that," Ulrik remarked. "They were totally inedible."

They stared at each other for a long time.

It was Karen who started. She actually wanted to say something but couldn't. They burst out laughing, tears streamed from their eyes, they held their stomachs, and several people in the train turned their heads and smiled at them.

They made love that night. Long and at times intense. Afterwards, they lay catching their breath in the bed in the all-too-small and crowded bedroom.

"Why don't you like Jonathan?" Karen asked, just to get some clarification, without that hint of criticism that accompanied it when she had brought up the subject on other occasions.

"You can't stand him either," he objected.

"I don't think he treats Sofie in the way she deserves."

Ulrik sighed. He searched for a long time for the right words. "Jonathan is so much that we are not," he tried.

"How?" She knew very well but wanted to hear how he would formulate it.

"Do you think he's ever read a newspaper? Has he read a book that wasn't about the internet or commandos?"

She chuckled. "Is that so bad?"

"Not really . . . It just doesn't have that much to do with us."

"He lives less than twenty kilometres away. He's married to our daughter and will probably be the father of our first grandchild. It has everything to do with us," she objected. "What do you think my parents thought when I met you? I'm sure Dad had imagined a doctor as a son-in-law, someone he could talk to."

"And then he just got a journalist," said Ulrik in a theatrical voice. "But that was something else. I simply don't know what to talk to him about."

"Then it's you who's the problem. Not him."

"Our rent is going up by two thousand from January first. Something to do with his accountant."

"But we can't afford it."

Ulrik writhed. "Don't you think I know that?"

"Then you'll just have to get a job, Ulrik. Something or other. Maybe you should also look for something that has nothing to do with journalism."

"Fifty-five years old and a wimp. Employers aren't exactly queuing up."

"You haven't really tried."

"The elite! For crying out loud, Karen, that's so far out."

She decided to save that talk for later. "Sofie is happy with him. Mostly. That's the important thing."

"It's just such a small country. It ought to be possible to understand each other."

They talked for a long time, made love once more, and fell asleep. Satiated.

CHAPTER 6

What is normal?

The threshold had changed imperceptibly for Ulrik Torp. He normally weighed eighty-four kilos. He had done so for twenty-five years until he left the *Daily News*. But he had lost five kilos pretty quickly without really thinking about it. His perpetual hitching-up of his old pair of trousers had become a habit. It had become normal to shop exclusively in discount stores, not to go on exotic holidays, and to spend the mornings when Karen was teaching on nothing. In the space of a week, it had become normal to have cancer. Did he even have cancer? It had become normal for extremist small parties to become popular centre parties, for people to question vaccinations, experts, advisers, and numbers. It had become normal for the President of the United States to behave abnormally.

Sometimes it happened in surges, other times softly, softly. But in a strange way, Ulrik was moving along with it. Was he the only one who was becoming immune to statements from politicians that five or ten years ago would have sparked outcry but now simply resulted in shrugs or support?

Ulrik didn't think he had had a single extreme or even radical attitude to anything in his life.

Sure, as a young man, he had been a supporter of nuclear power while everyone else was against it. That was probably a kind of radical view, but most experts said it was sensible and much better than coal. Today, saying yes to nuclear power was probably no longer radical, more irrelevant. The middle of the road, beans on toast, and lukewarm compromises were for him the whole point of the organisation of society. But had he become blind? Had what was considered normal shifted? Was he like the frog in cold water that comes to the boil so slowly that the creature eventually dies without even noticing? And if so, how hot was the water now?

He had often been puzzled about how quickly people adjust. If you are on holiday for a week, it is understood on the sixth day that the holiday is coming to an end. With a two-week holiday, you make the same adjustment the day before it is due to end. This was his third day at the *Daily News* on work activation after a five-year absence, and it was as if it had just been an extended holiday. It had suddenly become normal to cycle into town in the morning, enter the bulletproof glass sluice with his access card and code, nod to Charlotte at reception, and take the lift up to the newsroom. It was as if time had stood still when he walked past Arne Lund's office, where he—as always—had been sitting since seven in the morning to plough through all the bulletins, morning newspapers, and news broadcasts in order to cobble a news day together once again, as only an experienced craftsman can.

"Hi!"

The boy looked up, got to his feet, and held out his hand, but without showing any intention of vacating Torp's desk. "I'm Simon. I'm an intern in the culture department, but I'm going to be on reportage during the election campaign."

Katrine was still sitting opposite. Torp felt a flicker of betrayal or perhaps even jealousy. Why hadn't she told the boy to sit somewhere else?

"Torp," said Torp.

"What a funny name. Can you actually be called that?"

The boy had sat down on Torp's chair again, but was still looking up. He couldn't be an elementary school intern, reasoned Torp. So he had to be a journalism student intern. Did they send out such youngsters nowadays?

"The *Daily News* has been given permission to borrow Ulrik Torp during the election campaign," said Katrine, trying to rescue the situation.

"Cool. I'll just google you."

Simon turned to his computer while Torp looked around for a vacant desk. There was a single old one with no adjustable height function standing on its own behind a screen. Torp sat down. One of the five wheels on the office chair was stuck.

"You've always been here," came the Google result from Simon the intern. Torp ignored the remark, mostly because it didn't really make sense, turned on his laptop, which he had fetched from his locker, and saw that an email had come from outside to his newspaper address. The first one. From a Jette Mikkelsen. *Regarding the article about my brother* was the subject line.

Dear Ulrik Torp,

Jeppe Mikkelsen, whom you have written about today, is my brother. You write that his brother—that is, also my brother—is involved in drug investigations, and that it may have something to do with the murder. Jeppe has never had anything to do with such things. Never. Do you have any idea how hurtful it is—not just for me, but for the whole family? You journalists have no idea how much harm you cause to us ordinary people.

Kind regards,
Jette Mikkelsen

Torp read it twice. It had been sent several hours ago. Just wait until the *Express* picked up on his article, added a few extra details and guesswork, found her brother in the archives, and gave it the whole nine yards on the Net; then she would really have reason to complain.

At the editorial meeting, Neckhair welcomed Simon the intern, who—it turned out, to Torp's astonishment—was twenty-four. Did the boy even have a shaver? New at the table, proclaimed Neckhair, was also Christian Crash, as everyone called him. A gangly guy in his mid-thirties with skinny trousers and a man bun at his neck, on loan from the modest but growing editorial staff who wrote about celebrities and gossip.

The head of reportage looked around the table—Katrine Taber-Nielsen, Simon the intern, Emma the intern, Christian Crash, Grandma-Bente, and Ulrik Torp. It wasn't just the core squad, but the full squad of Denmark's second-largest newspaper that for the next fortnight was going to cover that part of the country which had nothing to do with the general election.

"We have a feature article in the newspaper today," began Neckhair, "written by the former Minister of Justice and Foreign Secretary Brathenberg. I'm sure he thinks that everything was better when he was in charge."

The others laughed, except Simon the intern. Up until ten years ago, Otto Brathenberg had been a powerful Foreign Secretary for eight years, and before that, interrupted only by a period in opposition, had been an equally powerful Minister of Justice. He was known for having unlimited confidence in his own abilities and insights, but also for having a feeling for new trends and young talents. He was now in his mid-seventies, but occasionally still got involved in the public debate. It was usually both insightful and opinionated "sermons from the mount" that he expected all normal people to take to heart—not only because they were so obviously true, but because he was vouching for them. Today's column in the *Daily News—Brathenberg: Don't believe in simple solutions*—should be understood as his manifesto in relation to the coming general election. Torp had always liked him. He had made himself available to journalists as a minister, had always been ready to give a little extra in an interview, had often spoken off the record, but had rarely been misused and even more rarely had himself misused professional relationships, which was a difficult discipline. He was, in Torp's opinion, a proper politician in the true sense of the word, one who had spent his entire adult life organising society. Otto Brathenberg was from the Labour Party, but it was a coincidence as much as anything else. He could equally well have been in the Liberal Party. It was even something he had flirted with. And, in addition, he was on the board of the *Daily News*.

"Arne Lund thinks we should do an interview with Brathenberg," said Neckhair without much enthusiasm. "It sounded a bit like the idea came from editor-in-chief Henriksen's corner office," he continued.

"That's a bit far out. Why not also interview Churchill while we're at it?" Simon the intern laughed.

Torp could see that he had quickly looked up Brathenberg on his smartphone.

"The Christiansborg office is busy today," continued Neckhair. "Rumour has it that the Labour Party is now guaranteeing a referendum on the EU if the Nationalists will back them after the election. The Liberals may promise the same thing. It will be the big story of the day. That actually fits very well with a Brathenberg chat one of these days." He turned to Torp. "That should be right up your street, Ulrik. You've probably interviewed him loads of times in the old days."

There were several things in the last two sentences that jarred with Torp. The order—for it was an order—that he should interview the old minister. Not because he objected to doing it, in fact on the contrary, but not as an order. Journalists should, if nothing else, have the illusion of themselves choosing and deciding. At least, that was how it used to be—Torp hesitated in mid-thought—in the old days. That the young and inexperienced middle manager consistently called him Ulrik was something he would have to get used to; but wasn't he aware that everyone else called him Torp? Finally—and the worst thing—was his "probably." "You've probably interviewed him loads of times." Of course he had! The idiot was in his mid-thirties. If he was a real journalist, he would have read the newspapers every single day for the past fifteen years. Then there wouldn't be any need for a "probably." He was guessing, he was groping in the dark; he was a half-grown boy and a clone of Torp's son-in-law. Everything had to be googled; the superficiality ran deep.

Torp sighed.

"I was actually intending to follow up on the murder of the young man in Ørstedsparken. The *Express* is making a big deal out of the story and there isn't much else of that kind around right now."

"Yes, you do that, by all means. There will hardly be space for Brathenberg tomorrow, but it would be great if the interview was ready to print. It can happily take up a bit of space. Two stories from you, Torp. Katrine?"

Katrine Taber-Nielsen hesitated.

"I'm following up a bit on the water wells, but I'll gladly help Torp with the murder in Ørstedsparken, if needed. I have a couple of good sources in the CID I can try," she said, looking at Torp.

"Great, you two get on with that, then. That murder may well turn out to be a really good story in the middle of all the politics," the young reportage manager concluded.

Katrine went to Torp's non-height-adjustable desk after the editorial meeting and laid her hand briefly on his shoulder. "Was that okay?"

Torp looked up. Sincerely happy. He liked her company. Unlike so many others around him, she was knowledgeable and talented, and stories often only got better when there were two. He assured her that it was more than okay, told her about the email from the victim's sister, and forwarded it to his writing partner. They could talk about a possible follow-up when she had got her water wells under control and he had contacted Otto Brathenberg.

It turned out that Neckhair had been right. The former Foreign Secretary and Justice Minister had himself been in touch with the *Daily News*'s editor-in-chief Asbjørn Henriksen with the proposal for both a column and an interview. He had, as he entertained Torp with this on the phone, actually been surprised that the appointment for an interview hadn't been made the day before, when he had submitted the article, so that the article and the interview could come out the same day, the first real day of the election campaign. All that stuff about an arm's length between the board and the editorial staff clearly wasn't something he took too seriously.

Otto Brathenberg was genuinely happy that it was Ulrik Torp who was to write the article.

"Your articles on financial support for parties cost us a hell of a lot of money, but hey, then the taxpayers had to take over," he chuckled once they had made the agreement over the phone and managed to spend five minutes talking about . . . well, yes, the old days.

Now Torp was standing in front of the functionalist villa in Hellerup, so famous in Danish politics, ready for his interview, as in the old days. As a young man, Brathenberg had written a book called *A Genuine Democracy*, which had become—somewhat unusual for its genre—a bestseller, regularly published in new editions. His thoughts on a living democracy were still used and discussed in educational institutions.

"I'm really concerned, for the first time in my life."

Brathenberg leaned back in his PK22 lounge chair and spread his arms out wide with a slight air of resignation. Torp sat opposite him in a matching chair and fumbled with the recorder function on the *Daily News*'s smartphone. How he missed a tape recorder. The political Nestor had kindly invited him inside with a *how nice it's you, Torp*. His wife, the emeritus professor of literature Lise Brathenberg, acclaimed in the finest circles, had helped her husband prepare a small table with plunger coffee, a carafe of cold water with a slice of lemon, and a bowl of small pieces of chocolate from the fridge. They were both older than they wanted to be, yet were so laid-back in their own self-confidence and kindness that they could bear their age. They were slim and tanned without being overly tanned. Otto Brathenberg was wearing a yellow shirt that hung out over his trousers; Lise was in a light summer dress that highlighted her upright posture—all precisely crumpled enough to be casual, and smooth enough to be classic. They could be dropped straight into a pension fund advertisement for the active, eternal life of retirement, thought Torp. There wasn't a single painting, not a piece of furniture, not a rug on the parquet floors that didn't fit in with everything else. As so often before, he was struck by the feeling of not belonging; of visiting a foreign country with unknown cultures and norms, like a weed in an ornamental garden, clear to all that he didn't belong here. He envied those journalist colleagues whose parents had themselves been writers or even editors-in-chief; how they so naturally referred to authors and acquaintances in the branch who had come into their childhood home, were godmothers to them, or with whom they had been on a road trip as children—names Torp only knew from newspapers and books. As a seven-year-old, Ulrik Torp had been able to reverse a tractor with a trailer perfectly, but that ability wasn't of much use in the world he had later become a part of. He envied politicians who had grown up in politician homes, who weren't at all surprised that they were on the top shelf—that it was almost inevitable to become a minister, top official, or leader of industry. Just as they had learned to walk, talk, and read, they knew which wines should be drunk with what, how to eat a lobster, and how to dress when going to the Theatre Royal. Everything that Torp had to learn and pretend about, they had as a reflex. Torp was considered an outsider less often than he thought, but the feeling of always being one wrong move away from being exposed never left him. *Come out now! Blue lights flashing. What were you thinking?*

Lise opened the glass façade out to the well-kept garden—it could almost be called a park—so that the balmy September day filled the living room, turned to her husband, and said she would be off now.

"It was nice to meet you again, Torp," she said with a smile, leaving them to each other.

"I'm really concerned," Otto continued when he could see that the *Daily News*'s correspondent had found the recorder function on his phone and was ready for the interview. "I didn't write anything about it in the article, so this is between the two of us, but I'm shocked that my old party will accept a demand for a referendum on the EU in order to be able to form a government. Pernille Hjort became party leader on the contrary view—that it was time for the demonisation of Brussels to stop. Goodness me, how spineless."

Brathenberg looked up in the expectation that Torp would nod in agreement with his analysis of the Labour Party leader.

"Just write that I'm shaken by the party. But leave out the spineless remark. This isn't personal. She is, of course, under pressure, but that's exactly where you have to resist as a politician."

"Are you worried about a referendum?"

"It can go both ways. Look at the UK." The old Foreign Secretary leaned forward in his Poul Kjærholm chair. "And it can spread to other countries. If it was just Denmark, then so what. But this populism is spreading. It's infectious. Like the Ebola virus."

He poured plunger coffee and cold water for his guest.

"This, Torp," he continued, "this can, in a worst-case scenario, overthrow everything we have spent seventy-five years building up."

"We?"

"Yes, all of us. The Western world. Liberal society."

Brathenberg briefly seemed irritated that Torp wasn't immediately on the same wavelength as him.

"I've always been fascinated by Truman—the President of the United States at the end of World War II when Roosevelt died."

Torp leaned back; now for the sermon on the mount.

"Truman was originally a haberdasher—he came into politics a bit by chance and just as randomly became President of the United States. Think of all the things he had to decide his position on—nuclear bombs on Hiroshima and Nagasaki, the creation of the United Nations, the airlift to Berlin, the International Monetary Fund, the World Bank, the GATT—which today has become the World Trade Organization. He launched the Marshall Plan to rebuild Europe and supported the formation of the European Coal and Steel Community that eventually became the EU. What we have often forgotten is that he also launched a Greco-Turkish aid programme to prevent the advance of Communism in those two countries and to ensure security in the Mediterranean and the Middle East. He recognised the state of Israel, he put his foot down when North Korea tried to take South Korea, and, oh yes, then he also just happened to create NATO. Imagine!" Brathenberg leaned forward again. "Just one of those things would have been more than plenty for an American president for an entire election period. None of this would have turned into anything if he—the haberdasher from Missouri—had shaken his head or let his hands tremble. All of it—as in, all of it—came from a nod from him."

Brathenberg looked at Torp's smartphone.

"Does that thing work? Does it record? Is there space for everything on the tape?"

Torp assured him that everything was being recorded, but refrained from remarking that, to his own annoyance, too, there was no tape in such a machine. The elderly man stood up in a surprisingly agile manner, gestured to his guest that he, too, should stand up, and walked ahead into the next room, which was filled with books from floor to ceiling. Brathenberg went straight to one of the lower shelves and pulled out a book.

"Here. David McCullough's Pulitzer-winning biography of Truman. He spent ten years writing it. It came out right before the 1992 presidential election. It was important to him that it came before the election so that voters—and candidates—could see what can be done with such an office."

He handed it to Torp, who felt compelled to take it. He flipped through it a bit to show polite interest and saw that it contained a personal dedication from the author.

To my great friend, Otto.

"It's a little popular. That was probably why it was awarded the Pulitzer Prize," he laughed to himself. "It formed the basis of a bad TV film about Truman a few years later."

Torp tried to give it back to Brathenberg.

"No, damn it, Torp. Take it home. Read it. You can always bring it back sometime. There needs to be some of us who can retain the big picture."

He said the last sentence almost to himself. They sat down again in their respective PK22s. The coffee had become cold and the water warm.

"Everything that Truman and others with him built up can collapse because of populists and ignoramuses. Everything." The old Foreign Secretary clapped his hands together as if to illustrate his point. "And Denmark is one of several dominoes that can topple it if we suddenly have to vote on something as ridiculous as our membership of the EU." The contempt was almost tangible. He snorted. "You'll have to formulate that last bit in a slightly more politician-like way, but that's what I think."

"Where do you see these dominoes?"

Brathenberg paused for thought before answering.

"Italy has been and is probably still close to being. It seems unstable, but with the new-old government back in place of that idiot who lost his life earlier this summer, there might be a chance." He spread his arms. "You know the landscape as well as I do. We gave the Visegrád countries NATO and EU membership. We pump EU support into them, they don't take a single refugee, and they love populists. There are some powerful forces that are undermining everything at the moment. I don't really know if we can succeed."

"You called it an Ebola virus. That is stopped by, among other things, burning down villages. But this isn't a virus. It's a democratic protest," objected Torp.

"I think it was the philosopher Bertrand Russell who said that the problems of the modern world are due to the fact that the stupid are convinced of their own excellence, while the intelligent are in doubt."

"Are you in doubt, then?"

"Ha! One can always discuss cause and effect, Torp," Brathenberg leaned eagerly forward and looked him straight in the eye, "but the great changes in society come from above."

"And democracy?"

Brathenberg changed gear. To a lower one.

"Of course, Torp. You're absolutely right. We all need to talk more about it. Together. Hence my article and this interview."

He gave the impression that the interview was finished. That suited Torp. He had plenty to use—even if nothing had been recorded.

They were standing by the stairs chatting when the taxi arrived.

"Do you know how it went for Truman?" Otto Brathenberg smiled.

Torp sensed that he wasn't meant to make a guess. There would now be one last message from the mount.

"He left the White House as the most unpopular president in history. That's the problem with politicians today. They dare not be unpopular."

Torp shook his hand and thanked him for the interview and for the loan of the Truman biography.

CHAPTER 7

W e have one demand for the next Prime Minister. One. He should be able to manage that."

Annegrethe Hulsig smiled, paused, and made sure to turn her head so that everyone in the audience saw her face. The Nationalist Party leader was trying to stoke public feeling this first Friday afternoon of the election campaign. A few hundred people were standing in front of the small stage set up on Kultorvet, most of them, in Torp's estimation, loyal party soldiers. In the periphery, there were passersby, some of whom stopped and looked, as if they were just checking if a street artist was worth the time and the coins.

"And what is it?" she continued, putting her hand behind her ear as a signal that the audience should now contribute the familiar line at all her meetings.

They obeyed: "Referendum!"

"Precisely," she continued. "And it seems as if both the current Prime Minister, Palle Enevoldsen, and the Labour Party's Pernille Hjort have understood it. We must have that referendum on the European Union."

She gave a characteristic toss of her long blonde hair and again put her hand behind her ear and turned it towards her audience.

"Because what will we do with the EU?"

"Leave it!" roared the most energetic of her audience.

"That's exactly what we should do. Have a nice day, and remember to put a cross for our grandchildren and Denmark on the twenty-sixth."

Ulrik Torp looked around the group of people. That was how she ended all her meetings. Now chocolate was being handed out, wrapped in Danish flag paper. Torp accepted a piece from an elderly man wearing a party T-shirt and a flat cap that matched the chocolate wrapper. Several commentators wrote that the average Nationalist Party voter was an unskilled and bitter elderly man from the provinces. Torp couldn't see that in the circle of supporters on Kultorvet. They were like the common run of people. The party was new, it was its first election campaign, it was hers, and it was bobbing around the 2 per cent threshold but gradually starting to look stable above it. Foreign journalists had also taken note of the pretty party founder who seemed to be able to force an EU country to a referendum on membership almost on her own. Torp recognised a long-standing German correspondent at Annegrethe Hulsig's side. She would probably get over the threshold, reasoned Torp, and became annoyed again at having to walk around in the middle of a general election campaign without being an active part of it. For a brief moment, the interview with Otto Brathenberg had given him the illusion of being part of the election campaign, but that bubble had burst when he saw it printed in the newspaper the same morning, squeezed in at the back, right next to the sport and cut by a third without him having been consulted. The whole part with Truman had been cut out, and there was only room for a two-column old photo of the former Foreign Secretary. Was it in India where the newspaper layout was done? That was probably only true of some of the weekly supplements. Then it must be a firm out in the city that did it, as a way of circumventing the newspaper's old, expensive employment agreements. Here sat young—at best newly educated—journalists who shovelled out words for the same pay that Torp had received as a starting salary at the *Daily News* twenty-five years earlier. Torp didn't know who to complain to, so he had already given up.

He had also almost given up on getting through to Rigshospitalet.

"We've had major problems with our electronic patient records," lamented the voice on the phone.

Yes, thanks, Torp had indeed read about it. Billions of kroner had been poured into a centralised system, which had extended the waiting lists in most of the country. How many billions of public kroner was it possible for politicians to pour down the drain? His IT son-in-law explained that it was predictable, given the foreign software company that had won the EU tender—southern Europeans, like the company behind the billion-dollar purchase of trains that also didn't work, as he dryly pointed out. The problem was that he hadn't yet managed to become a patient in the first place. The voice couldn't find the referral from the dentist, and without a referral, she couldn't do anything. She promised that he would be notified by Monday; she had neither the authority, education, nor software to be able to do anything now. He must surely be able to understand that, and he could. Monday, then.

Torp stroked his right cheek, let his tongue fall into place, and walked over towards Annegrethe Hulsig and her supporters by the small podium that had served as a stage. The German correspondent had finished with the Nationalist Party leader and her demand for an EU referendum, which in the first instance had indirectly triggered a general election, and in the second instance could send the entire panoply of EU cooperation into yet another crisis. Now she turned her attention to the other journalists. The correspondent looked up as he approached.

"Hi, Torp," he said in his Danish, which after fifteen years in the country was still pronounced as though he had a potato in his mouth. Torp nodded.

"What a story. It's going round the whole of Oi-ropa." He knew it sounded strange in Danish but persisted with his pronunciation for Europe. "Are you back?"

Torp mumbled his avoidance of the question.

"Poland, Austria, and Hungary may also want to hold a referendum if one comes in Denmark," he continued.

The Germans always had the big picture, as Torp had already read. Brathenberg had also mentioned those countries as the most likely.

"Exciting times, Torp. Exciting times."

The German correspondent shook his head slightly, slapped Torp on the shoulder in a friendly manner, and hurried off. It wasn't often that the correspondent's stories about Denmark sparked very much interest in the German media he delivered to. This election campaign could well give him half a year's income. A referendum on top of that would cover next year's as well.

Annegrethe Hulsig continued to answer everyone's questions. No, she wasn't worried about a Denmark outside the EU. If other countries wanted to follow Denmark's example, that was up to them, not her. Yes, she was doing this for Denmark's and her children's sake. No, she didn't have anything against Muslims, but they shouldn't put Danish culture on the defensive. Yes, she thought both the Labour Party and the Liberals had betrayed the country. Furthermore, the People's Party had, too—it wasn't until now that they dared to agree with her on a referendum, and they had been close to power while tens of thousands of Muslims had been allowed to enter the country and go on social security. Yes, she could actually understand Ulla and Poul Hasting's fight for not voting at all—a fight that had been spreading intensely on social media in the election campaign under the hashtag *#contra*. The established political system had failed, explained Hulsig. Fortunately, she was an alternative. She wasn't a politician; she was a Dane. You wouldn't get any influence sitting on the sofa, she stressed.

Everything was delivered with a patience and a smile that many politicians could learn something from, thought Torp. Suddenly, her smile changed. A twitch went through her slender body, and a frightened, hunted expression came over her face. Torp heard shouting from behind, in the direction of Nørreport. It came closer. Hulsig withdrew. He turned his head. About fifty young people, several masked with balaclavas, charged towards Hulsig, her loyal party soldiers, and the small group of journalists who were still standing near her around the Nationalists' small podium.

Fascist pigs, fascist pigs, they shouted as they ran straight at them. A handful of police officers, who had been observing the election meeting at an appropriate distance, tried with only partial success to intervene, but they were too few, the young people too many, and Kultorvet too wide. Two men with Danish flag caps resolutely grabbed hold of Anne-grethe Hulsig and ran, practically carrying her, down Købmagergade. Other Danish flag flat-caps took up the fight when the self-proclaimed anti-fascists reached the spot. *Where's the pig? Where's the pig?* came the cry from several of them. They looked around, desperately twisting their heads. It was her they wanted. Everything else was clearly immaterial; just her, the symbol of all that they imagined they were against. People ran away screaming, Torp managed to run with them; left behind were a dozen from the Nationalist's youth wing and just as many hooded oppo-nents in a brief fight with each other. It looked more violent than it was. A few kicks and blows of the fist, a couple of bloody noses, some black eyes, an overturned loudspeaker system, and, as if on command, they were gone again—in an obviously planned escape in as many possible and impossible directions as Kultorvet offered. Back on the battlefield stood and lay the not-quite-battle-ready combatants from the National-ist Youth and four police officers. Some placards—Vote for Denmark—bearing the party founder's happy face had been trampled on Kultorvet's architect-designed stone. Pamphlets lay scattered around, dancing in the light, still mild September wind. Some sat crying; some were holding each other.

Annegrethe Hulsig came back after a few minutes with her two res-cuers, who were now, with a degree of pathos, behaving like her body-guards. They had fled into a small clothing store. The journalists returned from the corners of Kultorvet. Torp saw one of the *Daily News*'s young political reporters; they nodded briefly to each other, and Torp imme-diately accepted that it wasn't his parish. This was the political story of the day; maybe the weekend, too. A Danish example of the division and confrontation that prevailed among the electorate—not just in Denmark, but in most Western countries. The different groups of voters lived sepa-rately; each used their own media outlet and had fun with each other on social media, which acted as echo chambers and didn't facilitate the interethnic conversation that the more naive at first believed in. Few people read newspapers, and the anger kept getting more and more pet-rol poured on it. Torp had felt it himself when he had been ordered into a month's work activation for 2,814 kroner, when Rigshospitalet's computer system threw him out, and when his son-in-law put up the rent in the flat he had himself once bought for his daughter. The feeling of injustice that couldn't be addressed, couldn't be sent anywhere, but was just allowed to simmer and then boil up and eventually boil over. He could taste the bitterness when Karen went to work, when his son-in-law bought a stupid gas grill, when he was turned down on a hopeless job application, and when the *Daily News* got him back after dumping him like a bag of garbage.

And then the idiots who fought against each other on Kultorvet with-out probably having any idea why. Psychological experiments showed that when you only hung around with others like yourself, you became more extreme, and then the borders of normality shifted. The so-called anti-fascists and the core troops of the Nationalists had once been in the middle, where the beans on toast and the compromises lie. Now they believed that they were enemies. How had that happened? Torp under-stood the bitterness and the feeling of injustice, but not the confronta-tion. And in this case, it was completely gaga, too. The parties to the fight probably completely agreed on opposing the EU and globalisation. But the pictures were good and current, and Annegrethe Hulsig was excel-lent television. They were already underway—live on the news channel.

Torp left the scene and Kultorvet and took the Metro from Nørreport. Katrine Taber-Nielsen was waiting at the station in Vanløse. Despite the small, or large, intermezzo on Kultorvet, they were in good time, enough to sit down at a café and chat about the election. Torp sensed that, despite their age difference, they pretty much agreed on most things. He enjoyed her company and enjoyed the fact that it was obviously mutual.

"Why did you choose to become a journalist after studying at univer-sities in both the USA and the UK?" he asked when he had finished tell-ing her about the fight between the anti-fascists and the Nationalists. The story was already out on the media websites as breaking news. *Hulsig: I feared for my life*, read the headline in the *Express*.

She hesitated.

"I didn't, actually. It's just something I am right now. I came back to Denmark six months ago and asked the *Daily News* if they could use me. And they could."

"Why the *Daily News*?"

"It was something of a coincidence. I didn't know anyone. It could just as well have been another newspaper."

Was she like him? An outsider on a visit?

"What sort of background do you actually have?" It sounded like a polite question, but Torp was genuinely curious.

"Nothing special," she laughed. "A small town in South Zealand, beans on toast, and the commonplace."

"And Harvard and Cambridge, some of the world's finest and most prestigious universities," Torp added.

She paused for a bit, tasted her café au lait, and looked down at the table as if protecting herself.

"When you find out that you have the abilities and the possibilities, you also have a duty, don't you?"

She looked him straight in the eye and paused for a long time before the follow-up came—concerned, not aggressive.

"It doesn't seem as if you are using your abilities and opportunities."

She stressed *your*. Torp was surprised by her directness, which at first felt intimidating. Then it slipped into an experience of confidentiality and intimacy that surprised him. He had known her for five days. He was about to answer—something along the lines that she was right and yet wasn't. That his abilities were no longer in demand, that he was innocent, that he had been overtaken, that he had given up, had taken it all for granted, that several of the explanations contradicted each other, and that that was the point—that there was no reason for his downfall, that it had just happened. Why does a human being grind to a halt? Why does a society grind to a halt? Why did the Roman Empire fall? Why does a married couple drift apart? Things just happen, damn it, if you don't take care. That was what he was trying to formulate.

"Sorry," said Katrine, putting a hand quickly on his arm, "that was too close to the bone. That wasn't my intention."

She looked at her watch.

"We should actually go now if we're to be on time."

They walked in silence the short distance to the flat where Jeppe Mikkelsen's sister lived. After her first email to Ulrik Torp, in which she had complained about his article mentioning the other brother's involvement with drugs, she had sent a new email suggesting that there might be another explanation for the murder of her brother. Katrine had immediately agreed to come along, and since the appointment was at four o'clock on a Friday afternoon, just half an hour before the editorial staff finished work for the day, Neckhair didn't care that two journalists were agreeing to do one person's work. They were allowed to spend their free time on whatever they wanted, but this wouldn't result in any time off for either of them.

"How do I know I can trust you? And why have two of you come?"

Jette Mikkelsen was a careful woman; single mother and big sister to both her brothers. She had accepted that the *Daily News* was coming, but as she stood in the half-open doorway to her small social housing flat, it seemed as if she was regretting the visit of the two journalists.

"That's not something you can know. You just have to believe it." Katrine took over the conversation, even though she was standing partly behind Torp.

"We should first offer our condolences. What happened to your brother is horrible," said Torp, trying to smooth things out a bit; he wasn't sure his partner's remark was the surest door opener.

Jette Mikkelsen opened the door completely, apparently without taking note of his condolences.

She found two extra mugs and poured hot water from a thermos over some unbranded instant coffee. She looked like someone who hadn't slept in the three days or more that had passed since her brother's body had been found in Ørstedsparken.

"It had nothing to do with Jens. Nothing," she said, pushing the mugs over towards her guests on the other side of the dining table.

The living room was filled with heavy, worn leather furniture, too many green plants, and a handful of cats. Jette, Jens, and Jeppe, thought Torp. The latecomer had clearly become the nonconformist.

"Jens has been in a lot of messy business," she continued, "but that was several years ago. Jeppe has never done anything wrong. Do you understand that?"

She looked up, almost in despair. They understood that very well. Torp tried to explain that he had simply written what was true, that the police were looking for a connection and had fairly quickly reached the same conclusion, and that neither he, Katrine—he nodded over to his partner— nor the *Daily News* was responsible for what the *Express* or other fast media did. She could safely trust them. Torp saw Katrine's grimace when she tasted the coffee. It had been some time since the water had boiled, and the coffee's taste was a long way from the café au lait with organic Jersey milk she had just enjoyed. Jette Mikkelsen lit a home-rolled cigarette.

"Jeppe came by last weekend. He often comes by. He's good at that . . . was," she said. Her tired eyes began to glisten. "He said there was something wrong at work."

"Was he scared?"

Jette Mikkelsen shook her head. "No, I don't think so. He was more unsure about what he should do. Whether he was even right about it."

"Right about what?"

"He didn't say anything about that. Only that it was completely wild if it was true. He said that several times. *Wild*, he said."

"Did he say anything else?"

Torp ignored the smoke that hung heavily in the stuffy living room. The door to the balcony was probably closed because of the cats.

"Whatever it was, it was important. He worked for the Prime Minister, you know," she said with pride in her voice.

"In a way, he did. You could indeed say that," comforted Torp.

"Did he say anything else?" Katrine had finally given up on the instant coffee.

"He said something about South Africa and Nelson Mandela. *Like Mandela*, he said several times. But Mandela is dead, as you know."

"Yes, it doesn't make a lot of sense," said Katrine, getting up and thanking her for her time.

"Have you told anyone else about this?" Torp asked.

Jette Mikkelsen shook her head. "A lot of journalists called the day before yesterday. After your article," she said, pointing an accusing finger at Torp. "But not so many now."

"You know what, Jette," said Katrine, who had now completely taken command in the living room and put a long, comforting arm around her shoulder, "you just slam the phone down when they ring from now on. Now you need to concentrate on yourself and the memory of your brother. When is his funeral?"

She shook her head. "I don't know. Dorthe, his wife, is taking care of it. I daresay it hasn't been decided yet."

"Thanks for the coffee," Katrine said quietly. "We'll find our own way out."

"She was completely crazy," laughed Katrine when they were walking briskly towards the Metro station soon afterwards.

"She was sad," replied Torp, "and a bit crazy."

He laughed along with her, even though he didn't think it was totally appropriate.

Torp was quiet for a while.

"But *wild* and *Mandela*—he must have said something along those lines. It's not something she would just make up."

They arrived at the Metro.

"What is it that Arne Lund says? Gaga?" Katrine shook her head. "That story is dead, Torp. The *Express* won't be writing any more about it either. Dead, finished, done."

Torp nodded. She was probably right. He was about to hitch up his trousers but stopped himself in the act. A new habit. Instead, he stroked his hand over his right cheek, which was perhaps hiding more. He went through his body—from his feet, up his legs, stomach, chest, lungs, heart, neck, head, and out into his arms—was it being filled with small cancer cells that couldn't be killed? Where were they hiding? He had googled tumours in the mouth, about how important it was to get it looked at in time. Was he in time? Karen was unhappy that he hadn't gone to the dentist long ago, but how was anyone supposed to know? It was probably nothing. My God, the imagination had no limits. But there was actually a little pressure on the right side. The dentist had criticised him for not coming in time. Or had it just been a general remark that wasn't specifically aimed at him? Many people got a lump without it being serious, the Google search had shown. But for some, it had been fatal. It was about arriving in time, doing something about it as soon as one got suspicious. And that was now. He couldn't have come when he didn't have any suspicions. It would probably work out okay. Monday. On Monday, he would be notified when he should come in for his examination.

He got off at Lindevang Station; she was continuing into town. They wished each other a good weekend. It struck him then that he didn't have the faintest idea where she lived.

CHAPTER 8

I t was raining on election day, and the political commentators on the news channel agreed from the early morning that it would probably affect turnout negatively. On the other hand, the wildcard of a possible referendum on the EU as a consequence of the election would perhaps pull in the other direction.

Enough.

So not even the brainiacs on television could pack more reservations into their analysis, thought Torp, as he sat in the waiting room at Rigshospitalet, waiting to go in. The clever dicks were convinced that the Hasting couple's contra-campaign to not vote at all was a one-day wonder that wouldn't have much effect on voters.

"The 1970s called; they want Ulla and Poul Hasting back," as one of the commentators rather jauntily put it to everyone's great amusement. Even the studio presenter had a hard time holding back the laughter that would compromise her impartiality.

Torp's appointment for an examination had gone from nurse to doctor, from system failure to computer crash, and from misunderstanding to negligence. It was like trying to change a contract with a mobile network operator. In the end, he had turned up personally at the hospital the week before, had found the right department, and proclaimed that he wouldn't leave until he was given an appointment. Date and time. Less than five minutes later, a nurse handed him a small note: *26 September at 10:00.*

"Sorry," she said, wheeling out a long explanation about the lack of doctors and the pressure of work.

Before he had cycled down to Rigshospitalet, Torp had been into Frederiksberg Town Hall to vote. Karen would be voting when she got home from work at the private school. He had actually intended to vote for the Labour Party and its new leader, Pernille Hjort, but then swung over to the Liberals. Truth be told, he liked the Prime Minister, Palle Enevoldsen. On the other hand, he was opposed to the referendum on the EU, which the Prime Minister had reluctantly accepted in order to be able to continue. Then he had returned to the Labour Party, even though he had never voted for them before. But the Labour Party had also bowed to the demand from the Nationalists and the New Radicals for a referendum, so in principle, it was the same for both. It was once said that there was congestion in the middle of Danish politics. That was no longer the case. He stood hesitating in the polling booth for so long that one of the election officials finally stood up against the curtain and asked anxiously if everything was all right. Torp recalled an old anarchist friend who, as a young man, had studied the Danish constitution and voting rules and couldn't find a place that said how much thinking time a voter was entitled to. His dream had been to block the election result by sitting in the polling booth with books on philosophy and politics, which he would flip through to find out where to put his cross. When the most senior election official theatrically rang the bell at 8:00 p.m. and asked if there were *any more people who want to cast their vote*, he would, in contrast to a child on the potty at kindergarten, shout that he wasn't ready. The culmination was meant to be that they would have to report on television later in the evening that there was still a polling station where the election process hadn't yet been completed, which was why the general election wasn't over. *That way we dismantle the state*, his anarchist friend had laughed. Torp had thought it was funny, but still hadn't understood at that time where the anger against the fellowship of the national state came from. Furthermore, this friend had later been hired as a civil servant in a high position and had been there ever since. That contained its own irony, thought Torp.

"Is everything okay?" The official repeated the question.

It made Torp jump. It was. He folded the ballot paper in a hurry and put it in the box, which was duly secured with a clearly visible padlock. For the first time in his life, he had returned a blank ballot paper. That hadn't been his intention at all, but he hadn't had time to decide, he argued to himself, as he trudged through the rain down Jagtvej on his way towards his long-awaited appointment with the hospital service.

The short election campaign hadn't changed much either, in terms of positions or support. If the Nationalists and the New Radicals—who had been scornfully called the *City Radicals* during the election campaign because it was only in the big cities that they got votes—crossed the 2 per cent threshold, the two parties would propose a referendum on EU membership, a proposal that neither the Labour Party, the Liberals, nor the People's Party would oppose. If neither of the two parties crossed the threshold, there would be no one to put forward the proposal, which would thus be dead. This had finally become clear during the last round of the party leader debates, when the pressure was especially directed at the large People's Party. *Why can't you make a proposal for a referendum yourselves? Why do you need others to do it?* the two studio presenters wanted to know. The question had been asked over and over again and got the same political nonsense answer that had permeated politics because politicians lived in fear of seven seconds of their answer being clipped out and sent in a tape loop on social media without context and reservations.

"*We think there is every reason to be critical of Brussels and won't stand in the way of a desire to hear what the Danish people think.*"

"*But then why won't you make a proposal for a referendum yourselves—why should others do it for you?*"

"*We don't have anything against referendums as such, and Brussels is itself responsible for the criticism, which we otherwise share.*"

"*You didn't answer the question.*"

"Well, we aren't going to get any closer than that we think referendums can be a good idea, and the bureaucrats in Brussels have acquired too much power."

However, the dilemma for the People's Party was obvious. The party harboured an EU scepticism bordering on opposition, paired with a burning desire to become the governing party. These two opposing forces could only unite if others got the ball rolling—i.e., the New Radicals and the Nationalists. They weren't going to be the ones gambling with Danish membership. And if a referendum ended with a vote for withdrawal, it would be a national task for a governing party to make the best of it. The People's Party, as so often before, found itself in the best of both worlds without the ultimate responsibility.

Torp flipped through a newspaper covering North Zealand that was several days old. It was a quarter past ten. He should have been called in fifteen minutes ago. The nurse had said the examination would take a maximum of one hour, an ultrasound scan to see exactly where the lump was, and at the same time a sample to determine if it was benign or malignant. It was really just to be completely, totally sure that there was nothing seriously wrong. He shouldn't be worried, and the very regrettable misunderstandings that had delayed it all for a few weeks didn't *really* mean anything. Even though he didn't like the *really*, he had almost believed it. Torp had agreed with the *Daily News* that he wouldn't show up until noon and had informed Karen that he would be working at the newspaper in the evening, not necessarily because he had to write something, but more because that was how he had spent election night throughout most of his adult life—at the newspaper. She would go to a friend, where they would sit on the sofa together shouting abuse at the Nationalists, she had announced.

His eyes fell on an article inside the newspaper. The newspaper's local Hillerød page had an interview with Svend, his daughter's brother-in-law and the Nationalist candidate in the Hillerød constituency. *"A hundred thousand bureaucrats in Brussels are not going to rule over my liquorice pipes and cucumbers. We want our Denmark back,"* the candidate stated in the introduction.

"Ulrik Torp!"

He looked up. A nurse was scanning the waiting room.

He stood up. This was it.

"Why do you all call him Christian Crash?"

Torp was sitting back in *his* seat in the editorial office at the adjustable height desk directly opposite Katrine Taber-Nielsen. Christian Crash was celebrating his thirty-fourth birthday and had gone out to fetch cakes. After the first day with Simon the intern's seizure of the seat, Torp had started clocking in at the *Daily News* a quarter of an hour before the others. For some reason or other, no one sat down at Katrine's desk, even though she came in a little later. Simon's regular seat had, therefore, little by little, become the old desk without adjustable height. The hierarchy, or whatever it was that did it, was in place. Everyone accepted their role and position. It gave Torp an inner peace, and after a week, he was able to arrive at his normal time without Simon taking his seat.

How had Christian Crash got his name? Katrine shook her head. She had never thought about it. They were all sitting in their respective seats chatting. Torp knew from experience that the day of the general election was strange for both journalists and politicians. It was like waiting for an earthquake. You knew it was going to be intense. You really wanted to be doing something after several weeks of hard work, but there was very little to do before the evening. Now it was the almost 3 million voters' turn to do just a little. Politicians, in particular, were restless and nervous—all of them. For good reason, the interns didn't know where Christian Crash had got his name from—Simon probably because it was one of the few things he couldn't google, as Torp remarked, regretting it the moment he said it. Simon was actually talented and energetic. No one laughed either. Neckhair, the young reportage manager who during Torp's three weeks of work activation so far had revealed his competent side several times, knew the story.

"Christian writes about celebrities and semi-celebrities. A few years ago, he was obsessed with getting an interview with Gitta Kjær, the great diva of Danish theatre. She had a new lover and was about to dump her fourth husband. At least, that's what the rumour mill was saying, but no one—not even the established gossip magazines—could get close to even half a confirmation, and Gitta was completely impossible to get hold of."

Neckhair was enjoying the story and the attention. He sped up the narrative a bit, as he wanted to finish before the main character came back with the birthday pastries. Christian Crash had accepted his nickname, but didn't like it when people laughed at the story. He thought he had done his job better than most and felt unfairly treated by management afterwards.

Neckhair continued. "The rumours were that one of the weekly magazines was going to print that Gitta was leaving her husband for a new one, but without being able to say who the new one was. They had no idea." It was clear to see from the storyteller that he was now approaching the climax. "So, Christian is driving in one of the *Daily News*'s cars on Strandvejen for a completely different reason, and suddenly, he sees Gitta Kjær sitting in the car in front of him, in the passenger seat. A Jaguar. She kisses the driver on the cheek several times and is constantly stroking the hair at his neck, but Christian can't see or recognise the man. He *knows* it's her new lover, but he doesn't know who it is. So what does Christian do next?" The head of reportage looks around. "Can't you guess? Christian Crash!"

No one guesses. *Tell us now. Get on with it, man.*

"So he only fucking drives straight up the back of the car, doesn't he? Like, as it's waiting at a red light. With dents in the bumpers and all that shit. Gitta Kjær stays in the car, but of course the man gets out so that he and Christian can exchange names and telephone numbers for the insurance companies. And ta-daaaa—Hilmar Ytzen, shipping company magnate, multimillionaire, Gitta Kjær's lover and future husband, after they both got their divorces later. Welcome to the front page!"

"What did the newspaper say?" asked Torp as the first to regain his ability to speak after the whole group had finished laughing.

"It was just before Asbjørn Henriksen became editor-in-chief. That was Christian's luck. The old one agreed that the newspaper would pay the insurance excess and gave an official apology to the shipowner, both for the dents and for the story, which was a clear breach of his—and Gitta's—privacy. He kept a lid on the whole thing and gave Christian a written warning, which will be in his personnel file as long as he's at the *Daily News*. And that's it."

"Why didn't he just say it was an accident?"

"Because he was proud as punch, for Christ's sake. In Christian's opinion, he had invented a completely new method of journalistic research."

"Cakes!"

Christian Crash came in from the far end of the editorial office carrying two long cinnamon pastries as if they were royal gifts. The whole reportage group roared with laughter. What was so funny?

Ulrik had begun to think about his body and his limbs. Piece by piece. Were his cells slowly but surely self-dissolving on a long, destructive march? Were the incipient liver spots on his arms an expression of rapid death or slow death? He had expected some form of release or clarification at the long-awaited examination at Rigshospitalet, but it had turned into just a stepping stone to even more waiting time, even more uncertainty. Yes, there was clearly a lump on the right side of the jaw. The ultrasound scan showed that the tumour wasn't very large. The consultant noted by examining it himself that it neither bled nor had discoloration. That was a good sign. On the other hand, the patient's observation that it had grown in size was a bad sign, but it didn't have to mean anything. Did it hurt when pressed? Yes, a little. Hmm. No clear answers. No clear answers at all. Just, thank you for today and you'll hear from us as soon as we have the results. When? You'll hear from us. But it's the weekend soon. Yes, indeed. A tumour doesn't have weekends. A friendly smile. Goodbye.

In the afternoon, without much commitment, he had written a few minor and, from whatever angle, indifferent stories; a little for the Net and for that small part of tomorrow's printed newspaper that wasn't about the general election. Now and then, he glanced sideways at the television screen. The same commentators who in the morning had been rejecting any possibility of the Hasting couple's contra-campaign to abstain from voting having any effect at all had now imperceptibly renamed the campaign a "movement," in step with the turnout at the polls being compared with the turnout at the most recent general election. There was a striking decline, but, as one of the commentators noted, the weather had also been different both four and eight years ago. Many would probably vote later than usual due to the bad weather.

Enough.

Late in the afternoon, he received an email from Jette Mikkelsen. She had written several times to find out who had murdered her brother. Her desperation that no one was writing a word about the murder in Ørstedsparken anymore now matched her anger about the stories in the media in the first few days. Were people indifferent? No, there was just nothing new, Torp wrote back. Anton, his source at Police Headquarters, was able to tell him that they had absolutely nothing to go on. Roger. No more. A secretary in the Minister's secretariat had stated that in the evening, an hour before he was murdered, Jeppe Mikkelsen had made a somewhat strange and untimely attempt to have a conversation with the head of department or the Minister. So far, they hadn't been able to use it for much, explained Anton.

The new email from the elder sister was along the same lines as the previous one. Complaints, frustration, no one gave a damn. And then a little addition in the middle of it all: *Jeppe had talked about Mandela and South Africa, something with 1994. And then a Spang-Johansen in the old days.* It made no sense. Spang-Johansen? He decided for the first time not to answer. That's how it was with readers. At some point, you just had to drop contact, otherwise they just went on and on and on. People with a case and lots of time were the worst. Torp looked over at Katrine. She was concentrating on writing a story, sensed that someone was looking at her, looked up, smiled, and looked down again. He would miss her when the four weeks of work activation were over. Today was Thursday. Next Friday it would be over. He would also miss Simon the intern, the boy who wasn't quite so bad after all. And Emma. Not Neckhair. He looked around and was surprised by how quickly it had become normal for him to come into the newspaper again. And how it would stop in an instant next Friday. Should he buy cakes? He probably should. He had no illusions about being able to stay. Maybe a little temp work once in a while. He had decided to mention it to Arne Lund that he was available. *Torp Communication—competence and experience*—he wanted to find his business cards. There must be at least 980 left.

There was suddenly a smell of food. Torp looked up. Some of the Filipino girls from the canteen were rolling food trolleys into the editorial office. At the same time, an email came out to everyone that there was election campaign food in the large editorial room—pizza and chilli con carne. At Christiansborg, there would only be pizza. Cakes and sweets in the large bowls for the rest of the evening. The time was 7:00 p.m. There was an hour until the polls closed and the television stations' two major exit forecasts would be announced. Contrary to opinion polls, where people were asked whom they intended to vote for, exit polls were primarily based on what people had actually done, like Torp, who had submitted a blank voting slip without really wanting to. And yet . . . the blank voting slip had at least solved a problem for him.

"Can we trust the exit polls coming in a little while?"

Simon the intern looked up from his pizza. Grandma-Bente had scuttled in on their table and asked the question between two mouthfuls of chili con carne.

"The short answer is yes," said Torp straight off. "The long answer is that we almost can. The polling institutes have become super good at that kind of thing. They practically get it spot on by now."

He told them about some exit polls from previous elections which had missed by a mile. That was rarely the case anymore.

It was two minutes to eight. Everyone turned to the two television screens, each showing a different channel. On the stroke of eight, both channels went through to two different polling stations in the provinces. Two mayors rang their bells in Herning and Aalborg, respectively. *"Is there anyone else who wants to cast a vote?"* Pause, head to both sides. *"I hereby declare the election complete."*

Then came the exit forecasts. Everyone leaned forward.

On both channels, the forecasts were showing 2.1 per cent for the Nationalists and 2.0 per cent for the New Radicals. The Nationalists had flourished after the trouble on Kultorvet, but Annegrethe Hulsig had been caught in the middle of the election campaign talking of several billion going to foreigners, which didn't make sense at all. It had gone completely wrong at the party leaders' closing debate on television two evenings ago. Here she had mixed apples, pears, and bananas, so that it had eventually become embarrassing—even for her opponents. The core troops couldn't care less, but a number of people had obviously jumped off the bandwagon if the two exit polls were to be believed. From the outset, the New Radicals had had problems explaining why they were in favour of a referendum on the EU when they were already big supporters of the EU. That had also cost votes.

Both TV channels were with the Nationalists at Christiansborg. Here the infantry was trying to keep its spirits up; that wasn't so difficult— they were over the threshold, after all. Annegrethe Hulsig couldn't hear the questions from the TV journalists, but that wasn't so crucial. Her smile was genuine. Getting over the threshold was enough for her. *"Now we just have to have the proper result, but it's looking good,"* you could hear her shouting into the microphones. She seemed relieved.

"And what about the demand for a referendum?"

She didn't hesitate for a second. She never did. *"It's the same. If you want to be Prime Minister with our votes, then you have to guarantee a referendum on our membership of the European Union."* Again, she lit up with the smile that Danes had seen on the party's posters and on television in recent weeks.

Torp scanned the numbers. The People's Party had gone back; the Labour Party had got a minor slap in the face. The Prime Minister and the Liberals had made some progress—on both channels.

"The Prime Minister will continue," said Torp, almost to himself.

The channels were still with the Nationalists. Annegrethe Hulsig turned to her party members and shouted the battle cry they had become known for throughout the election campaign. *"What will we do with the EU?"* She sank a little at the knees, put her right hand behind her ear, and turned her head a little. *"Leave it!"* they obeyed, everyone clapping and laughing. *"This is a party night for democracy,"* she confirmed to the microphones. Both channels switched, one back to the advance studio at Christiansborg, the other to the New Radicals. The party leaders from the Labour Party, the People's Party, and the Liberals wouldn't be appearing until much later, when the result was certain. There was no jubilation among the New Radicals, just concern over the threshold. It could go both ways, and the question was whether the exit poll took into account the party's support in the major cities, as the party leader explained. *"We'll have to wait and see,"* he concluded. Back to the Christiansborg studio and analyses. Now they would have to tread water until the results began to come in. First the very small and, in the broad context, unimportant polling stations on the small islands, then "proper" polling stations, so that the exit poll was gradually mixed with real results and eventually completely eliminated in favour of real counts. Around 10:30 p.m., there would be a clear picture, explained Torp to his audience of Grandma-Bente and the interns Simon and Emma.

As the real election results gradually came in, both the New Radicals and the Nationalists slowly slid further down. The New Radicals were quickly on 1.9 per cent and looked as though they were remaining there. The polling institutes had apparently overestimated their support in the big cities, where the counts typically came last. With the Nationalists, it was more of a slow slide: 60 per cent counted—still 2.1 per cent of the vote; 70 per cent—2.1 per cent; 75 per cent—2.0 per cent; 80 per cent—2.0 per cent; 90 per cent—2.0 per cent; 97 per cent counted—1.9 per cent of the vote.

"It's definite," was the verdict from an experienced presenter on one TV channel. *"Neither the New Radicals nor the Nationalists will get into Parliament."* At the same time, it had now become clear that turnout was historically low.

Whether it was Ulla and Poul Hasting's contra movement or something completely different was unclear, but 72 per cent—a drop of more than thirteen percentage points from the last election, which was also low—was *"a historic slap in the face of democracy,"* as several commentators formulated it. During the round of party leaders half an hour after midnight, it was clear that Prime Minister Palle Enevoldsen would be able to continue. Like the other party leaders, he deplored the shockingly low turnout, but at the same time made it clear that there would be no referendum on Danish membership of the EU. He saw no reason for this, and the People's Party didn't protest, even though Annegrethe Hulsig used her last TV slot this time around to accuse them of hypocrisy.

The news ticked in on the international news agencies. No referendum in Denmark. No domino effect in other countries. In Brussels, commissioners and top officials were sitting up watching, as they were in a number of other European capitals. The Tokyo Stock Exchange would soon open with a slight rise in share prices, and the trend would hold as stock trading gradually awakened along with the sun all the way to New York.

Phew.

CHAPTER 9

Svend was annoyed. At first, he thought it must be a mistake. Despite the Nationalists' surprising defeat, he had at no point expected to be elected to Parliament himself. It was of course sad that the party, with its 1.9 per cent of the vote, had been so close. But that was how it was when you were up against the elite, the media, reputable society, the politically correct, the mainstream, the deep state, and power. Despite his brand-new political commitment—politics had never really interested him previously—he didn't really believe there was much that could be done about it. The elite was in power, no matter what you did; it apparently loved Muslims and Brussels, didn't care about Denmark, and insisted on conflict with Russia. Besides, he was himself very well situated, didn't lack anything, and thought, first and foremost, it had been important to give them all a punch in the gut. The whole bunch. All of them. A gut-buster. Election night had also been something of a gut-buster. *If it had lasted a few hours longer, we would have ended up with less than 1 per cent of the vote,* as he sarcastically put it, referring to the decline from 2.1 per cent of the votes in the exit poll at eight o'clock to the 1.9 per cent at half past ten.

But no, the worst thing was that he had lost the bet to Jonathan. He was sitting at the table in his brother's garden, looking at the box with the twelve bottles of French vintage wine—a fantastic burgundy, Jonathan had said—and with difficulty pushed it back to his brother.

The night before, Svend had helped count the ballots in the Hillerød constituency. He could already see that there weren't many personal votes for him. Did he really not have more presence? On the other hand, there was a good number of list votes for the Nationalists. All in all, the number of votes counted for the party during the evening came to 1,036, he had noted on his pad before beer and sandwiches were served for all the officials. That was okay. Hillerød wasn't the Nationalists' stronghold; it was outside the cities that the party attracted support. And most importantly, the 1,036 votes were just enough to win the 1,000-plus bet over his brother. So he would have to live with his small number of personal votes.

Right up until his brother's irritating, know-all father-in-law had checked the numbers online. They were sitting in the garden, waiting for Jonathan's gas grill and tasting the wine. Jonathan had admitted defeat, gone down to the basement for the twelve bottles, and, proclaiming "a gambling debt is a debt of honour," had put the box on the table with a thump that had overturned a wine glass.

"Nine hundred ninety-four," said Ulrik at that moment. He had gone in on his *Daily News* smartphone to the Ministry of the Interior's website to check the number of votes in the Hillerød constituency.

"Nine hundred ninety-four," Ulrik repeated, looking up at everyone. Jonathan stopped his gastronomic endeavours at the grill; Svend stopped in mid-movement; his wife looked at him; Karen and Sofie interrupted their conversation.

"The Nationalists got nine hundred ninety-four votes in the Hillerød constituency. Ministry of the Interior's numbers." Ulrik handed his phone to Svend, who stared silently at the small screen. Jonathan came over, still with the grill tongs in his right hand.

"But there were one thousand thirty-six," said Svend. He looked up at Ulrik.

"You must have misunderstood."

Torp experienced the unexpected pleasure of sticking the knife in and twisting it. For goodness' sake, he couldn't have cared less. But then again, he did. Even though it meant that his son-in-law would soon understand that he had won their mindless, trivial bet.

"The number here is bulletproof. Reported to the computers in Denmark's Statistical Institute and the Ministry of the Interior. There's probably been an extra count that you weren't paying attention to. They've reviewed all the ballot papers today to count the personal votes."

Here, too, Torp was twisting the knife. He knew the reminder of the low number of personal voices would strike deep.

Svend had refrained from participating in the counting of the personal votes, which—even the day after the election—had still not been completed for the whole country. It would finally be decided which candidates in the various parties had been elected to Parliament during the course of the evening. The numbers last night just determined how many seats for each party.

Svend, retiring parliamentary candidate for the Nationalists in the Hillerød constituency, continued to stare at Ulrik's mobile.

Jonathan started laughing, not very much to start with, but with small grunts that slowly worked their way upwards through his throat in ever-increasing spasms, as if he was already having difficulty breathing freely. Then he emptied his lungs in a roar of jubilation, which startled everyone present. His brother looked up with the expression of a dog that was being beaten with a stick every time the winner managed to fill his lungs just to empty them loudly again.

"Jonathan," tried Sofie, half-heartedly without success. "Jonathan."

Svend handed the mobile back to Ulrik.

"I simply don't understand," came the meek response as the victory dance around the grill was ebbing out.

"This kind of thing happens," Ulrik assured him, in an almost sincere attempt to comfort the defeated candidate. "Some ballot papers have got into the wrong pile. It is eventually discovered, there is a recount to make sure, and the numbers are adjusted. It isn't unusual. You just got an early number, Svend."

Jonathan had put down the tongs and now went over to the table, took his reacquired box of twelve bottles of vintage burgundy like an actor overplaying his role and, with a slightly subdued grin, placed it inside the patio door.

"Don't forget, no merlot." He giggled as he lit his arsenal of patio heaters so they could sit in a garden in Denmark on September twenty-seventh without freezing to death.

"They think it's a conspiracy." Ulrik looked at Karen across from him on the train on the way home.

"They?"

"Svend and his wife. Jonathan, too, for that matter. Half of the population. Not just in Denmark."

"Conspiracy. What conspiracy?"

"They believe everything is pre-decided, directed, and controlled. That they don't have a chance. That we're living in a sham democracy. That I'm their opponent."

"Aren't you?" she laughed.

"They never read what I write."

"That's probably why," she comforted.

"Have you seen Facebook? It's completely gaga."

Karen had certainly seen the reactions to the general election on social media and several of the new online media that had their own narrow audience. *The deep state strikes again. The elite continues. The people have been cheated again. The Muslim lovers hold on to power. Brussels has monopolised Denmark. Media witch hunt against the people. Denmark's last chance wasted.*

She, too, was surprised at the anger that was drifting around in parts of the population. She looked at her husband, felt sorry for him for a moment.

"I think many people are afraid, Ulrik."

"Afraid of what?"

"Of losing everything. Everyone is, in fact, just a single step from falling into the abyss."

Ulrik stared at his wife.

"Everything we go around taking for granted," she continued. "Everyday life, independence, self-sufficiency. Have you ever thought about how thin the line really is? A divorce, a firing, a traffic accident—a single unfortunate event can overturn even the most comfortable of lives." She took his hand. "We're fragile. Maybe it hasn't dawned on us until now."

"Do you mean us as in us two, or us as in all of us?"

She hesitated. *Both. We two are also fragile. You're fragile, Ulrik.* That is what she wanted to say.

"All of us," she said, dodging the issue.

He grasped gratefully at her evasive manoeuvre. "And so the answer is to be angry at the EU, responsible politicians, and media people like me?" He maintained her swerve and got away from the land mines between them.

"Maybe it's just a wish for answers which are a little simpler."

"If the answer is simple, it's the wrong question," mumbled Ulrik.

It was their stop.

She took his hand as they were walking the last bit home to the flat. It was nice.

He couldn't find them.

Ulrik had got up unusually early for a Saturday and had taken a shower, shaved, had breakfast, and drunk coffee in almost one same movement. Karen had stayed in bed with a book and was following what he was doing with bafflement.

"I can't find them."

He rummaged in the IKEA boxes in the corner of the overfilled bedroom.

"My business cards," he said, clarifying for the bedbound.

"Have you got business cards from the *Daily News*?"

"No, damn it," came the irritated response from down among the boxes. "My Torp Communication business cards."

There they were. In the bottom box, along with the old photos from his school days and exam papers from high school. Four small boxes; only one had been opened and it was still almost full. One thousand business cards: *Torp Communication—competence and experience.* The address was their old five-room flat, but the phone number and email address were the same. He took a small handful and tucked them into the inside pocket of his blazer. Karen lowered her book, stayed in bed, but looked at him quizzically.

"I'm going into the *Daily News*," he answered to the unspoken question.

"On a Saturday? With your old business cards?"

She was a little surprised, but happy first and foremost at the fervour in his voice.

"Just in case," he said, bending down and kissing her on the forehead. Then he was gone.

Torp stroked his right cheek and felt with his tongue without thinking about it. He hadn't been able to escape his thoughts around Jeppe Mikkelsen, the young civil servant, found in Ørstedsparken, forgotten even by the *Express* and without leaving any useful clues for the CID. Anton at Police Headquarters assured Torp that there were people on the case, but also that it was difficult. When ordinary people are murdered and neither spouse nor close family seem to be involved, then it is difficult, he explained. If Jeppe Mikkelsen had had a secret mistress with a rejected boyfriend, then it was certainly an extremely secret one. They hadn't been able to find anything: no suspects, no motive, no clues—the gun had no record. Nothing. At Police Headquarters, they were now toying with the idea that it was a random sadistic killing, that Jeppe Mikkelsen just happened to be in the wrong place at the wrong time, confronted by an armed idiot who wanted to play the big guy or maybe thought Jeppe was someone else. The *Express* quoted a police source as saying that it could have been one of the Muslim gangs who had taken out the wrong person. Anton categorically rejected that.

Jeppe Mikkelsen's sister, Jette, had insisted to Torp that there had to be an explanation. What was he doing in Ørstedsparken in the first place? Her mutterings about South Africa and Mandela made no sense. But this morning she had sent a new email. He had actually cut off contact, but she clearly hadn't. *Have you spoken to Dorthe?* she wrote. And no, he hadn't. Despite several attempts, no journalists had got through to the widow. She didn't express it directly, but Torp perceived the email as a sign that she wanted to talk to him and that she had something to tell.

Dorthe Mikkelsen, Jeppe Mikkelsen, Vilbert Mikkelsen. It was one of those nameplates with matchstick drawings of mother, father, and child above the names. Looking happy. Vilbert? She hadn't had it changed, of course. Some—especially elderly—people never did; he knew that. Torp took a deep breath in front of the widow's Nørrebro flat and pressed the bell. He could hear footsteps in the hallway.

What does a grieving widow look like? What should she look like? Torp watched Dorthe Mikkelsen while she fetched mugs from the kitchen cupboard and prepared to brew some thin filter coffee. The flat looked like a catalogue from IKEA. Nice, tidy, sensible, and devoid of personality. There were flats in Brazil and Australia that looked exactly the same, thought Torp: sensible storage boxes, sorted and in order, no mess. Should a grieving widow be living in a mess? Dorthe Mikkelsen looked like what she was—a young mother who was getting too little sleep. The sad sheen over her face and her passive eyes were the only things that revealed it wasn't just lack of sleep that plagued her. Was the killing of her husband the disastrous event that would cause her to go to pieces? Hardly. The boy who was sleeping in the bedroom right now would keep her going. In a couple of years' time, she would have met a new boyfriend, roughly the same type, and moved to a terraced house in the suburbs, he thought. She would get over it, and Vilbert would have a new father and a little brother or sister. The real tragedy within the tragedy was Jeppe Mikkelsen's parents. Their lives had also stopped that night in Ørstedsparken, not clinically, but without a real possibility of resuscitation. His mother might go into a depression, lose her job, lose most of her friends, and isolate herself in the detached house in Jutland. In six months' time, her friends would be thinking, and maybe even saying, that it was about time she moved on. Later, they would fall by the wayside. His father would keep his job, bitterly and silently get up every morning and come home again, outwardly resembling himself, but inwardly as dead as mother and son. That is how it would go, thought Torp.

"Do you take milk?"

Dorthe Mikkelsen sat down at the kitchen table and gestured to Torp that he should, too. He shook his head. No thanks. No milk.

"Jette says you're different." She paused, looking for a reaction from Torp which didn't come. "Different from other journalists, I mean."

Torp mumbled something. He didn't want to throw his profession under a bus. The others were just doing their jobs, even his colleagues at the *Express*. They just had different jobs. He could have said that.

"Your sister-in-law says that Jeppe mentioned various things in the time leading up to his death."

"I had a burglary the night before last," she suddenly exclaimed. "Vilbert and I spent the night with a friend on election night. When I got home yesterday morning, someone had been in the flat." She continued without waiting for any reaction from her journalist guest. "The door wasn't broken in or anything. But Jeppe's old laptop was gone."

"Have you reported it to the police?"

She shook her head.

"The insurance company?"

She shook her head again. "The computer wasn't worth anything."

"And you're sure the computer is missing?"

He looked at the plastic boxes on the shelf above her head—*recipes, winter*—and realised how superfluous, almost insulting, the question might sound in her reality. She ignored it for the same reason.

"The police were here right after they had found Jeppe. They took his home computer—it belonged to the Ministry. The old one is—was—under the boxes."

She pointed to a thick shelf behind Torp. *Photos up to 2018*, it said on one of the boxes. They had probably set up a new box for pictures after the birth, he thought.

"Did he use it?"

"Sometimes. He didn't really want private things on the Ministry's computer." She made a slight gesture with her arms.

"That's how Jeppe was." It was a character trait devoid of criticism. Torp was in no doubt about who in the family had pasted explanatory labels on the IKEA boxes.

"Do you have any idea who may have killed your husband?"

"I was actually going to ask you that."

"I have a good source at Police Headquarters. They seem to have no idea." Torp leaned forward in the kitchen chair. "You ought to tell the police about the burglary and the computer."

She again got the dull sheen on her face that revealed more than tiredness. "You're welcome to tell them. I don't have the strength anymore."

She poured more coffee for herself but forgot her guest.

"Was your husband behaving differently in the days leading up to the murder?"

Dorthe Mikkelsen ran her fingers over one of Vilbert's pacifiers lying on the table. She looked up.

"Something had happened in the Ministry. He'd heard something. He wouldn't say what."

"Why not?"

"Because he wasn't sure." She felt it required an explanation. "Jeppe was very strict about following the rules. He felt very strongly that things should be in order. I often told him things that my friends had told me in confidence. She was unfaithful, he was unfaithful, he had done such and such, she had done such and such. Things that I'd promised not to tell anyone else." She smiled. "Of course, I told Jeppe. He always said that everyone has at least one person they confide in and that secrets are therefore impossible."

She paused and let the next sentence sound like a quiet triumph, a tribute to her late husband.

"Except with Jeppe. He never told anyone else. Not even me when it really mattered."

She shook her head as if she were in the middle of a monologue without an audience, as if she was arguing her way to a conclusion about the father of her son.

"He wanted to be sure first. Before that, he wouldn't say anything. Not to me either."

"Didn't he say anything at all?"

"Not really. He was sitting at the computer over the weekend and suddenly exclaimed that it was like South Africa and Nelson Mandela."

"What was?" Torp tried to sound more patient than he felt. Get to the point.

"And then he several times mentioned someone called Spang-Johansen."

"It sounds like the villain in all the Olsen Gang films."

She responded with something that almost sounded like a little laugh. "I said that, too. But he didn't think it was funny. That was clear. And then he shut up."

"The police say that an hour before he was murdered, he tried to have a conversation with the head of department or the Minister. Does that mean anything to you?"

The widow shook her head. Vilbert began to wake up in the bedroom, not with a wail, but in a way that was as orderly as the rest of the flat, where everything was in place, except Vilbert's father. She got up calmly, fetched the eight-month-old boy, warmed a bottle in the microwave, and sat down again in front of Torp with the sucking child in her arms, all in one calm, gliding, sure movement. Was it really possible to have a child that way?

"But it must all have had something to do with the general election. That's for sure."

She looked at Vilbert as she said it. It made Torp jump.

"Why the general election?"

"Jeppe was in the department in the Ministry of the Interior that has to do with general elections, so it was probably not so strange."

She looked at him.

"Didn't you know that?"

Torp shook his head.

Vilbert sucked the last baby formula out of the bottle and had almost fallen asleep again. Torp thanked her for the coffee and the talk, handed over his business card *Torp Communication—competence and experience*, explained that the address was wrong, but the phone number and email were correct, that she was welcome to call or write if there was anything—no matter what—and left them sitting there.

* * *

Torp let himself in through the terror sluice at the *Daily News* with his temporary employee card. At the weekend, it was the security company that took care of the building. The guard stared so hard at him that he felt guilty. The editorial office was practically deserted so early on a Saturday. The news editor had turned up, along with a couple of sub-editors; otherwise, it was empty. Most of tomorrow's newspaper would be written by the Christiansborg editorial staff. Tuesday was the first Tuesday in October, and in accordance with the constitution, the country's Prime Minister would begin the parliamentary year with his opening speech. The day before, with a little pretence, a government coalition had been negotiated with the People's Party. Then, as expected, the party leadership had withdrawn at the last minute and dropped government participation. What remained was a continuation of what Palle Enevoldsen had previously called *a narrow, manoeuvrable minority government*. It was newspeak for a government that had no friends and could accomplish nothing. As the commentator Jørgen Høegh had written in an analysis in the day's newspaper, that was how the situation was gradually becoming in most Western countries where the so-called old parties still held power. The parties couldn't use power for much more than administration. It wasn't power, it was powerlessness, as the Hawk concluded. He wasn't completely hopeless.

Simon the intern sat at Torp's desk, looking like someone who had been caught with his hand in the cookie jar.

"Stay where you are," said Torp, while happily noting the twitch in the intern's body, which showed that he acknowledged the crime. Torp sat down at Katrine Taber-Nielsen's desk, directly opposite Simon.

"Now, we two are going to get googling and search the media archive, Simon. The keywords are *South Africa, Nelson Mandela, general election,* and *1994* in different variations. And *Spang-Johansen*."

Simon seemed to liven up.

"What are we looking for?"

"No idea, Simon. Just search."

CHAPTER 10

He hadn't slept in the same bed as his wife for a good many years.

They had agreed to maintain appearances to the outside world, not so much for the sake of the children—their adult children had long ago seen through the unhappy relationship and were actually indifferent. No, they did it for the sake of the country and for the sake of his political career. His wife agreed with him that the two things couldn't be separated. His fate and the fate of the country were deeply woven into each other. Even though they didn't share a bed, they shared a political viewpoint to the outermost decimal.

Admittedly, Hungary was a member of the EU, NATO, the OECD, and Schengen—for some time—but it was the fellowship in the Visegrád Group—Poland, the Czech Republic, Slovakia, and Hungary—that had prospects.

He led the group. The others followed as best they could.

Muslims were to be kept out, the Gypsies down, their own citizens up. The EU could certainly be allowed to give money to infrastructure and agriculture, but Brussels wasn't going to be allowed to decide anything, especially not how the judicial system was organised. Russia was a useful partner, despite what they said in the West. And any political opposition had to be responded to firmly, immediately, and every time.

That was the only way it was possible to hold on to power. It also meant that he should have something done about Imre Arany, his deputy prime minister, who had become excessively liberal in his views, a little too popular within the party, and far too happy with his friends in Brussels.

The Hungarian Prime Minister could hear her taking a shower. Personally, he liked to wait a while before taking a shower after sex, loved the smell of juice and pussy. How old was she? Under thirty, half as old as him. He had no illusions. Were it not for his position and generous use of funds, she would find someone else. So far, this one had lasted the best part of a month. The free evenings in his flat in Budapest's old town with a succession of women kept him going, recharged his batteries, gave him the strength to lead the country and the movement that was growing in strength—in Hungary and the other Visegrád countries, but also to a lesser extent in the countries of Western Europe. His nationalist and anti-Muslim agenda had a pulling power in the populations that the old politicians had very little sense of. Several of them were old friends from the liberal honeymoon period after the fall of the Berlin Wall.

They were stuck in that time. He had moved on.

Now she had finished showering. He imagined her naked, smooth body, still wet. The short, dark hair, her clean-shaven genitals, and her small, firm breasts. He got horny again but stopped himself. The evening football match which he had been looking forward to all day was about to begin.

It was Saturday. He could relax. He turned on the television.

She came out. "Shall I make a cup of coffee, darling?"

She knew that he didn't like alcohol. Coffee would be nice, thanks.

Then she brought it in. Wearing only panties and a tight T-shirt.

The match had started.

Could a Saturday evening get any better?

CHAPTER 11

When the leader of the opposition, Pernille Hjort, came up the steps at Marienborg, it was Prime Minister Palle Enevoldsen himself who opened the door.

He had increasingly come to enjoy the Prime Minister's residence in the seven years he had been in the post so far. If the government could stay the course for the new electoral period, then it could add up to eleven years in one stretch; the second longest since the system change in 1901. He knew in advance that he didn't feel up to that. It wasn't so much the packed days, the large numbers of conflicts, or the loneliness of a job where you are surrounded by people all the time. It was the responsibility; the knowledge that everything was ultimately his responsibility—crises, defeats, unfair decisions, refugees, prisoner escapes, terrorist attacks—everything that was serious enough ended up on his desk and required a decision from him. It was intoxicating at first, but it was also corrosive, eating at him a little bit each day. He had to find a way out during the term, in a couple of years. For now, it was a matter of changing some ministers in his narrow government, working out a tolerable relationship with the People's Party, which had after all accepted that he should continue as Prime Minister, and finally clearing as much as possible with the Labour Party. It was the last item on his list this Saturday afternoon, just two days after the general election.

"Come in."

He stepped aside and let her come in to shelter from the wind that had picked up. Autumn had suddenly arrived and the wind contained drizzle. Even though the sun wouldn't set until around 7:00 p.m., it was already as if it had thrown in the towel. Enevoldsen showed with a wave of his arm that they would be going to the right.

Hjort was on her way to the left, to the public part of Marienborg, where she had been to several meetings over the years—mostly when her predecessor as leader of the Labour Party had been Prime Minister for a single election period, and she herself had been Minister of Employment. To the right were the private quarters. Coffee, tea, water, and cake had been served at the sofa arrangement in the small living room.

"In the more than ten years I was deputy leader of the Liberals, minister, and one of Erik's closest political assistants, I was never invited into this private part of Marienborg," the Prime Minister remarked after they had sat down. "Not even once."

Hjort smiled. She knew the stories of his predecessor, his self-discipline, and awkward, complicated dealings with other people. Palle Enevoldsen wasn't like that at all. On the contrary. Neither was she. While politically they were each other's principal opponent, they clicked rather well, understood each other.

The Prime Minister poured tea for her and coffee for himself and pushed the sugar bowl over. She took half a spoonful. He remembered that.

"So you avoided the New Radicals," said Palle.

"And you avoided the Nationalists," replied Pernille.

They both laughed loudly and at length.

"Goodness me, what a bunch of idiots," gasped the leader of the Labour Party.

She had tears in her eyes after their shared laugh.

"My Nationalists were worse, though," protested the Prime Minister.

"You clearly haven't been in deep negotiations with the New Radicals and been dependent on their support."

Palle spread his arms. His Finance Minister had made deals a few times with the New Radicals, but no, he admitted, he didn't have her experience in exactly that area. He suddenly became serious.

"Can't we shake hands on never doing this again?"

Palle Enevoldsen looked at the woman who had tried, and would still be trying, to overthrow him politically. Pernille Hjort knew of course what he was referring to: their common genuflection in the election campaign, their commitment to guaranteeing a referendum on the EU to please the two small parties and an indefinable popular sentiment.

She reciprocated his seriousness. "It was so close to going wrong. Palle—we'll never do that again. Never."

They didn't have to shake hands, have witnesses, or write anything down. This wasn't an agreement between the two leading parties. It was a personal and confidential agreement between the two of them. As long as they were both leaders of their parties, it was a firm promise: no referendum on EU membership.

After that, they discussed the issue of the historically low turnout. Seventy-two per cent was still high internationally, but Denmark was usually close to 90 per cent. Was it a vote of no confidence, a middle finger, an expression of people not really caring? Or perhaps the opposite, an expression that there was confidence that the system and the politicians could certainly handle things fine themselves? If people really wanted something new, then they would surely have voted, wouldn't they?

"I wonder if it's the contra movement—Ulla and Poul Hasting's claim to fame," ruminated the Prime Minister. He was sincerely in doubt.

"You know Ulla—you were a minister with her," said Pernille.

It was, in fact, a question. What was she like, the old Redstocking who had gone the whole trip from one political extreme to the other? Hjort hadn't been a Member of Parliament when Ulla Hasting was a minister in the Labour Party.

"She's dreadful. They both are. That married couple only think of themselves. They've never seen a team lineup without making a plan for how it can be dissolved to their own advantage. Never."

"But you took her in when she left us. Didn't you know?"

"As leader of the Liberals and Prime Minister, Erik was obsessed with the idea of taking over your voters. She was part of that plan. He knew damn well what she was like. Everyone did." The Prime Minister paused. "And her husband. Those two have always been a package deal."

Palle shook his head. It wasn't something they could do anything about, and certainly not on a Saturday afternoon two days after the election and three days before the opening of Parliament. There was a bit of work for both of them to get to grips with.

"We've spoken with the Ministry of the Interior, and it believes that all the counts and recounts should be completed today."

Palle sighed; he had never been the big vote-getter, but on Thursday he had experienced a dramatic drop in the number of his personal votes. Pernille, on the other hand, was well liked by the voters, both her own—she had had a fantastic election personally—but also by those who traditionally voted for Palle Enevoldsen, as was indicated by the opinion polls that compared the two. *Who would you most like to have as Prime Minister? Who would you rather have as a babysitter for your children? Who would you most like to go and have a beer with? Who do you most trust on economic policy?* Those sorts of questions. She won them all, pretty much. She was younger than him, she was prettier than him, she was a new face in her position, sharp and direct, and she hadn't been in power yet.

Pernille Hjort would no doubt be brought down to earth one day, Palle Enevoldsen thought dispassionately.

"I'm expecting to go to the Queen on Monday with the new ministerial team. The government hasn't stepped down, but I have a few changes in my inside pocket."

They both laughed. Pernille was sure she knew whom he was referring to. The rumour mill at Borgen had been saying for a long time that the Foreign Secretary had become too weak. Old, indolent, and arrogant—he was lined up to be fired. The Minister of Social Affairs had been in a fight for a year with the spokesperson in the People's Party and was thereby politically incapable of action. Maybe she could be given another ministry. Finally, the young, ambitious Industry Minister was in trouble.

His wife had some business interests that he had taken into consideration to a striking degree in his ministerial decisions. It could develop into a real scandal. A quick firing could ward it off and perhaps allow the Minister to return in three to five years. The Labour Party leader thought those three might just as well use Saturday to buy idiotic gifts for their successors at the handovers on Monday after visiting the Queen one last time, but she didn't say anything.

Pernille nodded. She agreed. All in all, it was good to move on quickly. Moving boxes and rubbish bags filled the corridors at Christiansborg this Saturday, and the reelected politicians were already in the process of making plays for emptied offices that were better situated than their current ones. Changeover days in politics were merciless.

"It would be nice if we could be completely confident in foreign policy," Pernille contented herself with saying.

"We will be after Monday," the Prime Minister assured her.

There was an extraordinary summit in Brussels on Wednesday on the conflict in Ukraine and new sanctions against Russia, he said. Heads of government and their foreign secretaries would all be there.

And so continued the conversation over the next few hours between the two political opposites in Denmark. Neither of them dared to agree on the refugees, even though they didn't really have any big differences about the issue, so they didn't touch it at all. She wouldn't be able to take part in a tax reform, but a reform of social services and more conversion to renewable energy wouldn't divide them; on the contrary. They had both gone to the polls on a reorganisation of the hospital system and the responsibility of local government for prevention and aftercare. Cancer treatment in particular needed a major service overhaul. They agreed to find a compromise on the last sticking points during the autumn.

"In reality, we agree on most things," droned Palle.

"Don't tell anyone," replied Pernille with a smile.

They were both engine room politicians, enjoyed fiddling with the knobs of the welfare society, were familiar with most of them, had been brought up in the same youth politics culture, had both studied political science at the University of Copenhagen, albeit ten years apart, and lived less than 800 metres from each other in the Østerbro district of Copenhagen. What was it about a political system that forced them to be political opponents, wondered Pernille Hjort when she left the Marienborg she herself dreamed of taking over.

The Prime Minister remained seated in his private room after having followed the leader of the Labour Party to the front door. The sun was setting; he shuddered slightly in the chilly wind that came in over Lyngby Lake. The draught could be felt in several places at Marienborg. It was an old property that Supreme Court Counsel Christian Ludvig David had bequeathed to the nation in 1960. It looked nicest from a distance. Imagine if you had ninety seats for yourself, a majority, for an entire election period; just for one parliamentary year. As the current President of the European Commission once said when he was Prime Minister of Luxembourg: *We know exactly what we need to do to solve Europe's problems; what we haven't figured out is how we get re-elected when we do it.* Palle Enevoldsen smiled to himself. Think of all the things you could do if you didn't have to take your constituents into consideration, the eternal grouching about special interests, misunderstandings, and ignorance. After all, no one had suggested the voters be allowed to manage the construction when the Great Belt Bridge was to be built. Politics was also a feat of engineering—complicated, intricate, and dangerous in the wrong hands. It was basically unsuitable for democracy, the Prime Minister thought in his quiet and completely private moments.

He was hungry, alternating between asking the housekeeper to rustle up some food and continuing to work, or getting his ministerial driver to drive him home to Østerbro and have an evening free; he couldn't remember when he had last had one.

His mobile rang. It was the Foreign Secretary. Argh, he wasn't in the mood for him. No minister had ever been rewarded for arguing for his post. All politicians knew that. Regardless of the relationship with one's Prime Minister, ministerial appointments—and dismissals—were the only thing one could neither ask for nor comment on. It was a no-go zone. This applied to all Prime Ministers, and even relatively new politicians knew it. It couldn't, for Christ's sake, be that the Foreign Secretary—who had

had a fine political career but had dropped off fairly heavily recently—
was going to start with all that just twenty-four hours before he was due
to be fired. That would be too pathetic.

"Yes." The Prime Minister sounded just as short-tempered as he felt.

"Palle, it's Ingvar; sorry about the timing on a Saturday evening."

"Yes."

"My department head just called."

"Yes."

Palle Enevoldsen's "yes" became a little softer. He obviously wasn't
going to beg for a continued ministerial car, anyway.

"He's just talked to the ambassador in Budapest."

"Yes."

Now a touch of impatience was becoming perceptible in his voice.
Get to the point, Ingvar, you've become an old windbag, he wanted to say.
Instead, he let the pause fill the conversation.

"The Hungarian Prime Minister is dead. Found in his private flat
where he reportedly entertained his mistresses. Died in front of the television while watching a football match. Presumably a cardiac arrest. The
death isn't official yet."

Palle Enevoldsen didn't say anything. Ingvar continued.

"You know what this means, don't you, Palle?"

The Prime Minister knew immediately. This meant that Wednesday's
summit in Brussels could have a completely different outcome. Hungary's first man saw himself as Russia's voice in the EU. He would impose
his veto if the resolution and sanctions against Russia on Wednesday were
too far-reaching. After Italy's Prime Minister had been assassinated in the
early summer and the country had a new and more normal government,
Brussels had thought that many things would be easier. But the Hungarian Prime Minister had immediately and personally filled the political
vacuum. Now he was gone, too.

"The Deputy Prime Minister, Imre Arany, and I are old friends. We
became friends after the fall of the Wall, as you know. We went on holidays together in the nineties—our wives became friends, too. It's possible
to talk to him," said Ingvar.

Palle Enevoldsen knew all about that. The opportunity to agree on a sharp resolution and new, harsh sanctions against Russia suddenly presented itself. And his Foreign Secretary and Hungary's future political leader were old buddies.

Ingvar had suddenly had his political life extended.

CHAPTER 12

Ulrik Torp and Simon the intern were standing on the pavement listening to the noise from the party in the flat on the fourth floor. Torp was regretting his hesitant agreement to come here. There was drizzle in the wind and it was chilly in an insistent way—no matter what you did, you froze a little bit.

"You know what, Simon, I think I'll shoot off home anyway."

He was shivering. Karen had been more than positive when he had called from the editorial office and explained that he just wanted to have a beer with the intern.

"You need a change," she exclaimed.

Need a change?

"Nonsense, Torp. Just come on up."

Simon took his arm. Torp regretted it for the second time when they shuffled through the coat-filled entrance into the flat. The music was pounding from the living room, so Torp sought refuge in the kitchen with Simon, his life jacket in these unknown and troubled waters. A woman, slender and tall with a pronounced jaw and a charming smile, came towards them. She kissed the boy. Passionately.

"This is Torp—I told you about him." Simon had managed to extract his tongue from her mouth and turned to Torp. "And this is My."

"Hi, My."

"Hi, Torp. Nice to meet you."

She gave him an—in his opinion—excessive hug, which he tried to reciprocate. Another girl stuck a plastic glass with a reddish liquid and ice cubes in his hand. He studied it for so long that Simon had to tell him what it was.

"Aperol Spritz," he laughed in a loud voice to penetrate the music and the buzz of chatter.

Torp nodded. He had heard about the Italian drink and took a sip. It tasted awful. He listened to the music pounding from inside the living room and could sense from the kitchen floor that people were dancing. He recognised the music from Sofie's and Søren's parties before they had moved away from home. Or rather, he was well aware it wasn't the same music, but he was conscious that music had become like cheap clothes from Bangladesh with an H&M label in the collar—something that could be used a few times and then thrown out. It just sounded like the same music.

He looked around. What was this generation going to do when, in twenty years' time, it was sitting around a campfire and wanted to sing something from its youth? Torp felt even older than he was, and naked because he didn't have as much as a butterfly tattooed on his body. He looked around for the life jacket. It was gone. Simon had vanished.

Torp was alone in a sea of youth.

It was Simon who, a few hours earlier at the editorial office, had come up with yet another of his "maybe there's something in this." They had been sitting all day searching the internet—*South Africa, Mandela, general election, 1994*—and in the media archive without success. *Spang-Johansen* made no sense at all. They had tried all sorts of variations to no avail. They had rummaged around without having any idea what they were looking for, and Torp was getting discouraged, he who for a while had otherwise felt alive again. The bitterness was forgotten, the tongue against the small lump in his right cheek had paused, Jonathan was suddenly okay—my God. He could have many more years as an active journalist even without the *Daily News*. Ane in the job centre had just been doing her job, and the work activation was doing its job—it was fun after all, and important. They had laughed together, the boy and him, read articles and headlines aloud from each other's screens, drawn another blank, carried on. The hours had passed and the world outside disappeared. They took boring vending machine sandwiches from the canteen, which was closed at weekends, and continued working until Torp found his old self again early in the evening, spread his arms wide, and declared that *this is a waste of time*. Simon had insisted on spending a couple of hours more. The party he was going to didn't really start until 10:00 p.m. at the earliest. It was a mystery to Torp that parties didn't get going until such a late hour, but he knew the phenomenon from the time Sofie and Søren were living at home. It was one of several reasons why they had bought the flat.

Okay, another couple of hours, but it was really only Simon working now, at the keyboard he had had between his hands pretty much since he was born. His fingers danced away in the global library he had always been in, like a modern version of the library in Alexandria, which in antiquity, several hundred years before the birth of Christ, had tried to collect every publication and thus became the world's largest, and the leading centre for knowledge and learning. Now the world library was at the tip of Simon's fingers. He had access to it all. *South Africa, Mandela, general election, Spang-Johansen, 1994*—he just had to find the connection. Torp had, unnoticed, slipped onto Facebook when Simon looked up.

"Maybe there's something in this."

Torp removed Facebook from his screen and turned his despondent attention to the boy. It was 9:30 p.m. Wasn't he going to that party soon? It was far from the first time he had come out with his "maybe there's something in this."

Torp had no illusions. This had been a hopeless task from the beginning. Some remarks from that Jeppe Mikkelsen fellow, which his wife and sister had fixated on. You can say a lot, even just a day or two before you happen to meet a psychopath in Ørstedsparken.

Simon alternately read from and referred back to the article. He had found his way into the *Los Angeles Times*'s database, which, unlike Danish and most foreign newspapers, had registered articles dating back to the early 1990s.

"Does the *Daily News* have access to the *Los Angeles Times*'s database?" asked Torp in astonishment. The newspaper didn't even have a subscription to *The Economist* any longer. Simon gave him a wry smile.

"I have an online article from the *LA Times*. It's from May 1994 and describes the general election that made Nelson Mandela president. The article is about election fraud."

"*Widespread indications of voters casting ballots under the legal age of 18*," he read aloud, "*and scores of full ballot boxes coming from polling stations that didn't officially exist*. The latter is a quote from the chairman of the International Electoral Commission, the IEC." Simon looked back at his screen. "*Growing evidence of other polling abuses, compounded by computer sabotage . . . someone had 'tampered' with the computer program used to tabulate the vote totals*."

"Well now, election fraud in Africa. What's new?" Torp was having a hard time concentrating.

"Nothing," continued Simon, without looking up. He was completely immersed in his screen. "The chairman also says that it is hardly deliberate cheating, but just *monumental incompetence*. That's what he says." Simon laughed as his fingers continued dancing over his world library.

"The ANC gets sixty-four point seven per cent of the vote in the first free election where Black people can vote. The new Parliament elects Mandela as President, the whole world cheers."

The last bit was just something he referred to while finding what Torp was to understand was the culmination of his search.

"Here's an article a long time later. It's not online. This is a more detailed explanation of the election fraud, or an attempt at it, which had previously been dismissed as monumental incompetence."

Simon the intern was working as if he had no audience. He was completely inside himself, as so often when he was sitting at a screen.

"Some white computer idiots somewhere or other had changed the computer program so that it forwarded different vote numbers than it had been fed with. It would have shifted a few seats from the ANC, probably to the whites' National Party. Mandela became President in any case, but a few extra whites were elected to Parliament. It was discovered when the votes were re-entered and counted once more, and then the election could be approved with a thirty-six-hour delay, but enough time for Mandela to be elected by Parliament as South Africa's next President in front of the whole world. End of story."

Ulrik Torp had only been half listening. It was now 9:45 p.m.

He wanted to go home.

"They held back from making it public because the whole world was looking at South Africa. That election simply had to be in order, and Mandela had to be made President on the day scheduled. There was too much at stake. Therefore, it was initially dismissed as *monumental incompetence*." Simon paused and stared out into space. "Which in a way it was, wasn't it?"

Torp held his tongue against the lump in his right cheek. "What does that have to do with us?"

Simon returned to the editorial office at the *Daily News*; back to *the real reality*, as his mother had often called it.

"Dunno . . . it probably has nothing to do with anything. I just got caught up in it."

"Would you like to dance?" Torp was snatched out of his thoughts. My stood in front of him with a big smile. He had no desire to dance at all—wasn't good at it, and certainly not to that music.

"Yes, why not?" he heard himself say, letting himself be dragged into the living room.

It was mostly girls dancing with each other, he noted. Nothing had changed there, then. He tried to find a rhythm in the music and let himself fall into it as best he could.

"Simon says he's learning a lot from you." She grabbed both his arms and almost had to shout into his face. She slipped back into the music with no problems and came back to him after a few steps.

"He says you were once a spearhead."

A spearhead? Torp hesitated while hopping a little from side to side, more or less in time with the music.

"Thanks," he said, shouting back. The noise level precluded anything else.

They continued dancing in silence, but she kept smiling at him. He reciprocated as best he could. She was probably around the same age as Simon but seemed grown up. Looked like what she was—a woman. How could a boy satisfy her? He didn't understand the youth of today, couldn't suss them out. He could barely see who was young and who wasn't. They weren't interested in politics and newspapers. At least, they weren't members of, or active in, political parties, and they didn't buy newspapers and therefore encountered advertisements in other places entirely. That was one of the reasons he had been fired five years ago. Even so, Torp could see that they were politically engaged and well informed. They bought goats for people in Malawi through international organisations; they volunteered at hospices and nursing homes. They applied themselves to their studies and their work to a degree that his own generation hadn't come close to doing at their age. It wasn't their generation that was about to fuck it all up in the UK. It was the Britons of his generation and those who were even older who still believed the country was in conflict with Germany. *We won the war but lost the peace* was a slogan they could come out with seventy-five years later. In a way, they were right, but it wasn't Germany's or the young people's fault. When Torp sensed that a musical number was about to end, he thanked My for the dance, got another hug from her, hurried out into the kitchen again, and was immediately supplied with some more of the Italian dishwater. He looked around. Wasn't there any beer?

Simon had said on the way there that most of the people present would be a mix of journalistic interns from various media and recent graduates. Torp recognised some of them, which only made him feel even more exposed.

"Ulrik!"

He looked up. It was Neckhair, the leader of the *Daily News* reportage group. He was wearing a pink shirt and a blonde girl. What was it now, that rule with younger girlfriends? Half of one's own age plus seven years—otherwise you were a cradle snatcher. It was Sofie and her high school friends who had introduced him to the "nausea rule" several years ago. Torp knew that Neckhair was thirty-eight. He halved that and added seven. The girl should therefore be at least twenty-six if Neckhair were to be absolved. She wasn't a day over twenty. Maybe the nausea rule no longer existed, he argued to himself. A lot could have happened in ten years.

"Hi," Torp said.

What the hell are you doing here? they both thought. Neckhair got in first.

"What are you doing here?"

Torp explained how he had come to be at the party, hearing himself almost apologise for being there, without expecting the same apology from his interim colleague.

"You're finished on Friday, aren't you?" Neckhair asked.

Torp nodded. His four-week work activation was nearing completion. He had planned to have a chat with Arne Lund on the last day to find out if there might be an opening, perhaps a parental leave position.

"A lot has happened in journalism since you were young, right?" Neckhair swung his head around to indicate the people present. One of his hands was moving up and down the girl's back under her crop top. The other was holding a glass of Aperol Spritz, and it clearly wasn't the first of the evening.

"What do you mean?" Torp hadn't yet seen the attack.

"Well, just in the five years you've been totally out."

"What's happened then?"

"Everything happens a little faster, right?" Neckhair released his hold on the girl. "It can be difficult to keep up with the pace."

"Do you think so?" replied Torp.

From inside the living room, there was something that sounded like a quieter number. It was possible to talk in the kitchen without shouting.

"I don't have any problems, though," said Neckhair.

Torp was fully aware of what this was all about. Neckhair was unhappy that his reportage group had been commandeered during the election campaign and replaced by a job lot of interns, Christian Crash, Grandma-Bente when it was really tight, and then an old journalist in for four weeks of work activation sent by the job centre, enforced by HR. Only Katrine Taber-Nielsen apparently fit into his picture of himself as the leader of a group of journalists. The man was right, thought Torp. Something had happened to journalism when a fool like him became a middle manager and might at some point be in the running for a job as chief news editor. He involuntarily thought of Arne Lund, the old chief news editor, who sat in his cage every morning at seven with his overview, integrity, and forty years' experience.

"You're right," said Torp. "Something has definitely changed."

He didn't feel a need to say more than that.

He withdrew, as so often, put down his Aperol Spritz, nodded to the young girl, and went out into the hallway looking for a toilet, a beer, and Simon.

Simon was standing in the queue for the toilet. Another person in the queue handed Torp his can of beer when he asked where he could find some. It was an Aperol party—you had to bring your own beer if that was your tipple. The can had just been opened, assured the lad, who was studying political science, and whom Torp estimated must be in his mid-twenties, the same age as he had been when he was hired as a new graduate by the *Daily News* and they had had Sofie.

The toilet queue was discussing fake news. The US President's attacks on the established media had sparked a heated debate about what was true and what was false in the Western world. Could you trust anyone or anything at all? A gangly guy in the queue, with a large knot of hair at his neck, began to speak.

"Everything is a construction. Gender is a construction," he preached. "What is the truth, really?" he asked over the heads in the toilet queue. He seemed sober, thought Torp.

"Argh, not more stuff from your half-baked philosophy studies," exclaimed one of the others with a tone of voice that revealed that it would actually be okay to hear more from that quarter. Torp got an elbow in the side from the boy who had given him the can of beer.

"Wilhelm's reading philosophy. At least, he's enrolled for it."

Wilhelm spread his arms in front of an audience bursting for a pee.

"There are lots of concepts of truth," he began. "In the eighteenth century, Descartes believed that absolute truth must be independent of us, but at the same time accessible to us. It was also him who gave us *Cogito, ergo sum*—I think, therefore I am."

"Yes, goddammit, Wilhelm, you sure are," came a response from the queue. The others laughed. The eternal philosophy student laughed along with them.

"No, seriously. There are actually many truths. We can, for example, speak of a martyrological concept of truth. What one is willing to sacrifice one's life for is true. This is true for the members of Islamic State when they blow themselves up for a higher cause."

Wilhelm had now gained his audience's attention despite the music from the living room.

"There is also a constructivist concept of truth. Truth is a construction that we know is a construction. There is the authoritative concept of truth—what authorities say is true. Ask parents or schoolteachers if they think this is a good concept." He laughed. "Then there is the consensus concept of truth. What we agree on is true."

Wilhelm was exultant. His study of philosophy didn't always pay off, but when it did, it was important to take advantage of the opportunity. Several people protested. Some of them were trying in vain to follow his thoughts. Torp's beer can buddy shook his head.

"Sometimes it's possible to become a lot dumber by getting a little wiser, Wilhelm. A broken watch tells the right time twice a day, but you can't use it for shit," remarked an older guy in the background, who—Torp understood—was actually a philosopher. Everyone laughed. Wilhelm, too.

Torp felt a vibration from the smartphone in his inside pocket. He gratefully took a sip of his beer, while pulling out his mobile. It was getting towards midnight; it could be a text message from Karen asking where he had got to. Not as a criticism, as he knew. She was never like that. More to hear if she should go to bed or wait for him a little longer.

The text message was breaking news—*The Hungarian Prime Minister was reported dead from a cardiac arrest on Saturday night*. British Reuters was the source of the story, and it was emphasised that the death hadn't yet been officially confirmed by the Hungarian authorities. Torp wasn't in any doubt, though. Reuters was such a well-respected agency that it wouldn't dream of sending the bulletin unless it was completely true. He passed the news on to the toilet queue. A long discussion ensued. Even with Aperol Spritz in their blood, the desperate pissers were completely up to date on the Hungarian Prime Minister, his intense flirtation with Russia, his outbursts against the EU and refugees, and not least his repeated attacks on Muslims, even though there virtually wasn't a single one among the country's 10 million citizens.

"And he was a liberal and a hero of freedom right after the fall of the Wall. Isn't it incredible?" This was from the political science student, now minus beer can, who was shaking his head.

Then they began to discuss the consequences of the death. Torp just listened, agreeing with most of it. Initially, it would probably mean a moderation of Hungary's policy in Europe, perhaps also its domestic policy. But in the long run, it hardly made much of a difference. The Prime Minister was more a result of developments in the country than the cause of it. However, this conclusion—about cause and effect—triggered a major discussion in the queue. Finally, Wilhelm looked at Torp. What did he think? Were these developments determined from above or below? Was it a result of popular masses and movements, or was it triggered and perhaps even controlled by individuals? Torp almost felt that he should provide the final and correct answer to their discussion—not as the oldest amongst them, but as the one with the most experience. He thought about his interview at the beginning of the election campaign with Otto Brathenberg, the experienced, wise, old diplomat—and experienced, cynical, old politician. He had said that great changes in society come from above. Without leaders to show the way, the direction becomes so diffuse that the crucial event rarely happens. Maybe he was right. Would the revolution in Russia have led to anything but violence and chaos without Lenin? Would the Soviet Union have developed so demoniacally without Stalin? And on another track—would there have been a structural reform of local government in Denmark without Palle Enevoldsen? Maybe. Later. In a different format. Would Sweden have become a great tennis nation for two decades without Bjørn Borg? Torp leaned most towards Otto Brathenberg. Leaders indicated a direction that made it possible to act. That was his answer to the queue that had now moved so much that he was the next man. Wilhelm the eternal philosopher didn't seem convinced, but accepted the argument.

When he had had his turn in the toilet, Simon grabbed hold of him. They went into the flat's bedroom, which was furthest from the living room and where they would be least disturbed by the music. There was a couple lying there, making out innocently in the bed between the pile of overcoats. It didn't bother them or Simon, so Torp decided that it didn't bother him either.

"I've been thinking all evening about that business with South Africa and the articles in the *Los Angeles Times*," said the intern. "I can't get it out of my head."

"But what exactly did they do, did you say?"

Torp tried to be friendly towards his persistent partner. Simon took a short, pedagogical pause and looked the old man in front of him in the eye.

"There was once an employee of a Danish bank who had deceived the bank and its customers for several years without anyone noticing. He had transferred several million to his own bank account by rounding amounts credited to customers' accounts." Simon was trying in his enthusiasm to explain patiently. "Let's say we're talking about five thousand four hundred fourteen kroner and seventeen øre; he had written an algorithm which automatically transferred the seventeen øre to his own account. No one notices it, but he takes thousands and thousands of customers' seventeen øre, month after month—it added up to several million. And it was only discovered by chance."

Torp was still having a hard time holding his concentration. It was probably the fiftieth time today that they had discussed a possible connection which they had no idea about. Forty of those times were because of something Simon had found. The kissing couple in the double bed got up and left the bedroom. They obviously didn't think they could move onto the next phase with an audience. In a way, Torp agreed with them, without seeing himself as prudish. Simon hadn't paid them any attention.

"The fraudsters in South Africa had programmed the computer doing the counting in their constituency to change the reported number of votes for themselves," he continued. "Each time a hundred votes were reported manually, the computer program changed it to, for example, one hundred four. There were loads of polling districts and constituencies, and they didn't think anyone would notice the small shifts. Like with the banker and the decimals." The intern clapped his hands. "But when there are consistent shifts in the same direction, it adds up. It was probably only because of a meddlesome international election commission that it was discovered in South Africa at all. By the way, that was the year I was born."

Simon laughed.

"Then you can also go the other way."

"The other way?"

"Yes, remove some votes."

"Can you?"

"Of course," said Simon, "Then you just multiply the reported number by, for example, zero point ninety-six and give the votes to some others. It's a simple algorithm."

"So, for example, one thousand thirty-six votes can become nine hundred ninety-four."

"Yes, if you want. It's dead easy. You just have to hack the system."

CHAPTER 13

They were sitting in Simon's car on their way to Hillerød. Since when had it become normal for interns to have a car? Torp watched the boy, who was giving a good impersonation of an experienced motorist as he put the Polo in fourth gear and let the small engine slog its way up to 110 kilometres per hour. They practically had the Hillerød motorway to themselves this Sunday morning.

He had escaped from the party at two in the morning. It turned out that the eternal philosopher Wilhelm wasn't into Aperol Spritz either, but on the other hand was very generous with the cut-price canned beers he had brought in copious quantities. Torp, without fully being able to understand the reason why, had in return given him his business card and explained that the address was incorrect, but telephone number and email correct. *Torp Communication—competence and experience*; Wilhelm had slightly nasally read it out loud and then put the card in his pocket, a pact between the two—the intellect and the experience, as he explained it, after which he doled out the obligatory hug to his buddy. It had actually been really pleasant, Torp had assured Karen as he had slid in to join her in the double bed with no chance of not waking her up. She mumbled and immediately fell asleep again, but he couldn't sleep. He thought of Simon's story of the banker who became a millionaire by rounding down the decimals. He thought of the election of Mandela and the advanced and, at the same time, amateurish attempt at electoral fraud with an algorithm in the computer system. Simon had become enthused, but also showed his youth when Torp had carelessly mentioned the bet his son-in-law had made with his brother to get over or under 1,000 votes in the constituency—and then told him about how the brother, Svend, first thought he had won, but the next day had to admit his defeat when he saw the final figures on the Interior Ministry's website.

"Can't you see? It's like in South Africa," Simon exclaimed, breathing Aperol Spritz straight into Torp's face.

The music had stopped by that time after several furious complaints from neighbours and a single friendly attendance by law enforcement.

That was too far out, Torp had argued. This is Denmark. But he had agreed to spend Sunday doing one final check. He might as well—it was his last weekend as an employee at the *Daily News*; for now, at least.

My, Simon's girlfriend, opened the door when Torp arrived. She gave him a new hug. Torp was getting used to it, but thought it was weird. They hardly knew each other, it was Sunday morning, and he was only going for a drive with her boyfriend.

The intern lived in a flat the same size as Torp's. Simon had suggested picking Torp up on the way, but that had been rejected very firmly. Torp didn't want to reveal his own two-room flat; he would rather take the Metro to Simon on Amager and continue from there.

My walked unaffectedly around the flat in knickers and a pre-washed and very small T-shirt. Even with morning hair and a hangover, she was beautiful, thought Torp. He had been seated on a wobbly chair in the kitchen with a cup of instant coffee, watching Simon, who was drinking cola with his oatmeal. The boy hadn't shaved, which didn't really matter.

They worked off both the tiredness and the hangover in the car with silence and the radio. The death of the Hungarian Prime Minister had been confirmed by the authorities, as had the fact that the Deputy Prime Minister would be taking over for the time being.

A political commentator was playing the wise guy over what would be in the Danish Prime Minister's speech when Parliament opened on

Tuesday. Torp thought it sounded just like him ten to fifteen years ago. Tightening up on immigrants, tax reform, and health care reform; she expressed it in simple, quick sentences. Torp would have said pretty much the same thing—also ten to fifteen years ago.

A ditched Member of Parliament for the New Radicals was interviewed.

"Personally, I had a better election than four years ago. But I'll still continue in politics," she explained. The presenter gently corrected her. All Members of Parliament for the New Radicals had lost ground at the election—including her.

"In any case, the New Radicals will be more needed than ever if the climate and consumption aren't going to ruin everything for us," she insisted.

Torp looked at his intern. They were both paying attention to the exchange on the radio. The journalist was right; all the Members of Parliament for the New Radicals had lost votes, which wasn't so strange. At the election four years ago, the party had received almost 3 per cent of the vote. This time it was 1.9 per cent.

Simon swung off the motorway when Torp told him to. They had reached Hillerød. Torp found the address on the road map in his smartphone and navigated the last bit out to a newly built residential area on the outskirts of the town.

Thursday's parliamentary candidate for the Nationalists was clearly surprised to see his brother's high and mighty father-in-law standing at his front door with a boy.

"Had a bit of a late night," he exclaimed, as if he owed them an explanation for his boxer shorts, bare belly, and morning hair on a Sunday morning at—oh yes—almost lunchtime. There were empty wine bottles and washing-up in the kitchen. The dining table and the coffee table in the modest terraced house both had glass tops with steel frames. The chairs were high-backed, the sofas deep. All in black leather. Torp and Simon sat on the big sofa, Torp with a feeling of never being able to get off it again, while Svend got to work on the coffee. His wife—the blonde, not quite natural—was nowhere to be seen. The door to what must be the bedroom was closed. She was probably sleeping it off.

"Jonathan and your Sofie were here last night with some others. Those twelve bottles, you know. *A gambling debt is a debt of honour.*"

Svend was trying unsuccessfully to sound like his brother. He coughed up some morning mucus, wanted to light a cigarette, but changed his mind in deference to his guests. He put the coffee and cups on the coffee table and pulled on a crumpled T-shirt. He then sat down on a leather-covered footstool, leaned forward, spread his legs, and faced his two guests. They were only separated by the huge glass table, and Svend looked defiantly at them.

"Now then, what is it you two want to tell me about my election result on Thursday that you think is so crucial?"

Svend immediately understood what it was all about. He worked in IT himself, agreeing with Simon that such an algorithm would be easy to write. The hard part, of course, was getting into the system. But if the Russians could hack into the American election and into presidential candidates, it could probably also be done in Denmark.

"Does that mean I won my bet with Jonathan anyway?"

He gave a crooked smile to show that in the bigger picture, it was of course a minor added bonus, but still a bonus.

Torp tried to dampen Simon's enthusiastic look with his own. There was absolutely no certainty that this was true. It was still a long shot.

"The reason we've come, Svend, is that we must begin by becoming more certain about the counting of the Nationalists' votes in the Hillerød constituency on election night. We need to get hold of some of the other officials so we know exactly what happened. There could be a minor error in many places in the system. Where were you on the night?"

"At the largest polling station in the municipality, Frederiksborg Centre. There are over six thousand voters registered there." Svend looked up. "But there are about fifteen polling stations in the municipality alone. It'll be completely impossible to get an overall view."

"Exactly," said Torp.

"Does each polling station report the vote totals to the Ministry of the Interior, or do the polling stations report to the constituency, which then forwards the numbers to the ministry?"

Svend thought Simon was asking him and looked completely lost.

"I have no idea. Listen," he said, "I was just a parliamentary candidate for a small party and this was my first time. I don't know about that sort of thing. Annegrethe Hulsig was standing in the larger constituency. She was supposed to be the one elected in North Zealand."

Torp took over. He had been working on these matters all his adult life except for the last five years.

"It's no longer the Ministry of the Interior itself that processes the figures on election night. Statistics Denmark has taken over, but never mind that." Torp shook his head. "There are almost fourteen hundred polling stations at a general election." He could see that they thought it sounded like a lot. "Yes, in the old days, there were a lot more. When I say the old days, I mean before two thousand seven and the structural reform."

Simon said, "Each polling station reports via Statistics Denmark to the Ministry of the Interior. First electronically, then over the phone. It all immediately goes onto the Ministry's website and to the media. The Danish electoral system is enormously transparent. There are about fifty people sitting in the ministry working on the numbers on such an evening," he concluded.

Simon continued, this time addressing Svend.

"Who gave you the number during the evening? The one thousand thirty-six votes for the Nationalists?"

Svend shook his head. He needed some breakfast, fluids, and a headache pill. He couldn't remember. It had been a little confusing and they were going to have sandwiches when it was all counted. It had been a really nice evening.

"Who was in charge of the officials in the Frederiksborg Centre, where you were?" asked Torp.

Svend seemed completely lost momentarily.

"It was the mayor. Hanne Østergaard from the Labour Party."

The mayor answered her phone right away. That was the advantage of mobiles and Sundays. No, she couldn't remember how many votes the Nationalists got in the Hillerød constituency; he could surely find that out on the Ministry of the Interior's website. No, she didn't have any notes from the election night counts; what was he actually trying to get at? It was actually the Sunday after a tough election campaign, her first day off in more than a month. And no, the number 1,036 didn't mean anything to her—have a nice day.

Torp carried on calling several of the officials that Svend remembered he had eaten sandwiches and drunk supermarket beers with on election night. His two-man audience in the terraced house in Hillerød followed him, full of suspense. The voices on the phone were all different variants of the mayor until he came to an elderly woman who represented the New Radicals. She didn't know anything about the numbers for the Nationalists.

"But I have written down the number for my own party. We received eight hundred fifteen votes in total in the Hillerød constituency." She sounded proud, both about her quick reply and about her party which, like the Nationalists, had ended up just below the threshold. "It wasn't an easy election campaign for us, but the grassroots work has always been the most important—for me, at least," she explained, and began talking about all the grassroots activities she had been engaged in for three decades.

Torp was only half listening. Sitting with Svend's laptop, he immediately accessed the Ministry's website and found the Hillerød constituency. He interrupted her somewhere between a women's camp and a nuclear march.

"According to the Ministry of the Interior, the New Radicals received seven hundred eighty-three votes in the Hillerød constituency."

"According to who?"

"According to the Ministry of the Interior. That's the official election result."

"That's not true. We got eight hundred fifteen."

"Are you sure?"

"Absolutely." She laughed. "We were all together at my house yesterday for lunch, where we compared numbers."

"Who are *we*?"

"All the officials from the New Radicals in the constituency. It's actually some of the small polling stations that gather the most votes for us.

Frederiksborg Centre, where I was sitting, didn't give many, but I knew that in advance."

"Are you completely sure?"

"Yes, of course. That's what I'm saying." She sounded a little annoyed at having the question repeated. "Is there a problem?"

Torp assured her that there was no problem, that he trusted her numbers, thanked her very much, and apologised for disturbing her.

Susse had emerged from her sleep. She was prettier than her husband when fresh out of bed, thought Torp. She said a polite hello but didn't seem to be particularly interested in the men's conversation. After making one more jug of coffee and finding a Swiss roll, which she placed on the glass table, she started tidying the kitchen without saying very much. She, too, was clearly affected by her husband's gambling debt from the night before.

Torp asked Svend to find the names and telephone lists of all the Nationalists' delegates and general election candidates. Then Torp and Simon started working their phones.

Sorry to disturb you. It's the Daily News. *Did you help count the votes on election night? Did you write down what your party got? Have you seen the official figure on the Ministry of the Interior's website? Is there anything you have been surprised about? No, we're just asking because there may have been some irregularities. Ah, that was a shame. Okay, then, I'll try him. Thanks for your help. Not at all, it was a great help.*

That's how they rang round for three hours. Svend lost interest at one point, took a shower, served more coffee, and found another Swiss roll—raspberry from Dan Cake. There are ninety-two constituencies in the country. In addition to the Hillerød district, they had made contact with twenty-four. Svend's list was neither complete nor updated, and it was far from everyone who picked up the phone as midday on Sunday turned into late afternoon. Simon gathered the notes together.

"Twenty of the constituencies have no idea what we are talking about or don't understand it. Two general election candidates had certainly been a little puzzled. They were sure that the party had received more votes on the evening itself, but trusted the Ministry's figures and didn't have specific numbers themselves. Just thought so. The delegates from the last two—smaller—constituencies were totally sure—as in *totally*. The Ministry's figures didn't tally with their own; seven hundred sixty-six votes for the Nationalists had become seven hundred thirty-five at the Ministry in one of the constituencies; thirteen hundred fifteen votes had become twelve hundred sixty-two in the other."

"But why haven't they said anything?" Svend asked.

Svend had again sat down at the coffee table, which was overflowing with papers, coffee cups, and the remains of what was now the third Swiss roll from Dan Cake. Torp could feel his stomach rebelling against not having had any real food all day. It was almost 5:00 p.m.

"Because they weren't worried about it. So why check the Interior Ministry's website? You didn't do that either," Torp pointed out.

"But we were so close to the threshold—one point nine per cent. We only needed five thousand votes, according to the newspapers." Svend looked completely lost.

"And then forty or fifty votes don't mean anything. Like the banker with the roundings down," Simon said. The last comment didn't make Svend any the wiser.

"But these are only the figures from two of the Nationalists' constituencies," Torp said. "Three, including Hillerød. It isn't much to draw a conclusion from."

Torp bit his lower lip. He didn't know what he had been hoping for. Yes, come to think of it, he actually knew very well. To begin with, he had, very unlike a journalist, hoped that there was no problem at all; secondly, that it would be easy to clarify. Three out of twenty-five. A few hundred votes. Meaning that it wasn't enough. Besides, it all seemed so unlikely. Election fraud was something that happened in other countries: South Africa, Russia, banana republics. And if something like that had happened in Denmark, was it the Russians, just as they had tried in the USA, France, and Germany? Why Denmark? What in the world could be the point of that? And if it wasn't the Russians—that is, if it was anyone at all, Torp warned himself—then who could it be? Opponents of the Nationalists? The woman from the New Radicals in Hillerød was also totally sure. It wasn't many votes, probably just a coincidence. But they hadn't followed up on that trail at all. Should they? Should he go to his chief news editor, Arne Lund? Maybe the editor-in-chief, Asbjørn Henriksen? That would be completely out of the question. They didn't have nearly enough to go on. He could see that Simon the intern was almost thinking of himself as Woodward or Bernstein from the *Washington Post*, the men behind the Watergate revelations and the reason why Torp himself had become a journalist. Imagine being able to overthrow Nixon—the President of the United States, the most powerful man in the world—with a typewriter. He had wanted his fingers on a typewriter, too, and had successfully applied for admission to the School of Journalism. Torp wasn't so sure that the typewriter could perform the same magic tricks today. Or rather, he was sure it couldn't. In some ways, that was good. In other ways, it was a disaster. If words and facts aren't able to challenge those in power—then what? No, it wasn't nearly enough. It could be anything from coincidence to sloppiness. *Monumental incompetence*, as they had called it in South Africa. Maybe this was a scandal in the Ministry of the Interior or in Statistics Denmark. Sloppiness, which could cost an office manager their job. Maybe the Minister, if he bungled it, which he certainly wouldn't, thought Torp. He was a smart cookie. Would he even be continuing? Presumably. Prime Minister Palle Enevoldsen could continue with the same government. The People's Party wouldn't dare bring him down. Thoughts were swarming around Torp's brain, cutting in, running back and forth. The story was obvious—it couldn't be a coincidence. Then he mentally shook his head—how could he believe such a thing? On three random sets of numbers.

"Arne Lund will just laugh at us—best-case scenario," said Torp as they sat in Simon's Polo on their way back to Copenhagen.

It was evening, and now he could just about make out that his partner hadn't shaved ten hours earlier. Svend had stood in the doorway of the terrace house and waved goodbye. A slightly touching sight, thought Torp. He had come to like the brother of his son-in-law a bit; he seemed so helpless as an amateur politician when the banal slogans were peeled away. Was he insecure and afraid, as Karen thought? Maybe. Or maybe he was just confused like everyone else.

Torp had given him his business card on the stairs and assured him that the telephone number and email were correct, even though the address was different. The last bit was unnecessary. Svend had visited his brother and Sofie several times when they lived in what was then the flat he and Karen had bought for Sofie to live in. Svend was welcome to call him if anything occurred to him.

"This story is way too thin, Simon. There is no story."

Simon took a bite of his burger while steering the Polo with his knees. They had gone into the nearest McDrive to suffocate some of today's three Dan Cake Swiss rolls, which hadn't worked on the morning hangovers at all.

"I'm sure Woodward also said that to Bernstein," said the intern.

"Woodward was the brain, Bernstein the writer," replied Torp.

"What am I, then?" He laughed.

"You're the intern, Simon. And I'm in job centre activation. We're a pretty couple, us two."

They laughed at each other between french fries, burger leftovers, and cola.

"Seriously though, Simon," continued Torp. We're nowhere near having a story. We don't mention this to anyone. And certainly not Arne Lund."

"So is he Ben Bradlee?" Simon laughed again.

Torp was pleasantly surprised that he also knew who had been the editor-in-chief of the *Washington Post* during Watergate, the man who, along with the newspaper's owner, Katharine Graham, had withstood enormous pressure for several years about the revelations which ended up overthrowing the President of the United States and—for a while— changed American politics and journalism.

"Arne Lund is a rock, Simon. When everything else is sliding, stick with Arne Lund."

The intern nodded. He understood that there was no story. That this was Denmark and not South Africa. That coincidences weren't the same as revelations. That sloppiness wasn't the same as fraud.

"Where do we go from here?" Simon wanted to know.

"Roughly speaking, there are two ways to research dangerous journalism."

Torp was preparing for a little intern tutorial. Simon briefly turned his face away from the direction of travel. He was ready.

"You can be very careful not to reveal to anyone what you are working on. Keep all your cards close to your chest about your sources. That's the classic way."

Simon nodded.

"And then there's the meterman method."

Simon sensed he wasn't meant to ask anything. He should just listen, so that's what he did.

"It comes from American journalism," continued Torp. "A meterman is—or was—the man who went from house to house reading gas and electricity meters. In order for people to know to lock their dogs inside or not to think it was a thief on the prowl, they would shout 'meterman, meterman' out loud to announce their arrival."

"And?" said Simon.

"Sometimes it is simplest and most effective as a journalist to shout 'meterman.' Here I am, this is what I know, and now you're going to answer my questions. There's no need to make it too complicated."

There was silence in the little driving compartment, except for the small, worn-out engine that was struggling to get back to Copenhagen.

"We just don't know who to shout it to," he said to conclude the tutorial. They had arrived at Frederiksberg.

"It's been a great weekend. Thanks, Torp."

Torp stuffed the last bite of the burger in his mouth to suffocate a lump in his throat—just a little one. And yes, Simon could just drop him off here on the corner of Peter Bangs Vej and Dalgas Boulevard. He didn't have to drive him to the door.

In five days, his time would be up at the *Daily News*. The work activation would be over and probably so would his days with the *Daily News*. Back to endless days with no real content and unstructured surfing around the internet. Back to the stalemate and the oppressive bitterness that had largely disappeared in recent weeks. Maybe he should write a novel. Karen had often encouraged him to do so, but about what? He didn't have anything to tell. Most journalists had at least one bad novel in them, as was scornfully said in "proper" writer circles. He had no ambitions to contribute to that idle talk. Torp pressed his tongue against the lump in his right cheek, all the way down to his jaw. Maybe Rigshospitalet would have the result of his test tomorrow.

He was still hungry.

CHAPTER 14

Katrine Taber-Nielsen allowed the red wine to oxygenate in her mouth, slurping it gently before swallowing.

"I love Austrian red wines," she exclaimed. "Don't you?"

She leaned over towards Ulrik Torp. They were sitting in the wine bar next to the Ministry of Employment just across the road from Christiansborg, where everyone was preparing for the opening of Parliament the following day. The sun was setting, the weather was noticeably better than the weekend's drizzle and wind, but there were still limits to what could be expected in late September. Some people were using thick blankets to defy the calendar and the latitude at the wine bar's tables down by the canal. Ulrik and Katrine were in no doubt. They wanted to be inside, also to avoid the sidelong glances after their slightly too dramatic arrival. Torp had gone on ahead before she came cycling at high speed on her Biomega bike, a Copenhagen designer bicycle that was trying to turn two wheels, pedals, and chain into a political manifesto for almost 10,000 kroner. Somehow or another, it had succeeded.

Torp recognised the bike as the same type as that which one of Karen's friends had also acquired in between a period of intense interest in meditation and one of fervent, but fortunately for her children, short-term resistance to child vaccinations. Was she like that, his temporary colleague at the *Daily News*, whose company he had come to increasingly appreciate? Maybe it was just a bike for her.

Suddenly, Katrine had slid on the slippery cobblestones in front of the wine bar and toppled over. Luckily, she hadn't been travelling all that fast, so she had escaped unharmed—the bike had got a slight dent on the front mudguard.

They had quickly gone inside.

Torp, who was sitting here for the first time in more than five years, nodded to a few old acquaintances. The wine bar was a popular meeting place for politicians, political journalists, spin doctors, and civil servants. It was close to Christiansborg and most of the ministries, and the place was so expensive that you didn't have to put up with outsiders. Political secrets were rarely exchanged here. The atmosphere was open, noncommittal, and relaxed, as it can be only amongst like-minded people.

Torp felt for a brief moment that he was at a barbecue evening and wine tasting with his son-in-law. He oxygenated the Austrian speciality between his lips, swallowed, and nodded. Yes, it tasted really good. But hardly good enough to justify a price of 500–600 kroner. And Katrine had probably ordered one of the cheaper ones. There was a "board" in front of them. A "symphony," as the owner had explained, of Italian sausages and Danish cheeses. Torp couldn't remember a word of the explanation of the individual parts of the symphony, but he had to admit it tasted good. He dipped the bread in the olive oil that came in a small clay carafe.

They had been working late at the *Daily News*, a little unusually until well after 4:30 p.m. A briefing from management on yet another threatening round of cost-cutting and a subsequent union meeting had delayed everyone's work. The newspaper was still losing money, not only because the readership was declining, as it had been for decades, but more because the lack of advertising was leaving gaping holes in the budget. Several of the adverts that were left were retail ads that Torp knew were being sold for a tenth of what a full-page ad cost in "the old days," which wasn't so terribly long ago. Half price on veal. There would soon be half price on everything. The newspaper's board was going to meet on Friday and make the final decision.

Katrine had insisted that they should go into town and that it should be the wine bar. She clearly knew that Torp's finances as an unemployed person on work activation weren't up to that kind of place, so she immediately decided that since the idea was hers, so was the bill.

"You can pay another time," she said, brushing him off and thus preserving his dignity.

They both knew that it was unlikely there would be another time unless he got an opening at the *Daily News* and she stayed at the newspaper for a long time, both of which seemed unlikely.

Today's announcement from management that savings of 30 million had to be found really quickly didn't leave much hope for Torp's already limited expectations of reconnecting to his profession and his old workplace.

And even if there was an opening, there would hardly be a reason for a new trip to town with Katrine. She made no secret of the fact that this was—still—just a period of transition, and that she had no timetable for when the transitions would end with marriage, children, permanent housing, mortgages, and a stable job—if at all. After all, she was only thirty-two, as she had pointed out several times.

"I might go back to England or the USA in a few months."

"And do what?"

She shrugged and smiled. How should she know that? She would probably find something. Torp was amazed at this easy approach to life. Had he been like that himself when he was young?

Definitely not.

Had others of his generation been like that? Maybe.

But this global outlook and lack of a fixed home was a new phenomenon, which the EU, cheap airline tickets, Airbnb, the internet, and excessive welfare had brought with them. The possibilities were endless for very many. It had created a new divide between the generations, a divide of understanding that some people thought had narrowed, but which in recent years seemed to have grown wider and deeper, thought Torp. How could anyone be so rootless and at the same time so rooted in themselves? It remained a mystery to him. It was as if she had guessed his thoughts.

"I can live anywhere as long as there is good red wine."

She laughed disarmingly, put a piece of extra-mature North Sea cheese made from organic Jersey milk in her mouth, and gently rinsed it down with the Austrian.

She had come a long way since the beans on toast of her childhood, thought Torp.

The day at the *Daily News*, apart from the announced round of cost-cutting and the union meeting, had been just another day at the office. Simon was already sitting at his non-height-adjustable desk when Torp showed up at 9:00 a.m.

"Good morning, Woodward," he said with a knowing smile.

"Bernstein." Woodward nodded back. The others looked up.

"What's all that about?" asked Katrine.

"Thanks for the other night," said Neckhair vaguely as at that moment he hurried past his editorial staff, which would soon be back to normal again.

One more week, Arne Lund had explained. Next Monday, his people would be returning from Christiansborg. Then they would be finished with elections and post-elections, the chief news editor promised. The government's new ministers just had to be introduced to the Queen today; there would be handover deals in the ministries concerned, the opening speech on Tuesday, and the opening debate on Thursday.

Monday. Promise.

"Thanks for the other night?" echoed Katrine. "Out with it—was there something I missed out on this weekend?"

She laughed but was clearly looking for clarification. Torp told her about the party on Saturday, which he had inadvertently been dragged to.

"So you were in here working on Saturday?"

Torp told her briefly about the email from Jeppe Mikkelsen's sister, the visit to the widow, and her repetition about South Africa and Mandela; about the burglary of her flat, where the thief or thieves had only taken Jeppe's old computer, which he used privately; and about their hopeless surfing of the Net on Saturday. He refrained from saying anything about Sunday's futile trip to Hillerød. Bernstein listened and didn't interfere in the drip-fed delivery of information.

"Did you really think there had been election fraud?" Katrine ordered a new bottle. "Let's try an Italian this time. A little more powerful. Surprise us," was the message to the proprietor of the wine bar. She briefly laid her hand on Torp's, just a little longer than necessary for a gesture of friendship, and giggled a little.

"That bit was out there. I'll give you that," began Torp. "But you have to admit that there's something mysterious about that guy Jeppe Mikkelsen, who was shot in Ørstedsparken."

"But what should that have to do with election fraud?"

"Well, you know, he worked at the Ministry of the Interior in the department that is responsible for conducting general elections."

"Oh, Torp." She laughed.

A waiter in the wine bar came with the powerful Italian. Katrine tasted it and nodded. "We should also have another board," she said. They oxygenated and slurped together. Torp could feel the first bottle. This one was going to hit harder.

"No clue, no motive, nothing. It was three weeks ago. Don't you think it's weird?"

She shrugged.

"Virtually all murders in Denmark are solved almost immediately," he continued. "This is more than unusual."

"He was probably just a random victim. That's also the police's theory at the moment."

"But then the burglary the other day at his flat. The only thing that was stolen was his old computer."

"Have you told the police about this?"

He shook his head.

"Has the widow?"

He shook his head again. "She didn't think the computer was worth anything."

Katrine leaned back. "Be careful, you don't become . . ." she hesitated, "what is it you call it . . . gaga!"

Torp ignored her quip. "It doesn't look like a random case. A professional burglary in a flat, no one at home, and the only thing they take is an old, worthless computer used privately. What was on that computer?"

He could really feel the red wine now. Torp was totally unused to drinking so much, and certainly not on a Monday after an equally unusual hangover at the weekend. Katrine, on the other hand, seemed completely unaffected.

"And the moon landing was recorded in a giant studio in Nevada, 9/11 was an inside job, and the Holocaust is a myth. Come on, Torp."

The way she put just as much concentration into saying each individual word revealed the level of alcohol in her blood. Katrine shared out the last of the Italian in their glasses. Torp ate the remains of a wild boar pâté, the origin of which he couldn't remember. Southern Jutland? Were there any wild boars left in Southern Jutland after that fence had been set up? They had only eaten half of the board.

"Do you have any children?"

She changed the topic abruptly, but made it seem natural. Torp nodded.

"A son in Brussels, and a daughter here."

"Shouldn't they be allowed to continue living in a world that is just as well regulated as it is now?"

Torp felt confused as he swallowed his wild boar pâté. What did she mean by that?

"It doesn't happen by itself," she continued. "You could help. Be a part."

"Be a part?"

Torp put his wine glass on the table. She looked at him for a long time. Concerned.

"You finish on Friday, Torp. Promise me you won't fuck up the chance to come back."

Again the abrupt change of subject. She had been initiated into his intention to have a chat with Arne Lund at the end of the week—despite the new round of cuts. There are always holes to be filled, as she emphasised. And yes, that was true; there were always holes, and the branch loved experienced freelancers who could be hired on low wages from week to week as long as the union accepted it, and the union was somewhat more compliant today than it had been ten years ago.

"You have to take care of yourself, Ulrik."

She'd called him Ulrik. It sounded funny.

Up at the wine bar's old, acid-washed grocer's counter, she told them to round the bill up to the nearest whole hundred and let the debit card take care of the rest. Eighteen hundred kroner. She didn't seem to pay any attention to the amount, just stuffed the receipt into her bag as they stood outside on the cobblestones and looked over at Christiansborg. A new parliamentary year would begin tomorrow—as if the old one had even ended. Right now, Palle Enevoldsen was presumably sitting in the Prime Minister's Office polishing up his opening speech. Civil servants were making the final adjustments to the catalogue of laws—the government's plan for the coming year, which would be changed and eroded many times as the opposition gained strength, support parties became frightened, journalists critical, and the population angry.

It was extremely troublesome, this democracy, he thought. Katrine took his arm.

"Torp." It was Torp again. No more Ulrik. "Drop that election stuff, drop Jeppe Mikkelsen, do good, solid work for the rest of the week, and then have that chat with Arne."

He looked at her, unsteady on his legs.

"Do you promise?"

He hesitated, mostly because of the half Italian.

"Promise me, Ulrik. Drop it. Drop that stuff about Woodward and Bernstein. Torp is more than enough for the next four days."

She held his head between both her hands, looked him deep in the eyes, and suddenly kissed him hard and wet on the mouth.

He remained standing and watched her as she hurriedly cycled away on her Biomega with the dented front mudguard. Had she used her tongue? A little, maybe.

Ulrik Torp was a little unsteady on his way down the stairs to the Metro when his phone rang.

"Woodward! It's Bernstein." Simon sounded excited. "I've found something. It's totally crazy. Where are you, are you in town?"

Torp told him where he was.

"Take the Metro out to me. You can be here in ten minutes. I'll make coffee. Hurry." He hung up.

Torp looked at his watch. It was nearly 11:00 p.m. He really needed to get home after a long day. It had gone okay at the *Daily News*; it had become everyday routine—almost like in the old days, except he wasn't writing about politics. Today, despite the internal meeting and the ensuing worried talk, he had turned out three stories. One about a Danish coach accident in Germany with injured Danes and then two stories about deferred maintenance costs in Copenhagen. They were his own stories that he had developed himself. The municipality faced a billion-kroner task with sewers and roads because the politicians had grossly under-prioritised them for more than thirty years. Torp found an external senior lecturer at DTU who compared it—almost—to the politicians in East Berlin, who had just let things slide during the years leading up to the fall of the Wall. For decades after, Berlin was Europe's construction site; everything was worn out, ruined, or broken down. That is how it goes when you don't maintain things, stated the lecturer. Torp had wanted to find a professor at DTU who would say much the same thing with greater authority, but Neckhair had thought that the external lecturer and a dissatisfied politician from Copenhagen's Citizens' Representation were more than enough for that story. Moreover, he would soon have to do an updated version of the coach accident for the website.

During the three weeks he had now been at the *Daily News*, his writing speed had increased considerably. It was nice to knock the rust off his fingers, to feel the experience and the craft in play together. He was fifty-five, but not at all as finished as he had managed to convince himself. He wasn't writing major, epoch-making stories, but doing solid craftsmanship. The problem, he knew, was that there was a regiment of young, newly trained journalists ready to give it a go for half the salary. He gave Simon and Emma several sidelong glances; they were talented and hadn't even finished their education yet.

Rigshospitalet hadn't been in contact. It was a simple test and a simple scan, they had told him the week before. There had to be an office where the results of the tests lay. Ulrik had been on the internet for God knew how long reading about the little lump at the bottom right side of his jaw. His tongue was gradually staying longer and longer down there without him thinking about it. The internet was both worthwhile and inadequate at the same time. But as long as Karen hadn't been told about something that was probably nothing, it was his only confidant.

The treatment depends on when the tumour is detected. If the tumour has not spread, it can be operated on. In later stages, when the tumour has spread, it is instead treated with radiation, chemotherapy, or both. Malignant tumours that are detected at an early stage are most often treated with successful results.

What was early? Was it even malignant? Were the politicians in Copenhagen who ten, twenty, and thirty years ago decided to postpone the maintenance of the sewer network and the roads aware of what they were doing? What they were postponing for the next generation? Had he come early enough? Why did men never go to the doctor? If he had been a woman, would it have been discovered earlier? These thoughts glided in and out of each other until Neckhair shouted across the room that it was now time for an update on the coach accident—the *Express* was way ahead.

After the update—there was nothing to update other than a few tweets from the German police, who also had nothing new to say—he went to a secluded spot in the editorial office to call Rigshospitalet.

They had to bloody well have a result by now.

Torp was put through a labyrinth of telephone connections. Some were answered but were the wrong extension. Others didn't answer. Back to the reception. Then he got cut off. So he called again. "It was me who called just now." The voice on the phone knew nothing about it. How many people answered the phones at Rigshospitalet? They must surely be sitting next to each other. Didn't colleagues talk to each other anymore? Eventually, he reached a phone and a nurse who had something to do with the department.

"We've had a system crash in our patient records and in the departments that work with tests," she explained.

It sounded like it wasn't the first time today she had reeled that explanation off. Torp pointed out that he had received roughly the same message several weeks ago when he waiting to be called in for the examination. The nurse routinely apologised but there was nothing she could do about it right now. If she could have his name and social security number, then she would certainly pass it on.

"So when can I expect to hear from you?"

She couldn't give a clear answer to that. It would happen as soon as possible. They would certainly contact him; she could very well understand his impatience, but there was no reason to be nervous. A few days wouldn't make any difference.

"A few days," exclaimed the ten-digit social security number. "It's been four weeks since my dentist referred me to you, and you made a total mess of it the first time!"

She understood that; it wasn't she who had written the software that all the hospitals on Zealand were subject to, and which didn't work despite billions of kroner in development costs and just as many years in delay. And now he would have to excuse her. There were four waiting on her phone. He shouldn't be worried, and she apologised profusely.

Torp stood in front of Simon the intern's flat. The Austrian and the Italian were charging around in his blood. The intoxication was about to be supplemented by a headache. My opened the door, still only wearing knickers and the same pre-washed and short T-shirt. Did she ever walk around in anything else? Torp got in first this time and gave her a big hug which became a little longer than natural because he was using My to keep his balance in the small entrance, but none of that seemed to bother her.

"He's in the kitchen." She smiled, stepping aside.

"Bernstein!" Torp waved his arm.

"Woodward!"

The boy sat bent over some papers at the kitchen table. There was a load of washing-up pushed down to one end. His eyes were bloodshot but shining with excitement.

"I've got it." He corrected himself quickly. "We've got it. We've fucking got it! Woodward and Bernstein."

Torp sat down heavily. "What is it you say we've got?"

The intoxication was clearly diminishing. But as an equilibrium, it was being offset by a headache that was knocking on the door. Oh, he was so tired.

"Take a look at these numbers." Simon pushed a sheet of paper across the kitchen table.

1,036—994

766—735

1,315—1,262

"Yes?" Torp looked at Simon.

"Can't you see?"

"See what?" Torp sounded more irritated than he felt.

"These are the vote totals for the Nationalists we found in Hillerød yesterday at your brother-in-law's, or whatever it is he is—Svend."

Ulrik Torp looked at the paper. He didn't know what to look for. Simon's voice was trembling.

"The big numbers are the number of votes as the election officials we spoke to remembered them. He—Svend—and the other two from the Nationalists we rang up."

Torp nodded.

"And the small numbers," Simon continued, "are the official vote totals from the Ministry of the Interior."

Torp nodded again. The examples were few, the numbers random, perhaps sloppy, but nothing more than that. That was what they had agreed on. There was no story.

Simon continued, putting a thin, pale index finger on the paper and forcing his partner to hold his gaze.

"It's an algorithm. We were right."

Torp said nothing. My came into the kitchen and stood behind her boyfriend, clearly proud of what would now come from him.

"It's an algorithm," he repeated. "The difference between the figures from the polling station and the figures on the Ministry of the Interior's website is four per cent."

"Four?"

"Four per cent has been deducted from all three locations. Four per cent exactly."

CHAPTER 15

Prime Minister Palle Enevoldsen's driver carefully rolled the large Mercedes past Slotspladsen, turned left towards Prins Jørgens Gård with the front pointing directly towards the Supreme Court's grand staircase and the more modest rear entrance to the Prime Minister's Office to the left of it.

Enevoldsen was sitting in the back seat flipping through the opening speech he was to deliver in a few hours from the speaker's rostrum in Parliament—the most distinguished rostrum in the country, as it was called. Now he wasn't so sure, and certainly not today. It was a defensive speech without any major initiatives for the coming year. At this moment, what was most important was keeping the propeller in the water and just steering the country. An unpredictable referendum on the EU had been averted almost by pure luck. A few thousand votes had kept both the Nationalists and the New Radicals out of Parliament. How lucky could you get? He and the Labour Party's Pernille Hjort had promised each other that they would never step out on that ice floe again. He was certain that both of them would keep that promise. But what about all the other, for the time being, not-all-that-dangerous policies that they had both flirted with in an attempt to bridge the gap with public sentiment? Handshakes from Muslims in exchange for citizenship, minimum criminal age for twelve-year-olds, ban on the burqa, intervention against Romanian strawberry pickers—did Danes have any idea that if it weren't for hard-working Romanians, there would hardly be any more Danish strawberries? The list of populist, frivolous, media-friendly, easy-to-understand, and, from the viewpoint of major political issues, degrading proposals seemed endless. What was the next thing he would have to embrace? That they should eat a pork meatball before the handshake with the mayor? That the Theatre Royal should be moved out of Copenhagen?

Pretty much everything on the seemingly endless list of meretricious proposals represented something he and Pernille Hjort had rejected ten years ago as frivolous nonsense and symbolic politics from marginalised politicians and parties. Now it was mainstream, something both of them had increasingly often had to accept in a desperate attempt to show decisiveness and popular appeal.

He sighed. Perhaps he could retire in two years' time. It would also give his successor time to sit in the chair before the next election. My goodness, what a difference there was between being number two and number one. The next Prime Minister would find out in the same way he had. It could neither be told nor handed over. It had to be felt. As when a decision had to be made—right or left, yes or no—and everyone was looking at him. He had a dozen of them a day, big and small. And then once in a while one of the big ones, where he was completely alone with the decision—before, during, and after.

Palle Enevoldsen had lost count of the large number of political friendships from back in his youth he had lost in his years as Prime Minister. The day before yesterday, it had been the Minister of Social Affairs who hadn't seen her dismissal coming at all. They had known each other for thirty years, liked each other, and had even been in bed together a few times during their time in youth politics. When he called on Sunday night to tell her that her time at the Ministry of Social Affairs was over and that he didn't have another ministry for her, he was met with a cold "oh really." In a way, it was a relief for Enevoldsen. He wouldn't have been able to stand a longer conversation. It was the curse and privilege of a Prime Minister to change ministers based on his own, private analysis of what served him, the government, and the party best. Not necessarily in that order, but a prime ministerial algorithm couldn't always be explained.

That was politics.

He informed her when the Queen would be ready for the farewell audience on Monday, and then it was over with that conversation, thirty years of collegial friendship and occasionally more than that.

Enevoldsen noticed a large gathering on Slotspladsen in front of Christiansborg.

"Did you see who was demonstrating, Michael?"

His faithful and discreet driver throughout the years carefully parked the shiny car at the entrance to the Prime Minister's Office. They were early, since he and most of the members of Parliament would first be going to the opening day's obligatory service in the palace church. According to the calendar, autumn had just begun, but it was slightly delayed. The morning sun was kind today and the sky almost blue.

"I think it's the contras," came the response from the front seat.

The contras. It sounded like those bloody Reagan-backed militias in Nicaragua in the 1980s.

The Prime Minister stepped out and noticed that his bodyguards in the car behind him were doing the same. He had half an hour before the church service and just enough time to make a round of those in his office, but he decided to walk the few hundred metres out to Slotspladsen first. The bodyguards followed him closely, without it seeming obvious or intrusive.

She was standing on the stage with a guitar-wielding folk singer, the name of whom Enevoldsen couldn't remember. Ulla Hasting—his former ministerial colleague from a distant past that wasn't actually all that many years ago—was shouting in her thin voice out to her audience, which was probably a few thousand, but he could see that more were streaming in from all directions.

"It doesn't matter who has the power in there. Doesn't matter one bit. That is why we say no, no, and no again. We are contras!" she yelled.

Her husband was standing below the stage with his unfathomable smile.

The Prime Minister saw some young people handing out broad, yellow ribbons to the audience. Only now did he notice that the whole thing was being held in yellow, and that Ulla Hasting herself had a yellow ribbon around her neck. People were copying her, tying it around their necks. Then the folk singer was given the microphone. He struck a few chords to attract attention and began singing, so that it resounded all over the square, almost down to the National Bank building.

The Prime Minister immediately recognised the hit about the yellow ribbon from the 1970s. Now came the chorus, which everyone could sing along to, as the folk singer had informed them.

They bawled as if their lives were at stake, which they, in some way perhaps, were trying to convince themselves was the case. People clapped, cheered, and laughed; many thousands of them and more were arriving. The folk singer waved and bowed.

It made no sense at all in Palle Enevoldsen's head. It was one thing that the Hasting couple, with a little help from the spirit of the times, had knocked the turnout down to 72 per cent, but something else completely that they were now cultivating their so-called contra movement as if it were Scientology. But what did that have to do with yellow ribbons and that song? Why were they demonstrating on the day of the opening of Parliament? And why hadn't his special advisers told him about this?

He stood at the corner of Slotspladsen near the entrance to Prins Jørgens Gård and looked around. No one had noticed that the country's Prime Minister was standing, if not among the people, then a little on the fringe. There were many young people among the protesters; that was the one thing that immediately stood out. What were they so unhappy about?

The song was over. Now someone else jumped up on stage. Judging by Poul Hasting's commissar-like expression, it wasn't part of the plan. Palle Enevoldsen recognised her immediately. It was one of the Members of Parliament from the New Radicals who had just been voted out of her seat. She was wearing a multicoloured sweater, so you could hardly see the yellow ribbon that she, like everyone else, had hanging around her neck.

"I'm with you," she shouted. "There is an energy here that we can use to shift things. I'm with you!"

The protesters closest to the scene also recognised her.

"It's Pia Troense from the New Radicals," some of them exclaimed. The name went round among the people, who started booing her, first testing the waters, then louder.

"Get lost!"

"You are the system."

"You're no better."

"Take your pension and bugger off."

"Nobody invited you."

"Traitor."

The shouts became louder and, in a matter of a few seconds, more aggressive. Enevoldsen looked at Poul Hasting in amazement, he with the commissar smile who was smugly watching the events from the foot of the stage. The dethroned Member of Parliament in the multicoloured sweater was at first confused that there was booing and shouting. Then it dawned on her that she was the target of the protest.

"But I'm with you. I'm also a contra. We have to say no to those in there," she tried.

The protests intensified. Ulla Hasting gave her a mild shove as a sign that she didn't belong there. A hunted expression came over the face of the multicoloured politician. Enevoldsen involuntarily thought of Romania's dictator Nicolae Ceaușescu when he stood on that balcony in December 1989 and the people began to boo—just before the state-run television compassionately shut off the signal. The next day, the genius of the Carpathians and his wife were executed after a show trial.

The outgoing Member of Parliament for the New Radicals jumped down from the stage, past Poul Hasting, onward, away, past the crowd, who let her go, booing her all the way, in the direction of the palace church. She made brief eye contact with the country's Prime Minister, shifted her gaze, and ran off like a wounded deer. Enevoldsen looked at his bodyguards. No one had noticed him yet, but it was clear that his faithful shadows wanted him away from the square and up into the Prime Minister's Office.

Maybe he could retire as early as next year. Maybe this would be his last opening speech.

He turned calmly and left the square.

In the *Daily News*'s editorial office, Simon the intern went and sat across from Ulrik Torp when he heard that Katrine Taber-Nielsen had reported in sick with a fever and what looked like the flu.

Torp had texted her the night before on his way home from Simon's flat and his 4 per cent. It couldn't be just a coincidence that the difference between their own and the ministry's figures was exactly 4 per cent on all three examples. As little as Torp had believed in Simon's paranoid thoughts about election fraud in Denmark, he believed in such coincidences even less.

There was probably a plausible explanation, but it wasn't down to chance.

Katrine had quickly replied in a text message that they should keep it to themselves until they had more solid evidence. Torp agreed with her, and he had immediately said that to Simon when they met at the editorial office, Torp with a Tuesday hangover that didn't fit well with his age.

"We have got enough, goddammit," the intern whispered too loudly across the desks.

"We have nothing, Simon. Nothing."

Simon threw out his arms in despair. He had not slept all night after finding the 4 per cent and summoning a drunken Ulrik Torp close to midnight to deliver his revelation. Simon had continued most of the night at the keyboard he had grown up with. He had searched on Google, dived into databases, cross-checked, searched again, new keyword, new combination. That was how it had gone until the early morning. And he had found more, but could sense that now wasn't the right moment.

"Who has nothing?" asked Neckhair casually.

The leader of the reportage group was on his routine "morning round"—
something he had learned on one of the countless leadership courses that
were apparently still affordable, which Christian Crash had remarked on at
one point when no one from the management was around.

Grandma-Bente rattled her amber jewellery as she turned up the
volume on the television, which was broadcasting live from Christiansborg's Slotsplads and the contra demonstration. The camera followed the
former Member of Parliament for the New Radicals fleeing the square
and the cameras.

Grandma-Bente's eyes were glistening. She had been a neo-radical
long before the party was founded and was best friends with the now
fleeing and dethroned Member of Parliament, Pia Troense. She sat completely still on her chair and stared blankly at the television.

Several of the journalists, who were used to earthquakes, refugee disasters, and terrorism being work that you have to relate to soberly—and therefore sometimes also cynically—at first began giggling over the incident.

"Whoa!"

She had thought she was among friends.

"Did you see Poul Hasting's smile? That's the commissar we know
and love."

But soon there was silence in the editorial team in front of the TV
screen.

What exactly had they just seen?

"Next time they'll bloody lynch her," muttered Christian Crash.

"Did anyone mention the Bastille?" wondered Arne Lund out loud
but almost to himself, referring to the day in 1789 when angry French-
men stormed the Parisian medieval castle that served as a prison and
beheaded the commandant as the prelude to the French Revolution.

Ulla Hasting had again grabbed the microphone.

"We can't trust the politicians," she yelled.

The demonstrators cheered.

"Have you read," exclaimed Christian, "that she has proposed that
Parliament should only consist of Danes selected by drawing lots, and
that they should be replaced every six months?"

"Someone in Italy has also come up with that proposal," remarked Emma the intern.

"The Italians may also have more reason for it," laughed Christian, waiting for the others to join in.

Neckhair shushed him.

"The system has broken down," said Ulla Hasting next.

She had always been good at speaking in sound bites, thought Torp—the five or ten seconds that tasted like whipped cream both for journalists and for busy citizens, sound bites that had increasingly become the guide dog in the public debate. If a problem couldn't be boiled down to five to ten seconds, it was just a pity for the problem.

"So it *was* just me," remarked Arne Lund.

"Just you?"

"That thought about the Bastille," mumbled the chief news editor as he walked quietly back to his office.

Torp followed him. He wanted to have a chat with Lund about whether—despite a new round of cuts—there could be an opening for him later. A temporary job or his name on a phone list as on call when necessary. Something or other.

"Arne, do you have two minutes?"

Arne always had two minutes. It was one of the many things that made him such a good chief news editor. Torp stood in the doorway to mark that he actually meant only two minutes, maybe even less.

"Friday is my last day after this"—he was looking for the right name—"this work activation."

Arne Lund gave him a wry smile.

"It's been nice having you, Torp. Nice to have some people in the house one has always known."

"Could we have a chat on Friday? A little longer talk?"

Lund hesitated. Just long enough for Torp to feel that there was something he was not saying.

"Of course. My calendar on Friday is very tight," he said, looking in his papers.

"Let's say right after lunch. One o'clock."

Torp nodded. They both knew what it was all about. There was no need to go further into it now.

"Arne."

Arne looked up from his cluttered desk. "Yes?"

Torp was about to begin the sentence he had formulated in his head. *I have a suspicion that something totally irregular has occurred in the general election. Something we have to write about, even though we don't have the whole story yet.* That was how he had formulated it. The old chief news editor would understand. If there was going to be any point at all with the fourth state power, the free press, control of those in power, and all that Watergate talk, then this was the moment. And the possibility of a firmer connection for him to the *Daily News* would increase. If nothing else, as long as the story was able to run. And after Friday for real pay, not 2,814 kroner.

"Nothing. We'll talk about it on Friday. One o'clock."

He gave a thumbs up and left.

Simon was sitting opposite Torp in the canteen. His eyes were glowing; he had been trying to tell him something since they had arrived at work without anyone else hearing it. Torp had been aware of the unrest in the boy intern with the adult girlfriend since this morning, and also while they were following the peculiar demonstration at Christiansborg's Slotsplads on television. At the reportage group's editorial meeting a little later, Simon's legs had been bobbing impatiently up and down, while the others discussed the contras and the Hasting couple. That had to be covered, of course. The only question was whether the Christiansborg editorial staff could handle it on top of the Prime Minister's opening speech and the political reactions to it. The young editor-in-chief, Asbjørn Henriksen, stood close to the door, as usual, so he could escape at any moment. As always, he was immaculately dressed in a modern suit and casual unbuttoned shirt without a tie, and his "hi there" seemed even more out of place now that everyone knew he was currently looking for thirty to forty people he could fire. Henriksen cut through with pragmatism. Christiansborg had plenty on their plate; the reportage group would have to take care of the contras and the Hastings. And also get an interview with Pia Troense. It was a good story, he stated, tiptoeing out shortly after.

Neckhair gave the fleeing New Radical to Simon, who looked up in surprise when his name was mentioned. He was clearly only listening sporadically. Torp was to write an archive portrait of the Hasting couple with the reasoning that he knew them, after all, and knew their story down to his fingertips, which was true enough. Although Ulla Hasting had been a minister in two different governments for the Labour Party and the Liberals, respectively, Poul Hasting was the more interesting of the two. An intellectual as few others were, extreme as even fewer were in the seventies, when he expounded and supported violent political struggle. His breakthrough in the public consciousness came when he exposed his father as a member of the alternative, private, but US-backed intelligence agency known as The Firm, which was set up after World War II by former resistance fighters. They may have been missing the excitement, but above all, they didn't trust soft Danish politicians to dare to use the means necessary to keep Communism at bay. The exposure of the private intelligence agency had been a national scandal. Several former top politicians knew about it; some had even worked for The Firm in their youth. That one of them subsequently turned out to be Poul Hasting's conservative father gave the exposure yet another special colour. Torp thought the story was insanely exciting but could see from the participants in the editorial meeting that he was losing their attention even as he was telling them about it.

"What does that fucking song mean?" interrupted a young journalist.

Arne Lund took over. "The Americans used it in 1980 and '81 when Iran had the American hostages at the embassy in Tehran," he explained. "Relatives tied yellow ribbons around a tree in their driveway or front yard as a sign that they were expecting their son, daughter, or whoever it was, to come home. In the end, it was almost as if all Americans with a tree were relatives of one of the fifty-two American hostages."

"How did they get released?" asked Emma the intern.

"They were held for four hundred forty-four days. Minutes after Ronald Reagan took the oath of office as the newly elected President, they were in international airspace," continued Torp.

He remembered the day clearly. Emma was impressed to have a colleague who knew something so detailed about such really old days.

"But what does the yellow ribbon symbolise for the contras? A change of regime?" asked a journalist out into the room.

Arne Lund shrugged. That suggestion was probably as good as any. "It's gaga in any case," he said.

A liberating laugh ended the editorial meeting.

After the meeting, Torp tried for the third time that morning to text Katrine, while the Prime Minister delivered what was quickly hailed by commentators as "the most boring opening speech of the decade." No reply. She was probably trying to sleep the flu fever off.

"Torp, we have to have a chat."

Simon wanted him away from their desks, away from the others. It suited Torp fine to not talk about the general election and the vote counts when others were listening, but this was not a good time. He had to get going on his archival portrait of the Hasting couple—a small piece of uncomplicated journalism that he was actually looking forward to. Simon was also busy, surely.

"Aren't you going out to find Pia Troense, unless she's fled the country completely?"

"On my way. Torp—it's important, I think."

"I thought it was Woodward."

Bernstein smiled. "Sorry, Woodward. May Bernstein be allowed to talk—sort of a little Deep Throatish in a multistorey car park?"

"Can we use the canteen?"

They could.

Simon leaned forward. The canteen hadn't opened for lunch yet, so they had it to themselves except for some workmen sitting at the far end drinking Automat coffee with their packed lunches.

"I've found Spang-Johansen."

Torp felt lost for a moment.

"Spang-Johansen. The name that Jeppe Mikkelsen from the Ministry of the Interior mentioned several times to his wife and sister."

Torp was with him. He had completely forgotten the villain from all the Olsen Gang comedy films. A quick Google search had yielded nothing. After that, he had almost forgotten the name in favour of *South Africa, general election*, and *Mandela*—the other things that the murdered clerk had allegedly recited.

"I've found Spang-Johansen," repeated Simon, "in an old database back from the early 1970s."

"And?"

"He was also a civil servant—in the Ministry of Justice."

Torp was having a hard time sharing the excitement.

"He's dead!" exclaimed Simon, as if to emphasise the point his partner hadn't yet grasped.

Torp was going to make a cheeky remark that there were actually many from the 1970s who were no longer alive.

"He was murdered," continued Simon, "in 1973. Shot. The murderer was never found."

Woodward looked at his Bernstein and narrowed his eyes.

CHAPTER 16

Ulrik Torp had many reasons for being in a bad mood when he sat down at his desk at the *Daily News*, still his workplace for another three days, and turned on his computer. A red drop fell onto the space bar. He turned his arm and saw that it was full of scratches, several of which were bleeding a little.

Argh.

The bad mood had already begun at the breakfast table when he had been eating his muesli. Karen had entered the living room, swinging a piece of paper from an outstretched arm and uttering a disbelieving "what's this?!"

It was Rigshospitalet's cancer booklet, taken from the pocket of his new designer trousers, which she had long been threatening to wash. Ulrik laid out his cards straight away. He told her about the dentist, the small lump in his mouth, the biopsy, and the scan at Rigshospitalet and the awaited result of the tissue sample.

Now for the verdict.

Ulrik sat leaning forward at the dining table like a naughty teenager.

At first, she was shocked, then sad. Then she got angry. Then she wasn't any longer. Now it was the reproach phase.

"Of all the dry old sticks in this country, you are the most gnarled of them all, Ulrik."

He accepted it; his experience was that it was the best way to get it over and done with. In a little while, it would move into the concerned phase, and then it would fade out gently.

When would they examine the sample of the lump in his oral cavity? The tumour, as they called it. Was it today? He preferred to call it a lump. There had to be an answer soon.

"Had you intended that I should just be kept in the dark about it? Tell me, what the hell do you think marriage is all about?"

Karen had swung back a little to the anger phase. Her eyes glistened. Torp looked down and said nothing.

She had sensed that something was wrong, that he was holding something back, but had convinced herself that it was due to the *Daily News*, his interrupted career and identity as a journalist, that it had nothing to do with them. And she had been so glad that, despite everything, he had seemed happier the last few days, coming home late smelling of beer like other people with a life and a circle of acquaintances. The dismissal from the *Daily News* five years earlier had changed him. It was so trite to say that you lost confidence from not being of use, a cliché so overused that you hardly took any notice of it. But that didn't make it any less real. Karen couldn't stop once she got going. This is what she should have said several years ago. How his pride and vigour had slowly but steadily been decimated. How the sense of humour she had fallen for many years earlier had disappeared. How he seemed to be making himself more stupid, stifling his analytical power, his overview, and his insight. How he stayed indoors during the day so no one would think that there was an unemployed man living here. How he less and less often felt like going out somewhere in the evening. How he had withdrawn—not only from friends and their children, but also from her. Which was exactly why she had become so happy that he was working late at the *Daily News* several nights in a row and was naturally tired. She had seen the hint of a man again.

Her man.

And then this. She felt deceived, as if he had been unfaithful to her, not with another woman, but almost as bad, and yet—maybe this was worse.

He first tried to stutter his way through an explanation of his several-week-long silence. He didn't want to worry her. Didn't think it was anything serious. Didn't think about any deeper repercussions. Forgot it for periods, even. Had been busy. But the explanatory engine had quickly run out of fuel. There wasn't really any explanation, he explained in the end, waving his arms, saying that she was right and coming out with the redemptive apology, which didn't serve its purpose in either the anger phase or the blame phase. It didn't work until the concerned phase. Were they there now?

They were.

Karen sat down.

"Name. Phone number," she commanded.

Ulrik looked up.

"Rigshospitalet."

Karen grabbed her mobile phone and took her adult schoolteacher voice into Rigshospitalet's telephone labyrinth. Five minutes and a thank-you later, she had a name and department written down.

"Friday at one o'clock. I'm coming with you," she proclaimed, pushing the piece of paper towards him.

The scolding from Karen hit him first and foremost because he knew she was right. He had become a piddling version of himself in recent years, and his brief spell of flourishing at the *Daily News* had, funnily enough, reminded both Karen and himself how much he had changed. He was relieved in a way that Karen had taken the lead on the lump and insisted on going with him, but at the same time, he felt deprived of authority over himself.

Friday at 1:00 p.m. was unfortunate—it was the only time Arne Lund had available for the conversation which could be Torp's slender bridge back to a dignified everyday life.

Katrine Taber-Nielsen was still not responding to his text messages. How sick could she be? He was missing her common sense and sparring in the cacophony of indications that pointed to irregularities in connection with the general election. *Irregularities.* Simon had sneered at the word. The boy thought it was much worse, and maybe he was right. His most recent discovery of a Spang-Johansen, civil servant in the Ministry of Justice and killed in the spring of 1973, was another coincidence that couldn't just be chance. That was what he wanted to talk to Katrine about. She was rational, sober, and gifted. He enjoyed her company and had come to trust her despite their brief acquaintance.

Then they would have to go to Arne Lund. Regardless of his own conclusion—was there a story, or was it just coffee grounds?—the chief news editor should be brought into it. It was already a little too late.

It had been quite the start to the day. First Karen, then the missing Katrine, and then Simon, who in his youthful recklessness and exquisite lack of experience was putting increasing pressure on him.

All of that made it hard to be very happy this Wednesday morning.

Finally, there were the contras and their yellow ribbons. He hadn't realised until that morning how offensive he found the movement. Wearing his old, several sizes too large jeans, Torp had shuffled belatedly out of the flat after his session with Karen. On the small lawn in front of the property stood something in between a bush and a tree. The bush—because that is what it had to be, after all—was evergreen and had jagged, patterned leaves. Torp had never paid much attention to it but had immediately seen the yellow ribbon which had been wound around some of the branches. He had run his gaze over the other entrances to the property and the surrounding growth.

All of them had been draped in yellow ribbons. What the hell were they up to!

He had angrily tugged at the ribbon, discovered that there were thorns in the branches, scratched himself, tugged even more, scratched the underside of his left arm, but got most of the ribbon off at the second attempt. He had angrily tried to crumple it up, but it had an ability to sort of uncrumple itself again. An elderly man with a dog and cane had been watching the proceedings from the pavement. Torp had become slightly flustered, tossed the torn yellow ribbon onto the grass, stamping on it to show it who was boss, hitched up his trousers, ran his tongue over the lump in his lower mouth, mumbled a "good morning," and walked briskly towards the Metro.

Now his computer had finally booted up. It took forever because of the plethora of programs and security measures that the media house's computer department had fed it with.

Torp had received an email from Poul Hasting; it was probably a reaction to today's archive portrait of the couple. Torp could once again feel the anger washing through his body at the thought of their contra-campaign and demented proposals for a Parliament consisting of random citizens chosen by lot and replaced every six months. If anything promoted the loathing of politicians, it was that sort of thing. And the Hastings were far too clever not to know what they were doing. So why?

To Torp's surprise, the email was friendly.

Dear Torp,

It is a pleasure to see your pen again in the Daily News. *I have actually missed it. Regarding your otherwise excellent and reasonably honest article in today's newspaper about me and my wife, I would like to be allowed to make a few corrections and additions. I would very much like to offer you a cup of coffee in private. Shall we say at 3:00 p.m.?*

Kind regards,
Poul Hasting
P.S. Greetings from Ulla.

Torp read it through a couple of times. The couple had over the past decade become known for never, as in never, giving interviews. They expressed themselves on their own internet media about Muslims, globalisation, and Europe, had their loyal followers, wrote books, and gave lectures to the believers, but no longer spoke to journalists.

The wording of the email wasn't random. It wasn't an invitation to an interview. It was an invitation for coffee, some corrections and additions. He didn't believe the *greetings from Ulla*. She wasn't the greetings type.

And yet Torp could feel his mood lightening. He emailed back saying *thanks* and *see you at 3:00, kind regards, Torp*. If nothing else, it could be fun to see them again in the old family villa in Hellerup, which had previously played a major role in Danish politics, not least when Poul Hasting's father had been a prominent conservative politician back in the 1950s.

A new email landed in his Outlook inbox. It was from the shop steward. In connection with next week's expected redundancies, quite advantageous terms for voluntary resignation had been agreed with the management. The shop steward urged people to consider them carefully; the offer was, if not generous, then at the sizeable end, and the voluntary resignations would reduce the number of redundancies one for one. Roughly the same words had been used by the shop steward's predecessor five years earlier. Torp remembered his thoughts from that time— that it had nothing to do with him.

This was followed by the shop steward's long review of options for crisis help and psychological preparedness "during this difficult time." He looked up at the TV screen. The news channel was broadcasting live from the summit meeting in Brussels. It seemed that the Musketeers' Oath had been restored in the Union; first with the change of Prime Minister in Italy before the summer holidays, and now with the Deputy Prime Minister of Hungary, who had taken over the baton from his more nationalist predecessor, who had died over the weekend from a sudden malady.

Prime Minister Palle Enevoldsen was being interviewed by a couple of Danish journalists at the entrance to the meeting. Behind him stood Malta's young, energetic Prime Minister being interviewed for German television. He was in top form and finally seemed to have wriggled free of months of rumours about secret accounts in Panama and million-dollar transfers between the daughter of the Azerbaijani president and his own wife. He was the guarantee that Malta, despite Russian pressure, was a solid and loyal EU member.

"I expect that we will agree on a sharp resolution and a continuation of the sanctions against Russia," was the Danish Prime Minister's take on things. He looked tired after three weeks of election campaigning, government negotiations, ministerial dismissals, his opening speech, and tomorrow's opening debate in Parliament. A journalist wanted to know what to expect in connection with the plans for comprehensive and massive aid for the reconstruction of Syria. Did he still expect opposition in EU circles? No, the Prime Minister believed that there would be agreement on a fairly comprehensive aid package for the devastated country, so that millions of its citizens had something to return home to.

Foreign Minister Ingvar Kristoffersen stood obliquely behind his Prime Minister and, despite his voluminous stomach, looked as if he was reborn. A German journalist asked him in English if it was true that the new Hungarian Prime Minister and he were personal friends from back in the 1990s. The Foreign Minister was able to confirm this with forced seriousness. In fact, their wives were also close acquaintances, the friendship having arisen immediately after the fall of the Wall. Would the personal friendship have any influence on Hungary's new and more Union-friendly position? Ingvar Kristoffersen reflected on how he could take the credit without actually doing so. A quick smile and a *no, no, international politics doesn't work that way* could send the signal—don't listen to what I say, but take notice of how I look. The smile should precisely indicate that he, Ingvar Kristoffersen, was one of the key players during today's summit. His Prime Minister smelled the rat before the Foreign Minister managed to fix his smile.

"Now we will begin our meeting. You must ask Hungary about the Hungarian position, but I feel confident that Europe is united—also on this issue. Thank you, gentlemen."

The last remark from Palle Enevoldsen was just as much addressed to Ingvar Kristoffersen. Nothing more should be said. Europe was standing together again. That was the message.

The text message finally came from Katrine. She apologised for not answering, was simply so sick, still lying in bed with a high fever, and unlikely to come back the rest of the week. *Best wishes, Katrine*. Not *warmest wishes*.

No remark about him having finished at the paper by then and that they wouldn't have time to say goodbye to each other. Not a word about having a beer or visiting a wine bar together later when she was fit again. Torp sent a *get well soon* reply back with a smiley anyway.

"Was that Katrine?" Simon wanted to know.

Torp nodded.

"You're bleeding." He pointed to Torp's arm.

Torp tried to wipe it off with a sheet of A4 which wasn't absorbent and thus only helped a little. He wiped off the rest on his trousers and indicated that he couldn't be bothered to talk about it.

"She probably doesn't need to worry about being fired," continued Simon after he had seen the email from the shop steward.

Torp looked at him.

"I mean—when she actually has the editor-in-chief's father as her godfather, then she has her connections totally in order, right?"

"Godfather?"

"Asbjørn Henriksen's old father, the former top civil servant— Katrine's godfather," explained Simon, before asking, "What does that actually mean, godfather—except when it's Marlon Brando?"

"Why do you think old Niels Henriksen is Katrine's godfather?"

"I saw it on the internet. An ancient article."

Simon switched to whispering across the desks. They were alone, so there wasn't really any need for such a precaution.

"Emma is working on getting us hacked into Statistics Denmark's election computer."

"*What* did you say?" exclaimed Torp.

"Shh," he said, putting a finger to his mouth. "If someone has fiddled with it, changed the reported vote numbers, then you can probably see it if you dive in deep enough, she says."

"Emma?" Torp looked over at the desk where she usually sat. It was empty. "Where is she?"

"She's ill." Simon grinned, making air quotes around "ill" and muffling his voice even more. "She's sitting at home giving instructions to some computer hackers she knows in Estonia. They think they can easily get into the system and see what has happened."

"Emma?" Torp raised his voice.

"She's ill," said Neckhair, who was further away but had heard Torp's outburst. Torp nodded to the leader of the reportage group.

"Emma!" he repeated in a quiet voice, ducking his head to face Simon.

"Why is that so strange? Did you think that just because she's quiet, that she can't do anything? Emma can do lots."

Simon shut up when he saw Neckhair and Christian Crash approaching.

It was time for an editorial meeting.

The October weather continued to play at being late summer. Torp decided to cycle out to Poul Hasting in Hellerup.

During the day, he had followed up with another article about the lack of maintenance of the sewers in the municipality of Copenhagen.

"I warned about this for all of the twenty years I was department manager," explained a retired civil servant. "But as long as the shit was flowing, no one took any notice, neither the citizens nor the politicians."

The story was good and had in recent days given birth to several Ritzau bulletins, quotes in *Radio News* broadcasts, and a single TV news feature. Arne Lund urged Torp to check the phenomenon in a number of the country's large municipalities. It was certain to be the same picture in most places.

Simon had gone to the microfilm archive to look for articles about the civil servant Spang-Johansen, who tragically passed away in the spring of 1973. It was hardly a coincidence that his fate was so similar to Jeppe Mikkelsen's so many years later, but the common thread was hard to see. Simon had to agree with him on that at least.

Neither Neckhair nor the others protested that he was slipping off several hours before he had actually finished work for the day. Firstly, it was a kind of work, even if it wasn't an interview. In addition, the worst pressure in connection with the general election had subsided. Finally, everyone was aware that Torp, on work activation, would be gone in two days. He was, in principle, already off the roster.

"Remember the countrywide story on the sewers," Neckhair urged him. He certainly would. It would be ready for the weekend.

On his way out to Poul Hasting, Torp wanted to pop in to see former Minister of Justice and Foreign Secretary Otto Brathenberg with the book about US President Truman, which Brathenberg had practically stuffed down his throat during the interview at the beginning of the election campaign. It was just a small detour. Torp had leafed through the book a little. It was actually quite impressive what Truman had accomplished in the uncertainty of the postwar years, something rather different from the current president of the superpower.

Torp stepped on the pedals. He felt the wind whistling through his hair and the little beads of sweat on his forehead. It had been a long time since he had cycled so far, a long time since he had used his body actively at all. He would do that when all this was over—Jeppe Mikkelsen, vote count, Spang-Johansen, the work activation, Arne Lund, the *Daily News*, the tumour—when everything was sorted out and in place, he would get more exercise. Running or cycling. Maybe both. He didn't want to be a *mamil*—middle-aged man in Lycra. They looked silly, and he couldn't afford the equipment either. A pedal up to his old garden gate; out to Amager nature reserve and back; up to Dyrehaven, past Sofie and Jonathan—he wanted to be reconciled with Jonathan. And run around Damhus Lake. It wasn't so far, but run he would.

Torp couldn't remember when he had last addressed his future. Karen hadn't just declared her love for him by scolding him, she had committed to him, to them.

He was past Østerbrogade, past Svanemøllen, now Hellerup and Strandvejen. The clouds were playing with the afternoon sun; first it was out, then it was hidden. He pedalled harder than he should and could feel his heartbeat rising a little too high and the sweat pouring out under his shirt. Otto Brathenberg's villa was up on the left between other large houses; a few of them had yellow ribbons around the giant trees in the front garden. Even wealthy people could be fools—Torp had always known that. The frequency of political ignoramuses and idiots was at least as high in the upper echelons of society as in the lower. It was nice in a way to get it confirmed—*the pleasure of disgust*, as Karen's late father had called the kind of realisations that one was both satisfied with and disgusted by. Ahead lay the severe, functionalist villa belonging to the former Minister of Justice and Foreign Secretary. Torp slowed down, coasted the last bit down the exclusive road, and wiped the sweat off his forehead with his left arm, noting that the scratches from the morning's fight with the yellow ribbon and the bush in front of the flat were no longer bleeding.

He parked the bike on the pavement and took the Truman book off the carrier. If Brathenberg wasn't home, he would put it on the steps by the back door with *thank you for the loan* written on his business card.

Torp went up the driveway.

Brathenberg's Jaguar was parked in the garage. He was home. A bike stood up against the railing by the main steps. Torp went closer but stopped abruptly five metres before the steps.

The bike.

He recognised it.

The expensive, trendy, strange, and Østerbro-modern Biomega, with a small dent on the front mudguard—right where it had hit the cobblestones in front of the wine bar.

What was Katrine Taber-Nielsen doing out at Otto Brathenberg's house? Torp took out his mobile and looked at the last text message from her. It was four hours old. *Still lying in bed with a high fever. Unlikely to be back at the newspaper the rest of the week.*

It made no sense. Torp dropped his first instinct to go up the stairs, call, and get a natural explanation. So she was playing truant from her job at the *Daily News* for a few days—most of the week. She wasn't the first person in the labour market to do that. Goodness me, no. But why with Brathenberg? And why did she feel she had to lie to him?

Torp tried to recall what they had talked about when they sat at the café in Vanløse prior to their visit to Jeppe Mikkelsen's strange sister. She had come from nothing—beans on toast in South Zealand. That is what she had told him. If you were brought up on beans on toast, how did you get one of the last half-century's most powerful civil servants as your godfather? Old Henriksen was more in accord with Katrine's Cambridge and Harvard.

Torp stood in the pea shingle and took small dance steps back and forth. One moment he wanted to ring the bell. The next he wanted to hurry away. He weighed the Truman book in his hand; he could just put it by the back door. No, that would look strangest of all. Torp withdrew without it being a real decision formulated in his head. First backwards, one step, two, three, five. Then he turned around and hurried out onto the pavement, onto his bike, away, still with the Truman book in his left hand. He struggled to get it fastened in the carrier as he cycled back to Strandvejen, his thoughts rushing around wildly in his head. This made no sense. Nor did that.

He swung left. Poul Hasting lived barely a kilometre further up the road.

CHAPTER 17

Words make a difference.

The difference between a freedom fighter and a terrorist is monumental, although the actions seen *from* the outside may seem reminiscent of each other. Ulrik Torp had been taught about the meaning of words and manipulation by an old foreign editor when he started as a trainee journalist. A rebellion movement or a guerrilla movement is in principle the same movement, but with different signatures. Revolutionary, resistance fighter, partisan, rebel, saboteur, radical, activist—much depends on the eye that sees.

Poul Hasting leaned back in the uncomfortable designer chair. His lifelong relativisation of political concepts, his eternal struggle to explain and defend, was, as Torp had envisaged, the real reason for the coffee invitation.

"You wrote in the *Daily News* today that I defended the Rote Armee Fraktion and the group's actions in the 1970s—that is simply not true."

He was friendly and well dressed and smiled at Torp. The German terrorist organisation, also known as the Baader-Meinhof group, was at that time justified and defended in parts of the far left in Europe. Poul Hasting had been part of that grouping, and this was pointed out every time he was written about. Torp observed him with sincere interest: the healthy, slim body, the discreet designer glasses, the clear blue eyes, and the smile—the commissar's smile—reminiscent of the Mona Lisa's. Was it a genuine smile or just a superhuman's arrogant and intellectual way of looking at a world that didn't deserve better? Was it a smile that suggested that here was a man with more privileges than others, with the right to decide, judge, and execute?

Torp had always had a hard time figuring him out. How was it possible to swing so wildly in a political life—from one extreme to the other? Hasting, as written a few years ago in a portrait on the occasion of his sixtieth birthday, *had hardly had a moderate viewpoint in his life.*

"You say 'actions.' Why not use the right word—terror, murder of innocents?"

"Ah, come now, Torp," protested Hasting. "They weren't exactly innocent. They were carefully selected people from what we then called the ruling class. Several of them had been active Nazis during the war."

"What does that have to do with assassinations, kidnappings, and full-blown executions?"

Hasting leaned forward. He had had this discussion hundreds of times over more than forty years. Several times with himself. Had he been too far out? Yes, along with many others. They had cultivated the theory of the armed revolution, that it was the only possibility for the people—the proletariat—to gain power. Those in power would naturally never give up their privileges. Violence was not a desire, but a possibility you couldn't renounce as a revolutionary. The flirtation with the terrorist groups in Italy and especially West Germany was a mistake. He had realised this quite quickly at the time, but still too late, although several polls in West Germany had shown that he had been far from alone. An astonishingly high level of understanding prevailed among the German people about the political worldview of the Rote Armee Fraktion. The historically big mistake was that the country hadn't taken on a confrontation with the Nazi era. With the acceptance of the Americans, many Nazis from Hitler's time had been allowed to continue working untouched, building the German *Wirtschaftswunder.* People had just carried on as usual and didn't talk about it. *Daddy, what did you do during the war?* That wasn't a question that was asked during the German miracle, as the nation incorporated into the EC and NATO.

"I was in good company. The French philosopher Jean-Paul Sartre regarded West Germany as a continuation of Nazi Germany, and therefore the Rote Armee Fraktion in his view was a resistance movement."

"Was that your view, too?"

"Ah, Torp. That's too easy. Sartre visited Andreas Baader in Stammheim Prison in 1974. He subsequently criticised the West German government for actually using torture against Andreas Baader and Ulrike Meinhof. That isn't at all the same as paying homage to terror. On the contrary, in fact."

"Forget Sartre. Back to you. You later wrote that as a socialist there was no reason to join the bourgeois howling chorus over the Rote Armee Fraktion because it would obscure the political content of the struggle."

Torp had done his homework. The quote from the mid-1970s was referenced almost verbatim. He knew it was a sore point with Hasting— the one he had always retracted the last forty years or more when it was touched on.

"And at the same time, I distanced myself from their activities. In the same sentence. Remember that." His index finger was stuck out warningly.

"What a balancing act!"

"Yes, that was back then."

Hasting smiled again. He had delivered his message. He never let a handling of his embarrassing writings go unchallenged.

"Is it that easy? 'That was back then'?"

Torp felt his mobile vibrating in the inside pocket of his blazer. He had put it on silent. It was the third time.

Hasting got to his feet. "Come with me. There's something I want to show you."

He had received Torp as if he were a prodigal son when he had opened the front door. Yellow ribbons were hanging around the trees in the front garden. There were several boxes with yellow ribbons in the hall. Some young contras were sorting them into bags to be distributed throughout the metropolitan area later in the day. They looked up at Torp with light in their eyes, but quickly sensed that he wasn't part of the movement, and immediately lost interest in him. If they had been bald and dressed in loose robes, they could just as well have been spending this Wednesday afternoon at Hare Krishna, he thought.

"This is becoming a whole movement," said Hasting contentedly while shuffling past the boxes and indicating to his guest that he should just follow him. The coffee was ready in the modern, compact, and stylistically consistent living room. This was Hasting's childhood home and the villa was part of Danish political history. Both of his parents had been prominent resistance fighters during World War II and several acts of sabotage had been planned in the villa.

His father had later become a long-time Member of Parliament for the fringe of the Conservative Party, a political standpoint doomed to clash with a rebellious, long-haired son incited by youth rebellion, Marxism, and opposition to the United States and the Vietnam War. The clash between father and son had become a public affair in 1975. And it was a corner of that story that Poul Hasting wanted to show his guest.

"Down here," he explained, going on slightly insecure legs down the stairs to the cellar.

Torp took the opportunity to check who was so eager to get hold of him on the phone. It was Simon the intern.

They stepped down into the cellar, the first part of which served as a laundry room. It was neat and tidy like the rest of the house. The washing machine and the tumble dryer were both spinning. Torp could just about stand upright. Hasting had to bow his gangly body a little. They went on, deeper into the lit cellar to the next room with cupboards, storage boxes, and shelves filled with books, further into the next room, all lying in a line with each other like pearls on a string, with no doors in between.

"Here," said Hasting, pointing towards the last room, which was a square of four metres per side. The ceiling was a little lower, there were no small windows at the top of the walls as in the other rooms, and the entrance was a little narrower. "This is where they lay, the weapons."

Torp could well remember the story. He had the iconic press photo of the room filled with old weapons fresh in his memory.

It was after the death of both of Hasting's parents, a long time after, during Ulla Hasting's first term as a minister for the Labour Party. Water damage in the cellar had forced the builders to break down some of the wall, and behind it they discovered the secret room filled with old weapons: pistols, machine guns, hand grenades, boxes of ammunition, and even gas masks. It had been part of a fairly extensive so-called stay-behind stockpile built up in the late 1940s and 1950s as a defence against the Communist occupation of the country, which even high-ranking politicians at times believed was imminent.

No one had known about the huge stockpile in the Hellerup villa. Or it would be more correct to say that those who had were either dead, demented, or kept their mouths shut.

"It was primarily former resistance fighters who were responsible for it. They feared that the politicians, as in 1940, would prove weak and cooperative. At the same time, they doubted the willingness in parts of the Danish defence forces."

Hasting again looked at his guest with his commissar smile, as friendly as a calm sea, where you have no idea about the depth and what is hiding down there.

"So explain to me, Torp—were they freedom fighters, or were they a guerrilla movement? Was there really such a big difference between what they were prepared to do and what the Rote Armee Fraktion did?"

"I don't acknowledge your relativism," said Torp.

His phone vibrated again. It was about time Simon calmed down.

"And the Blekingegade Gang? Their arsenal was barely larger than my father's. Was there really any difference between them and my father?"

"You can't mean that question seriously," exclaimed Torp.

"Nah, not quite," admitted Hasting. "But they each sincerely believed that what they were doing was right. We can probably agree on that much."

This last comment wasn't meant as a question. They had both inched into the room, which was completely empty except for a broken wooden tennis racket that lay dusty and overlooked in one corner. Torp forgot the lower height to the concrete ceiling and bumped his head slightly.

Hasting was clearly amusing himself. This wasn't a battle of emotions for him; it was an intellectual game, a battle of words.

"You've never held an extreme opinion in your life, I guess. Always in the middle of the road, always the status quo."

"Ha. I was a supporter of nuclear power," exclaimed Torp with an expression on his face that showed that he, as the guest in the cellar, accepted the premise of the discussion.

"But that was exactly the tune the ruling class was playing."

"You and your ruling class. For me, it was a climate-friendly energy source. Nothing else."

"But that means your eyes are closed. Everything is politics. If you don't acknowledge that, then you are yourself politicising things."

"And thus I am political, no matter what I do," protested Torp.

"Exactly, Torp. You're learning."

They left the cellar, back to the living room. Torp checked his phone again. This time it wasn't the intern. It was Anton, his long-time source at Police Headquarters.

"More coffee?" Hasting was signalling that the game was over and that he had won.

"Did you ever actually reconcile with your father?"

Torp took the opportunity to change tracks. He could feel the phone vibrating again. What could be so important?

Hasting shook his head. "He died in 1987. Twelve years after the scandal that followed The Firm's exposure. I didn't even attend his funeral." The older, well-kept man spread his arms. "I regret that immensely today. Not because of my father, but because of the pain it caused my mother that her eldest son didn't come to his father's funeral. I should have done that. For her sake."

"Have you forgiven him?"

Hasting twisted in his chair. He wasn't used to that kind of intimate probing of his emotional life. He was into rationales, plans, strategies, analyses—his whole life had in a way been centred on that. He and his wife had opted out of having children, first because of their political commitment and unwillingness to bring children into a world close to nuclear war and annihilation or, at the very least, bourgeoisification. Later, the opt-out became just as much an expression of comfort. In addition to a marriage, Poul and Ulla Hasting were also half a century of an unbreakable work and ideas fellowship.

Few knew of his inner struggles.

"Forgiveness. That's a big word."

He thought for a long time and began unusually cautiously.

"I think I see my father more as a historical figure, someone you read about, like Stalin or Martin Luther King."

He stopped, realising the odd couple he had lined up.

"Without comparing them, of course," he said before continuing. "It's easy to both disagree with and be angry with Stalin and everything he did, but it's difficult to be personally offended. That's how I feel about my father today."

He looked up uncertainly.

"Do you understand what I mean?"

Torp nodded. He could easily understand that.

"In 1975, when our former Prime Minister, in a drunken state, told a journalist about The Firm, I didn't know that my father had been a part of it."

Ulrik Torp knew all about the story of The Firm. He could faintly remember the fuss but wasn't even a teenager when it was first written about. Since then, he had read about it several times with equal parts fascination, astonishment, and disgust. A number of former resistance fighters had got in touch with the CIA after World War II and agreed to set up a private intelligence service. Several of the members had also become employed by the Danish Military Intelligence Service, the FE, but didn't say anything to the leadership. Several changing Prime Ministers and a few other top politicians had known about The Firm and left it at that. The message had been that if they were exposed, then they would stand alone; nothing was in writing and no one would come to their defence. The CIA, several employers' organisations, and individual parties had paid for The Firm's not entirely insignificant expenses via brown envelopes with cash that couldn't be traced.

Torp thought that The Firm had an element of naive cops and robbers about it; a feeling that many of the members had substantiated through their involvement in the Home Guard, which for the first many years after the war had been dominated by the thinking of the resistance movement.

The members of The Firm—no one actually knew to this day how many they were—had observed, noted, made lists, and conducted conspiracies. They had made sure to recruit new members in key parts of Danish society, in the central administration, among politicians, at the top of the business community, and in the media. Many people had acted as listening posts and had had, to put it mildly, an exaggerated notion of the importance of their own efforts.

But The Firm's position in a vacuum between official intelligence and ordinary civil society had nevertheless been so unique that it had also provided an opportunity to do some of the things that a legitimate intelligence service under parliamentary scrutiny could not, may not, or dare not do. Among other things, it had carried out a seven-year wiretapping in the home of the deputy chairman of the Danish Communist Party, who had also had a seat in Parliament. Everything had been passed on to the CIA.

The Firm had created "fake news" in the form of letters to party members with information from the wiretaps to divide the Communists. And it had succeeded. Division and paranoia had spread further in the party, and The Firm had been instrumental in the Communists' long-standing and dethroned chairman initiating a collaboration with—of all organisations—the CIA.

And at the same time, several of the members had been active in "stay-behind," which—again with the approval and support of the Americans—had set up large and small weapons depots around the country, including the secret cellar room in the Hasting villa in Hellerup, in order to be ready if the Communists came and the official Denmark again betrayed the country.

The scandal that emerged after an alcoholic ex-Prime Minister's slip of the tongue revealed the existence of the organisation should have been much bigger than it was, thought Torp. But in some way or another, too many people had been directly or indirectly involved for it to really get off the ground. It had come to light much later that a subsequent minister and top politician in the Labour Party had even taken an active part in the wiretapping of the Communists' deputy chairman. As part of a trusted student job, he had sat in the flat underneath and—for 400 kroner a month—faithfully pressed start and stop on the tape recorder when the talking above either began or ended. Far too many people in far too high positions in far too many different parties, organisations, and ministries had had an interest in hushing up the case.

It was extra-parliamentary, it was thumpingly illegal, and it had involved the top echelons of society. And no one had been prosecuted.

The fear of the Communists had been real, as several people explained. It was another time.

Ulla Hasting entered the living room, saw Torp, and greeted him reservedly. She was more private than her husband, and thus also more vulnerable. As a minister for many years—for two different parties, to boot—it was probably inevitable. Torp had written quite a few critical articles about her, and he could see from her facial expression that she remembered a number of them.

"Torp is back at the *Daily News*," her husband explained. "Isn't that nice?"

Ulla Hasting didn't comment on how nice it was. "I think we're going to run out of yellow ribbons. I'll order some more boxes."

"You do that, darling."

She nodded and left them.

"Had you never sensed that your father was in The Firm?"

Poul Hasting shook his head. "Not for a second. But when the story broke back then during Christmas 1975, I could see from his demeanour that something was up."

Hasting was staring blankly in front of him. He remained in the same living room, but he was more than forty years back in time.

"So I asked him. I was sitting in a chair—over there." He pointed over at the fireplace at the other end of the living room.

"And what did he answer?"

"That they hadn't trusted the politicians. That April ninth, 1940 showed what could be expected of them."

"But they bypassed everything—democracy, the institutions, the Danish population. Everything they had fought for in the resistance movement," argued Torp.

"That's not how they saw it. My father quoted the German author Thomas Mann and asked me if one should be so tolerant that one tolerates one's own downfall. A step to one side violates democracy. A step to the other side opens you up to totalitarian regimes. He thought he had been keeping the balance."

"What did you say to that?"

"I left." Hasting looked up. "And told the press about him. That was the last time I saw my father."

"And then shortly after, you defended the Rote Armee Fraktion."

"To give him something to think about, yes."

Hasting was talking more to himself than to his guest.

"What really happened to The Firm?"

"As I recall it, it had been exposed internally as early as 1963. The head of the Military Intelligence Service found out that it existed and that several of his closest staff members were involved. But its time was already over by then. The fear of an immediate Soviet invasion had gone, the Danish Communist Party had been repulsed, the Labour Party was heavily in power in the country and in the workplace." He spread his arms again. "It had become a bit of a family business or fraternity. Several of them came and went here in the house. If I had been a little older, I might have been lured into it as a youngster. When I was old enough, the youth uprising was slowly beginning, and the length of my hair didn't really fit The Firm. It's my impression that it slowly faded away during the sixties. That was also the official communiqué in 1975."

"And now you've become a contra."

Hasting leaned back and let out a loud laugh. "You have to admit that it's become a hit, with the yellow ribbon and the ridiculous song."

"But why?"

"Why what?"

"Why contra? Why campaign for not voting? Why the drawing of lots among citizens to fill Parliament?"

Hasting became serious. "Things are at breaking point, Torp. There are no authorities. No hierarchies. And worst of all: no faith in the future. Inequality, refugees, Muslims, pollution, climate, terror—it's all piling up."

Torp suddenly felt a surge of anger in his body. "And in that situation, it helps to undermine representative democracy?"

"My father didn't think that representative democracy was sufficient in either the 1940s, '50s, or '60s, even though he was himself a Member of Parliament for part of the time. I didn't think it was enough in the '70s, I admit that. Maybe I'm back to the same conclusion now—just in a slightly different way."

"You were against the ruling class. Then you were against Muslims and left-wingers. And now are you just against everything?"

Hasting leaned forward. "I'm against change, Torp. That's something completely different."

"What became of the revolution?"

"Are you familiar with the concept of uncertainty reduction?"

Torp shook his head.

"Uncertainty reduction—we're looking for ways we can reduce uncertainty in our lives. Look around you, Torp. Look at yourself and your own life. We're all doing it in our small, petty lives. We're trying to make everything safe and secure and shield ourselves from outside upheavals. Migrants across the Mediterranean and population explosion in Africa. The pressure on our Royal Danish welfare state, this small country club we're no longer allowed to have in peace. The great politicians of the coming decades won't be the ones promising reforms or revolutions. The future belongs to politicians who can *hinder* reforms and revolutions. Those who can promise renewal without change. That will be the political demand. Seen in that light, Prime Minister Palle Enevoldsen's opening speech yesterday was brilliant. The most boring of the decade, it was called. I say thank you very much."

Hasting was warming up to his theme.

"Look around in Europe and the United States—the whole Western world. Today's summit in Brussels and the resolutions against Russia. Do you really think that is what the people are demanding? Enmity with a neighbour because of a peninsula far away? Come on, Torp."

Hasting leaned forward. He let his listener understand that this was important, handing him a book lying on the table.

"Oswald Spengler, *The Decline of the West—Der Untergang des Abendlandes*. It was written a hundred years ago, but it's more urgent than ever. It can all go completely wrong."

Torp took the book in his hand, mostly out of courtesy.

"People are tired of experiments, tired of being told what to think, tired of taking responsibility for the whole world, tired of having the white man's chronically bad conscience, tired of intellectuals, insecurity, robots, and migrants. They just want to be allowed to live a quiet, safe life." Hasting spread his arms. "Is that so bad?"

Torp tried to nod and shake his head at the same time.

"The yellow ribbons, the song, the support for not voting, the provocation of filling Parliament with members selected by lottery, Torp. This isn't politics. It's anti-politics."

"Everything is politics, if you remember," replied Torp.

"Touché." Hasting took the shot without allowing himself to be affected by it and struck back.

"What about you, Torp? Is there nothing at all you're ready to fight for? Apart from your quiet life, I mean?"

Torp dodged the question. He was about to become entangled in a personal political discussion with Poul Hasting, and he had no desire to be. On the other hand, the intellectual cynic fascinated him. His mobile was again ringing in the inside pocket of his blazer.

"And now you're back at the *Daily News*?"

Torp hesitated; he couldn't be bothered to explain about the work activation and the municipal benefits department. He remarked that his guest visit to the *Daily News* was initially just in connection with the election, and that he had his own business. As a kind of documentation of that, he presented his business card.

Torp Communication—competence and experience.

"The address isn't correct, but the phone number and email are fine," he pointed out, as if he owed him an explanation—of that, too.

Hasting looked up. Torp felt like he had been rumbled. How could he think he could hide his downfall from the commissar?

"You're welcome to write on our online media if you're lacking a platform."

Torp suppressed an outburst. The Hasting couple's realnews.dk admittedly received financial support from the public purse, but it was only taken seriously by the self-righteous crowd around the couple, which admittedly was quite large. The overarching tenor was that a ruling class and deep state was controlling society, and that the established media was a part of that conspiracy.

"I know what you're thinking," said Hasting, stealing a march on him. "Take it as a standing invitation; we have many readers."

He shifted to the front of his chair as a sign that the session was coming to an end.

"Ah, well—but since you're at the *Daily News* a little longer yet, you can probably find out more about The Firm from one of your journalist colleagues at the newspaper."

Torp put his business card on the table.

"Katrine Taber-Nielsen," continued Hasting.

"What about her?"

"Her grandfather, Arne Taber, was one of the founders of The Firm and was in it till the end. Didn't you know that?"

CHAPTER 18

They were in Emma's room in a flat in Østerbro, which she shared with two other students.

Torp looked at her world in wonder. The large desk that occupied half of her home was filled with PCs, monitors, large and small boxes, a tangle of wires, and small lights of various colours that were flashing incessantly.

In the middle of it all was Emma, the *Daily News*'s quiet intern with the blonde hair and the harmless articles. She had two keyboards and three screens going at the same time and was mastering them as if she was the conductor of a symphony orchestra launching into the most difficult version of Wagner.

Simon sat back to front on an unsteady wicker chair following what she was doing. Torp was standing up; there wasn't room for any more chairs. An unmade three-quarter bed filled the rest of the room. The only light came from the computer screens and a dusty, dented Poul Henningsen lamp hovering close to Emma's head. A skewed black roller blind prevented the light from the late afternoon sun from penetrating through the room's only window and reflecting on the screens.

Torp had cycled from Poul Hasting's Hellerup villa with a feeling of being repulsed and attracted at the same time. This ability to turn things upside down was both intellectually alluring and frightening. How could he possibly cram the resistance movement, his father, the Rote Armee Fraktion, and the Blekingegade Gang into the same box? The man was rhetorically seductive to weak souls, like the two young people who were currently handing out his yellow ribbons in the metropolitan area instead of working in a supermarket or helping as volunteers in the Danish Red Cross.

And yet he had hit the spot with several of his analyses. Poul and Ulla Hasting had been part of the backdrop to Danish politics for almost fifty years, periodically right at the front of the stage, both as personal actors and as a sign of the times. She had been a minister for the Labour Party when it had a tailwind. Then she had been a minister for the Liberals when their time came. Now it was the rebellion against everything that the couple had tuned into with the accuracy of a seismograph. Torp was in no doubt that Poul Hasting meant every single word. It was a characteristic of almost all intellectual populists throughout history—they knew what they were doing and meant it.

That Katrine Taber-Nielsen's grandfather was Arne Taber, one of the founders of The Firm and active in it to the last, only added to the list of strange information about his journalist colleague at the *Daily News*—this beans-on-toast girl, as she herself referred to her background. Why had she reported sick when she obviously wasn't? What in the world was she doing with the former Minister of Justice and Foreign Secretary Otto Brathenberg, the ageing member of the board at the *Daily News*? Or at least her bike was there; that didn't necessarily have to mean that she was there. *For goodness' sake, Ulrik, you're fooling yourself; of course she was there.*

And then Simon's information that she was the goddaughter of Henriksen—*that* Henriksen; father of editor-in-chief Asbjørn Henriksen; Mr. Slotsholmen, as he had been known, the powerful, long-standing head of department in both the Ministry of Justice and the Ministry of Foreign Affairs.

Had she concealed the information or just not told him? Did it mean anything? And if so, what?

Torp saw neither right nor wrong in any of it. He had got off his bike a few hundred metres from the Hastings, texted Katrine, and asked her to call him. It was important.

Then he had rung Anton at Police Headquarters.

"Hi, it's Torp. You called?" Normally, the traffic went the other way.

"Yes, I promised to call you if anything new came up about Jeppe Mikkelsen in Ørstedsparken."

"And?"

"It's not much."

Torp's pulse was already going down again. "Not much." There was nothing about his family or circle of friends that indicated anything—not even his brother. He didn't owe money to anyone other than the mortgage company; none of his colleagues in the Ministry could say anything at all unfavourable about him. Quite a few were barely aware of his existence. Jeppe Mikkelsen was so straightforward and deadly boring that it was enough to send a criminal investigator mad.

"But we have traced the Neuhausen, the gun that was used. The one we found in a rubbish bin."

Torp said nothing. He thought it was the quickest way for Anton to get to the essentials.

"Yes, it was a little difficult. It had been ground down so that it couldn't be traced. But that happened many years ago. We've got a new technique for something like that," he said, embarking on what could become a long technical explanation.

"Anton. Get to the point," exclaimed Torp as kindly as he could. He was standing with his bike on Strandvejen by the Tuborg Harbour and needed a pee to boot. The coffee from Hasting had run through.

"It doesn't have to mean anything, but we don't have many clues. The murder weapon was a service pistol in the Military Intelligence Service back in the 1960s."

"And?"

"And nothing more. That was all. I mean, I told you it wasn't much," said Anton defensively. "You can't get much out of it. The Neuhausen had been used as a service pistol for officers and others, also in the Army for a number of years back then. But now we at least know that it originates here, in Denmark. Not from abroad."

Torp could feel the disappointment. More than three weeks had gone by since Jeppe Mikkelsen had been shot in Ørstedsparken. It wasn't much.

"Now I have you on the line, Anton. Unsolved murder cases are never dropped, right?"

"It hasn't even been four weeks yet," he protested.

"I'm not talking about this one. Back in 1973, a Spang-Johansen was murdered. He was also a civil servant, and that murder has apparently never been solved. Could you check it out?"

"Seventy-three!" protested Anton. "Do you think we have too many employees at Police Headquarters, since you think I should spend time on that?"

"Exactly."

Anton sighed. "I can't bear to ask why. I'll go down to the archive and dust it off, if I have time. No guarantee."

"Roger. More?"

"Roger. No more."

Torp had to pee even more now. He would have a headwind going into the city, he realised, and answered Simon's text message. The intern had called a total of four times in the hour and a half that the visit to Hasting had lasted. Finally, there was just a text message with Emma's address in Classensgade, asking him to come as soon as possible. Torp wrote that he would be there in ten minutes.

It took almost twenty.

Emma's thin fingers danced across both keyboards while she took control with two wireless mice. One computer screen was filled with numbers and characters that didn't mean a thing to Torp.

"Could someone explain to me what we're looking at?" he tried.

Emma looked up, stopped working, and shuffled around a bit in her office chair, which was just another wonky kitchen chair with broken wickerwork in the back.

"This," she said, pointing at the screen, "is the mainframe at Statistics Denmark. It's hard to believe, but they're still using it—along with a normal cloud setup, of course."

Torp said nothing. Emma could see that he understood nothing. She had to start further down.

"It's about which system is being used. Mainframes are from the awful old days when computers filled a wardrobe or more. Lots of big companies still use mainframes—in combination, of course, with other systems."

"Of course," Torp heard himself say.

"There is typically a lot, and I mean a lot, of work invested in the infrastructure and processes in one of these, so there's no way it can pay for banks, shipping companies—old companies—to start all over again only with cloud services and modern architecture such as Google or Facebook. And then also good old Statistics Denmark with this EC12er," she said with a smile.

Torp remembered that Simon had talked to Emma about getting into the election computer which Statistics Denmark was using in collaboration with the Ministry of the Interior. The boy intern had firmly believed that someone had cheated with the Nationalists' votes in the election ever since the visit to Sofie's brother-in-law, Svend, in Hillerød. His 4 per cent discovery was remarkable, but he had to be hiding an explanation, a mistake. Torp had been startled by Simon's remark that Emma would ask some hackers from Estonia to break into the system but didn't frankly take it seriously. People said so much.

"Is it the hackers from Estonia?"

Emma nodded.

"How?"

"It turned out to be a piece of cake. It only took them a few hours. I could have done it myself. It would just have taken a little longer," she admitted.

It was clear that the hackers from Estonia were at the top of a hierarchy that Torp knew very little about.

The old man in the room looked at the young girl and her fine, pale parchment skin that testified to far too little light and far too poor food.

She was, Torp knew from the *Daily News*'s canteen, a discreet but inveterate vegan, first and foremost because of climate change, not so much because it was a pity for the animals. Her life was serious.

He may often have been uncomprehending towards that generation and its music, but he was equally safe in the knowledge that they were the ones who were going to take over the globe. They could neither spell nor use commas, but what did that mean in the bigger picture? They had a firm, secure compass for what was right and wrong.

Parents and elementary school were better than their reputation. Much had been achieved, as was the case with Simon and Emma.

"They owed me a favour." She gave a slight shrug as an explanation for the unspoken question.

"Owed you a favour?" Torp was both shocked and impressed.

"Did you think it was only pale boys who can be computer programmers?" Simon looked at Torp, obviously proud of Emma's abilities. "Emma can program a Ford Mondeo to drive down Gammel Kongevej without a driver."

"Ah," said Emma, suddenly looking a little shy. "Preferably not during the rush hour and without too many cyclists." They laughed knowingly.

"What did you do for them since they owed you a favour?"

Emma shook her head.

"You don't want to know anything about that, Torp," said Simon. It was meant quite seriously, he was made to understand.

Torp sensed the seriousness and suddenly became curious.

"So, is there anything to look at?"

He looked at Emma. She nodded. "I'm looking for an algorithm. It's always wrapped in the part of the application that handles input and output. Do you understand?"

"No." Torp shook his head gently but indicated that she should just continue.

"You can always see if a program that contains an algorithm has been changed. A hash was created when the system was put into operation." She looked up and tried to translate. "That's a checksum of the file. A digital fingerprint."

The last bit meant a little to Torp. He nodded. Continue.

"The most commonly used is md5sum, but md5 is no longer secure enough for important files. They've found that out at Statistics Denmark despite everything." Emma shook her head. She was clearly not impressed. "They have therefore used a newer hash—sha256sum. You either save the fingerprint or compare it to a copy. Here is the fingerprint that has been saved."

"Emma. I understand nothing. Nothing." Torp stood bent over anyway and looked at the screen in astonishment.

"They've used a high-level programming language. Here in Java. We could find Fortran or C elsewhere on this old grinder." She typed a few times, clicked with the mouse, and got a new screen picture that was just as incomprehensible to Torp. "I've decompiled it and used a debugger to see what happens to data while running the program. They've hidden it well. The algorithm is only activated in operation, not during testing. Impossible to debug without access to the mainframe."

"Emma! Look at me. I don't understand a word of what you're saying."

She took a deep breath, thought for two seconds, and sighed at the wall of ignorance and the generation gap she was being confronted with.

"Someone has been fiddling with the computer in Statistics Denmark that received and calculated the number of votes on election night so that the Nationalists and the New Radicals both received fewer votes."

Emma said it without any passion in her voice. That's just the way it was.

"We were right, Torp. All along. Also with the four per cent."

It was probably mostly Simon who had been right all along, thought Torp without correcting the intern. He was still having a hard time believing it. Election fraud in Denmark? It had never happened before. According to researchers, the Danish electoral system competed with the Finnish to be the safest in the world. Above all, it was transparent.

It is difficult to pull off a massive swindle with a pencil, as the election experts often put it when they had to explain why Russian interference in other Western countries wouldn't be possible in Denmark.

The pencil in particular had its limitations. Torp recalled that twenty years ago, a local politician had been accused of putting extra ticks by her own name on ballot papers that had simply been ticked off for her party. It had happened during the count that she had been assigned to. She was accused of giving herself a few handfuls of extra personal votes. Torp didn't remember how the case ended. That was the level it was at in Denmark.

"When did that happen?" he asked Emma.

In explanation, she pointed to the middle of the screen, but, as far as Torp was concerned, she could just as well have stuck her hand in a pile of sand.

"Here in the access log. They are in on Thursday last week between eight fourteen and eight thirty-three p.m. Again from ten oh four to ten seventeen. Finished. Then they're out."

Thursday was election night.

Suddenly, it all fell into place in Torp's head. Of course.

The exit polls came on both TV channels at 8:00 p.m. and were amazingly similar. The Nationalists and the New Radicals were both just over the 2 per cent threshold. If you assumed that those numbers were almost accurate—and exit polls were these days—then you knew how much had to be deducted to land below the threshold. Then it was just a matter of changing input and output, or whatever the hell Emma had called it; in with one vote total—out with another. They corrected once and both parties landed just under 2 per cent of the vote; all in all, 7,000–8,000 votes.

In the United States, less than 100,000 votes distributed differently in three states would have given another President at the last election. Power had become tissue-thin at more and more elections in the Western world. The last two governments in Denmark had held power by just one or two mandates.

Small numbers, small corrections that the individual candidate might wonder about, but who would have an overview? And when? There were 1,400 polling stations in Denmark. That was six to seven votes on average per polling station. Like the banker who rounded the decimals to his own account and became a millionaire until someone stumbled upon it. Like the white Africans who tried to pinch a few extra seats in the 1994 South African general election. That was what Jeppe Mikkelsen—the young civil servant in the Ministry of the Interior—had got wind of and hinted at to his wife and sister a few days before he was shot in Ørstedsparken. Fragments of a telephone conversation in the ministry or overhearing a discreet conversation in a meeting room about the plans. Enough for him to surf the Net a bit at home and then the futile—and fatal—attempt to talk confidentially with the head of department or the Minister about his suspicions.

But why the Nationalists and the New Radicals? They each in principle supported their own prime ministerial candidate, stood in their respective blocs, and disagreed on pretty much everything. Ulrik Torp was looking for an explanation.

Simon interrupted his thoughts.

"Now we can write the story."

Simon looked excitedly at his watch, Emma, and Torp at more or less the same time.

"It's not even five o'clock. If we call Arne Lund and say we're on our way, we can have it in the newspaper tomorrow." He got up, his eyes shining with excitement.

Torp shook his head. "We're onto a story, but so far we're only onto half of it." He corrected himself. "Less than half."

Emma just looked at him. Simon wanted to protest. Torp pointed at the computer screen.

"We have an algorithm that has been changed. We have four examples where the candidates remember a number other than the official one. Three of them are from the Nationalists and the difference is four per cent for all three. Can we see who's been inside the election computer?" He looked at Emma. She shook her head.

"No chance. They've used a VPN to get in, so there are only tracks for the first proxy. That's all. It could be someone in the Ministry, but it could also be someone from outside."

Torp knew nothing about VPNs but understood the conclusion. "We don't know who's behind it, we don't know what the purpose has been, we don't know if there is a connection to the murder of Jeppe Mikkelsen in Ørstedsparken."

"But we know that the algorithm has been tampered with. That someone has cheated with the election," objected Simon.

"Precisely, Bernstein. Someone. We don't know who, why, how much, or how. Those are way too many unanswered questions for my liking. Didn't you learn that at the School of Journalism?"

"I'm at the University of Southern Denmark."

"Whatever!"

Woodward shook his head. No story yet.

Torp cycled from Østerbro along the lakes before turning right along Gammel Kongevej towards Frederiksberg. Could Emma really program a car to drive without a driver? It was an exaggeration, of course, but it made him wonder about how he had been able to overlook her. How the entire editorial staff of the *Daily News* had overlooked her. She was quiet, but maybe it would have been different if she had been a boy. How many girls with unusual abilities were overlooked in the boys' club that the media branch still was, despite the large number of female journalists? Maybe it suited her perfectly to be a little overlooked, a little invisible, a little different. Simon was the opposite type—firmly convinced that he could change the world. He wasn't *that* good, but, as he remembered from some teen TV from when Sofie was young, you could come a long way with self-confidence, charm, and gorgeous hair. Not that there was anything particularly gorgeous about his hair, but the self-confidence and charm weren't lacking in the very young Bernstein.

Ha!

Watergate!

Was this his Watergate or his Waterloo? The story could tip both ways. It could be really big. It could also be the misunderstanding that Torp was constantly looking for, the natural explanation that would checkmate the whole paranoia.

Simon had found out more about Spang-Johansen, an eighty-two-year-old widow who now lived in a nursing home in Valby. She had apparently not remarried, had no children and no family, for that matter.

Torp had great confidence in Simon's abilities on the internet. If Simon said there was no family, then there was no family. He wasn't hacking, not in the true sense; at least that was Torp's impression. But he took full advantage of the opportunities that existed and arose online. The boy was born with it, when it came to the internet, fast search engines and powerful computers. He had never experienced anything else and took what deeply impressed Torp for granted.

Spang-Johansen's widow was called Martha. Full stop.

Torp looked at his watch. It was getting on for six. The sun hadn't set yet, the shops on Gammel Kongevej were closing, the rush hour was over, and now that he had a tailwind, he arrived just as fast as the cars. Karen had gone to a literature evening with her book club, Erik Aalbæk Jensen's *The Chalk Line*.

He made a quick decision and turned left at the City Hall—towards Valby.

He didn't notice the little red Peugeot that had been following him faithfully since the lakes.

CHAPTER 19

The stone was the size of an adult fist. Pitched hard, arcing upwards in a precise, straight line, it shattered the double glazed window of the flat, continued through the room, and thudded into the opposite wall.

The crash also shattered the silence of the night in the property, which with its two-room flats now had the character of a hall of residence for upper-middle-class children. The noise lasted a few seconds as shards of glass fell to the floor, leaving particle-size glass splinters lying evenly spread in the living room. A large piece of glass hung from the top of the window frame, before dropping like an icicle and hitting the radiator with a crack. A figure quickly moved away from the street, out onto Finsensvej, and disappeared.

The odd person turned in their bed, checked the time on their mobile, which was a quarter to three at night, and then slept on.

So much happened these days.

Karen wanted to call the police. Ulrik argued against. What use would it be? When the police were barely managing to investigate cars set on fire, what good would it do to involve a police force that clearly didn't want to be involved?

"Maybe there are fingerprints on it," she exclaimed.

Karen stood in bare feet and a short nightgown in the hallway with her head into the living room. She looked at the stone that had bounced off the wall into the middle of the floor.

"We could have been killed if the bedroom had been in here."

Ulrik had put his slippers on and was dressed only in underpants in the living room.

"This is a gross boyish prank."

His gaze went from the stone and up to the smashed window pane. He hoped he was right—that it was just a prank. If Jeppe Mikkelsen had been killed due to the suspicion or certainty of election fraud, then the same thing could surely happen to him. But no one knew about his research—except Simon and Emma. He pushed the thought away. Of course it was a prank.

The chilly October wind was blowing into the flat. Ulrik could already hear the radiator's thermostat turning up the heat in a futile attempt to compensate. He had to get hold of a glazier with a round-the-clock service so that a board could be put up immediately. Tomorrow he would have to call the owner of the flat. Such a thing should be taken care of by the owner and the owner's insurance company.

So there were a few benefits of not owning the bloody flat anymore. Jonathan would have to sort it out.

Karen had come home a little later than he had. It had been a lovely evening at the book club. Erik Aalbæk Jensen's *The Chalk Line* was excellent, she had explained enthusiastically as they shared a bottle of cheap South African red wine.

"Just imagine a thin line between doing the right thing and the totally wrong."

Karen had begun talking about the book in more detail, about the two Danish Waffen-SS volunteers, the farmer's son Bertel Jørgensen and the smallholder's son Hardy Bunken, who had fought on the Eastern Front and had then absconded from the regiment, just wanting to go home, and about their treason and the happenstance that made them traitors.

Torp had pretended to listen, had actually done so for short fragments. No, he had never read it. He wanted to, but he didn't read as much as she did, as she knew. Yes, the line between right and wrong could be thin. But his thoughts had been with Martha Spang-Johansen, the widow at the nursing home in Valby.

The place had refused to let him in.

"Are you a relative?" a brusque female voice on the door phone had wanted to know when he had rung the bell that evening.

Torp had been tempted to say yes. A distant nephew would have been an open sesame, but it was a mortal sin as a journalist to lie about his role. You could only go undercover or otherwise hide your identity as a journalist in very special cases and with the permission of the management. This was nowhere near such a situation.

"Ulrik Torp from the *Daily News*. I'm a journalist," he explained, bending at the knees to be sure to talk clearly into the microphone at the complex.

"We aren't going to have any journalists in here."

"I just need to talk to Martha Spang-Johansen. It's not about the nursing home."

"You must be joking," said the voice, rejecting his request.

Torp took a deep breath. "Couldn't you just open the door? Then perhaps I could tell you a little more about my errand."

"There's no chance whatsoever," was the reply, after which the connection was switched off.

Torp briefly considered ringing again but dropped the idea and at the same time hoped that the old people were being treated better. He sat down on a bench next to the entrance and shuddered slightly. You had to be very weak to get into a nursing home nowadays, as he knew from his father's last days. Maybe Martha Spang-Johansen was senile, so it didn't really matter. On the other hand, if she wasn't, then it was crucial to talk to her.

Jeppe Mikkelsen's remarks to his wife and sister about South Africa, elections, and Nelson Mandela turned out to have something to them. Both of the women had explained that he had also mentioned the name Spang-Johansen in the days leading up to his death. It could be a coincidence that the only Spang-Johansen Simon could find was a civil servant in the central administration who had been murdered—like Jeppe Mikkelsen. Admittedly, it was almost fifty years ago now, but even so. It could also be that it wasn't a coincidence.

Torp looked at his watch. Less than ten minutes had passed. The sun was setting and it wasn't even half past six. The summer was officially over, without the autumn having really taken hold. He really liked these intermediate phases that Denmark was so full of. There was rarely a clear answer to the weather in this country.

All in all, there was rarely a clear answer to anything. That suited him fine.

A middle-aged woman nodded kindly to him, went up the stairs to the nursing home, pressed the intercom, and said, "It's Birthe," whereupon the glass door slid aside and she disappeared. Torp made a quick decision, jumped up, and, without being noticed, just managed to get in before the door slid back again. He turned right, away from what looked like the staff department, down the hallway through a common room where some residents—all women—were sitting around a table.

How much time did you have left as a man when you had turned fifty-five and were in normal health apart from a lump—tumour—in your mouth? Six months? Twenty years? Thirty? Thirty if he was lucky. Friday at Rigshospitalet. With Karen.

Two of the old women were staring blankly into space. One of them was drooling a lot. Another had fallen asleep in her wheelchair. A young girl was feeding a piece of cake to an old woman. There was community singing of some kind on television that no one was paying any attention to. The flat screen looked like the only thing from the present. Everything else—the heavy furniture, the grilles in the floor for the probably slightly defective heating system, the bulging orange Poul Henningsen lamps— all seemed to be from the 1970s. It wasn't only the old people who were worn out and sad.

"You're late," shouted a resident. She was sitting in a comfortable armchair, diagonally behind him, with a cup of coffee in one hand and the saucer in the other.

"It's not your son, Anna."

"He's late," she repeated, now addressing the girl.

"Your son was here yesterday. He comes every Tuesday, you know that."

"Then you're late, too." She looked up at Torp again and wanted to reach out to him, which the cup and saucer prevented.

Torp felt a little awkward as he looked first at the old woman in the armchair, then at the girl. Old people and very young children had never been his forte. He didn't know what to say or do and always came across as gawky. He envied those who could relate to people quite naturally in such situations. The girl, *Christine* it said on her name tag, could clearly do that. She was guaranteed to be good at condolences, too. That was another thing Torp was useless at.

The old woman spat the cake out and the girl bent down to pick it up from the floor. Torp went on unnoticed, down the empty corridor that felt stuffy due to the building's dark red bricks, looking at the worn, bland linoleum floor and recognising the nursing home smell from his father's last days: a mixture of strong detergents, bad food, and old urine. He had a brief moment of nausea—not because of the smell, but because of the reminder. It was the first time he had been in a nursing home since his father's death, and he hadn't given the smell a thought, neither then nor since. In fact, it hadn't struck him until now.

Torp checked the name tags by the doors in the corridor. With the exception of a single Erik, they were all women.

Finally: *Martha Spang-Johansen.*

Last door on the left-hand side. He knocked and opened at a loud and clear "come in." There she sat, Martha Spang-Johansen, a widow since 1973, in the process of eating meat loaf with cranberry jelly, boiled potatoes, and a thick brown gravy that was swimming in fat. On the side was a glass of weak red squash.

She looked up, smiling and curious.

"Hello, young man. What can I do for you?"

Torp got his bearings in the room. It was small but bright and friendly. A piano filled one wall. The opposite wall consisted of a small shelving arrangement. On the wall above hung a series of framed black-and-white photos. One of them depicted a three-winged farmhouse taken from the air. Half of the country's nursing home rooms would contain an almost identical picture, he thought. Most elderly Danes had a farm in the family. A yellowed picture showed a wedding couple—presumably herself and Spang-Johansen. No children. No grandchildren. The church would be empty when she died.

Torp introduced himself, sat down, and complimented her on her room. She thanked him and continued eating her meat loaf. She skipped the potatoes but helped herself to good portions of the jelly and gravy. Torp would have done the same, he reasoned. He sat down in a chair close to her and let her finish eating in peace. When the last remnants of jelly and gravy had been mopped up with the meat, and the squash had been drunk, she looked at Torp with a smile.

"Who are you?"

"Ulrik Torp. I'm a journalist at the *Daily News*. I'd like to ask you some questions."

"It's not a good time right now. We're going to eat soon," she explained pedagogically. It was these moments that he found awkward, he thought. Should he tell her that she had just eaten? Should he ignore it or agree with her?

"Erm . . . You've just eaten," he replied.

Martha Spang-Johansen looked down at the plate, where there were two single pale potatoes left.

"What a fool I'm making of myself. So I have," she laughed politely.

She had been a fine lady, and still was. Her hair sat nicely in a bun, the skirt and blouse suited her and matched, and he could see that she had a little makeup on her face. Her nails were well groomed and clean except for a bit of gravy under a couple of them. The only discord was the rancid smell of urine. It must have been hours since she had last been changed. Martha Spang-Johansen turned her head away from the two lone potatoes and looked up at her guest.

"So who are you, then?"

Torp introduced himself again. This wasn't going to be of any use. He looked around the room.

"Is that you and your husband?" He pointed at what he guessed was their wedding photo.

The whole of Martha Spang-Johansen's face lit up.

"That's my husband, Johan, and me. We were so young." Torp wanted to say something to keep the conversation going, but she continued undaunted. "We were married in Holmen's Church in the autumn of 1963, just before President Kennedy was assassinated."

She got lost in her own thoughts, and Torp let her.

"And you are?"

Torp explained who he was and where he came from. She gently took hold of his arm and squeezed it.

They sat like that for a while.

He could just reach the bookshelf while keeping their arms linked. Torp reached out for the only photo album and guessed that no new photos would have been added for almost fifty years. The first pages were clearly pictures from her childhood on the farm: the milk churns and farm machinery of the '30s, parents and grandparents with straw hats and sticks lined up in the courtyard. At a distance, a carefree time, but it was in the middle of the Depression and unemployment, without penicillin and with a devastating world war just around the corner. He couldn't see that little Martha had any siblings. A photo with bicycle, school bag, big smile, and plaits. Maybe her first day at school in the middle of World War II.

He looked at her. All alone in the world and all alone in her own universe of dementia. He flipped on while she followed every page.

"Is that your husband?"

She nodded at the young man in military uniform. "Isn't he handsome?"

Torp agreed. He took a photo with his mobile.

"There he is again."

A slightly older Spang-Johansen was now sitting in an armchair in a living room filled with teak furniture, smiling at the photographer with a glass of wine in his hand.

"That was in our flat in Bellahøj. Johan had just been taken on at the ministry."

"The Ministry of Justice?"

She nodded. "I'm a little in doubt as to the year. It was after Bobby Kennedy's death. Shall we say 1968?"

Torp nodded. They could easily say that.

"Who are you now?" she asked, squeezing his arm.

It was lovely to have company.

"My name's Ulrik," said Torp. That was enough.

They went on turning the pages. Christmas Eve with parents or parents-in-law in the flat in Bellahøj. A package holiday, probably to Mallorca. She was beautiful in a bikini. And happy, thought Torp. Naturally happy, not just smiling at the photographer.

"Who's that?"

Torp stopped at a picture with her husband and another, slightly older man. They were both in white shirt and tie, not for a special occasion, just for work.

Martha Spang-Johansen narrowed her eyes a little. She wasn't wearing glasses.

"That's Johan with . . ." She let the part of her brain that still worked work. "They met each other at Kastellet. What was his name now?" She took a long pause. Then she relaxed.

"Met at Kastellet?"

"You know what, you'll have to ask my husband about that."

Torp nodded. He used his mobile to take a picture of the picture. They went on turning the pages. Now the black-and-white images had changed to faded colour photos. More package holidays. Something resembling a car holiday down through Europe in a blue Fiat 850, presumably from a time just before the oil crisis, landslide elections, and unemployment, a time when everything was possible. He stopped at another summer picture. The woman on the far left was Martha Spang-Johansen; the chair by her side was empty. They were sitting in a garden. It was summer and the picture was taken in backlight. Everyone had wine glasses in their hands and was looking in the direction of the photographer, well dressed verging on casual, the men without ties. Torp recognised the man from before along with what may have been his wife, a slightly stiff woman.

The other man was a young Otto Brathenberg, the later Minister of Justice and Foreign Secretary. The woman by his side was the—also back then—beautiful and upright Lise Brathenberg. The photographer would have to have been Johan Spang-Johansen.

The future belonged to them.

Three young couples in the middle of the welfare state's engine room with progress at full steam, just before it all started to boil over. Like the picture of Martha as a child in the courtyard with family and straw hat, some would see this picture as a testimony of a carefree time without the problems of today, before globalisation, upheaval, division, and climate change. But Torp knew that that too was a big, fat lie. The Vietnam War, the Cold War, the Soviet invasion of Czechoslovakia, Nixon, Watergate, environmental problems, youth in revolt, famine in Africa, oil crises, unemployment, high inflation, balance of payment deficits.

All generations were given one or more tasks to solve. The path back to la-la land didn't exist.

The only thing that was undeniably better once was the music.

"I think it'll soon be time to eat. You know what, young man, would you like to eat with me?" Martha Spang-Johansen pulled Torp out of his train of thought with a small tug on his arm.

"Can you remember this picture?" he asked, pointing at it. She looked at it for a long time.

"It's Lise and her husband. They are so sweet," she said, putting her finger on each of them. She paused, hesitated. "And that is Ingrid Henriksen and her husband. I can't quite remember his name. He was my husband's superior in the Department of Justice. They met at Kastellet." She looked up at her guest. "You know what, you'll have to ask him yourself." She looked around. "I wonder where my husband's got to. We're going to eat soon."

Torp grabbed his mobile and took yet another picture of a picture.

"Excuse me, what are you doing?" She looked at him, sincerely curious.

"I'm taking a picture with my phone. It's not a problem, is it?"

"Taking a picture with his phone." Martha Spang-Johansen chuckled, resembling for a brief flash a flirtatious eighteen-year-old.

The door opened. An uptight woman in her mid-forties stood menacingly in the doorway.

"Who are you?"

Torp got up. He recognised the voice from the door phone. She had already guessed the connection and wasn't waiting for an answer.

"You can't just come wading in here. And certainly not as a journalist. This is a private home."

Martha Spang-Johansen looked frightened. She didn't care for the bad atmosphere and hurriedly pulled her arm away from her guest's, as if she had been exposed getting up to no good.

"We're looking at pictures," she said.

The nursing home manager, or whatever she was, took three brisk steps over to the table, snatched the photo album out of Torp's hands, and slammed it shut. She was the manager of the nursing home; he could see on her name tag. *Heidi Antonsen.*

"I have to ask you to leave immediately. You can't just sneak into a private home."

She gave no indication it was a matter for discussion. Torp was perfectly aware that she had the upper hand. He got up, looked down at Martha Spang-Johansen, and took her hand.

"Thanks for the chat. It was really nice to meet you."

She smiled carefully, knowing full well that she had done something she wasn't allowed to do. Torp took a business card out of his inside pocket and handed it to *Heidi Antonsen, nursing home manager,* as a defence weapon.

"Torp Communication—competence and experience," she read aloud. "Just a minute, didn't you say you came from the *Daily News*?" Her hostility was now supplemented by suspicion.

"I come from the *Daily News*."

He tried to point to the card. She perceived it as if he wanted to take it back, which made her pull it close to her. This could be used as evidence.

"The address isn't correct, but the telephone number and email are," he tried.

"If you leave right now, I won't call the police."

She stared him straight in the eye. She wasn't afraid of him. He was supposed to be scared of her, which he was a little bit. Imagine being old under such a commandant. She took a step to the side so he could get past, and followed him all the way to the glass door, which slid open when she tugged a string while pressing a button in the wall. He turned to her.

"Martha Spang-Johansen should have had her nappy changed several hours ago."

She remained silently watching at the glass door to make sure the man left the grounds completely. She didn't notice the figure in the car in the nursing home's almost empty parking lot furthest away from the streetlamp either.

CHAPTER 20

Ulrik Torp was woken up at seven on Thursday morning by two phone calls and three text messages.

The twenty-four-hour glazier had come by during the night just an hour after he had called. Torp looked up at the wooden board that had been quickly put up as a replacement for the broken pane. It made the living room look even smaller and even more shabby. Karen stood in the background, ready with the vacuum cleaner. She again tried to argue that they should report it to the police.

One of the three text messages, the one he didn't mention to Karen, had so far settled that case. No police.

The first call was from Jonathan. What the hell was all that about a broken window? Then the glazier, who said he couldn't come until Friday morning. Between the calls, the text messages came rapidly one after the other.

Anton wanted to meet up, but not at Police Headquarters. Nine o'clock a.m. at Café Europa? He impressed on Torp that it was important. Okay.

Katrine Taber-Nielsen finally came out of the woodwork. She wanted to meet up, but not at the *Daily News*. Two p.m. at Café Victor? She impressed on Torp that it was important. Yet another okay.

Finally, the text message that Karen shouldn't see.

That was a friendly warning, Torp. The next one will be different. Stop! The sender was secret.

It must have something to do with the hacking of the election computer. How on earth could they know that Emma had entered the Ministry's computer system the day before and exposed the hacking on election night? And why did the threat come to him? He had a sudden thought and texted Simon to ask if he and Emma were okay. Simon responded quickly.

Why shouldn't we be okay?

Never mind. See you, Torp quickly wrote back. He hesitated a bit and added a smiley on a fresh text message. He hesitated again before sending a new text to Simon.

Spang-Johansen knew old Henriksen and Otto Brathenberg. See if you can find out anything. New smiley. This time in the same message. Torp had never really cared about text messages and even less about smileys or the damned emojis—an entire civilisation had regressed to childhood. Adult communication with each other abounded with fire trucks, hearts, cows, and yellow faces. It would be understandable if text messages had come before voice phone and emails. But they had come afterwards. It was a damned step backwards, except right here it was actually an advantage.

Old Henriksen, the king of Slotsholmen, was the father of the not entirely new editor-in-chief Asbjørn Henriksen, who, with his pale pink shirts and his "hi there," was trying with some success to kick new life and more savings into the *Daily News*. Apart from being godfather to Katrine Taber-Nielsen, he was also Spang-Johansen's boss in his young days in the Ministry of Justice, and the two of them formed a three-leaf clover friendship with the ambitious youth politician Otto Brathenberg—the man Katrine had visited on a sick day.

This was no longer a matter of coincidence. These things had to be connected.

Torp was looking for the common thread, as he explained to Anton, who was already sitting at Café Europa, when Torp, a couple of minutes before 9:00 a.m., parked his bike in Amagertorv on Strøget and walked in. He had decided in advance not to mention anything about the window being shattered during the night and this morning's threat by text.

The café was already filled with politicians, lobbyists, consultants, and a few media people. Some of them were having the house brunch—*skyr with fresh berries, maple syrup, cheese with quince jam, omelette with bacon, porcini, and cranberries, Nordic hot dog with mustard and glazed onion, smoked salmon with smoked cheese cream, rye biscuits, and fresh fruit.* Others had taken a vegetarian variant with kefir. Organic, naturally. With coffee and freshly squeezed juice, it ran up to 250 kroner or more.

How could these people, thought Torp for a brief moment, believe that they were on the same wavelength as a population that ate oatmeal and went to work at 7:00 a.m.?

Everyone wanted receipts. No one paid for themselves, he knew, or they could deduct the expense without worry—the control by the taxman was virtually nonexistent. And should they finally be summoned, the expense would be accepted. Everyone in the room knew it, and those who ate oatmeal at 7:00 a.m. knew it, too.

"I have no common thread, but I do have a breakthrough," said Anton. They each sat with a cup of smooth coffee, "Jutland coffee," as the waiter remarked with great bravado when they asked for filter coffee.

"You asked me to look at a Spang-Johansen, murdered in 1973."

"And?" Anton suddenly had Torp's full attention.

"It's a bit wild, Torp. A bit wild, this."

"Really?"

Anton leaned forward over the filter coffee, half whispering. "I went to the archive and found the box with evidence and papers from that time."

"Get on with it!"

"Nothing of the old rubbish has been put in the computer system."

Torp shook his head impatiently.

"There was broadly speaking nothing noticeable when you went through it."

"No?"

"But then I had a thought . . ." Anton paused. Not to prolong the suspense, he wasn't like that, but because he himself had such a hard time believing it. "Torp, for Christ's sake. It turns out that the bullet that Spang-Johansen was shot with comes from the same Neuhausen that Jeppe Mikkelsen was shot with."

"Really?"

"No doubt about it."

"How can you be so sure?"

Anton tried to be patient. "The barrel of a pistol gets small grooves, which set themselves in the projectile. Each pistol is unique—it's like a fingerprint. It's the same fucking pistol! More than forty-five years later."

"And what does that mean?"

Anton spread his arms wide. "I don't know. I was sitting at headquarters last night and discovered it by accident. There doesn't have to be a connection—weapons are exchanged, traded, and stolen. But it's one hell of a coincidence if the two murders aren't connected in some way or other."

"I no longer believe in coincidences," said Torp brusquely.

Anton shook his head. Nor did he. He drank the last of the coffee, which had become less than lukewarm, and pulled a face. "Now you know. I thought that was most fair since it was you who put us on the trail. I'm going to send this further into the system in a little while, and then a completely different kind of investigation will begin."

He looked up.

"We know that the pistol was an officer's pistol in the Military Intelligence Service in the 1960s, before it disappeared."

Anton leaned forward so that no one at Café Europa except Torp could hear him, even though no one would be able to hear anything. Not for nothing were the clientele called the talking classes.

"I would appreciate it if you would just hold your horses on the internet and don't write about it until your printed newspaper tomorrow."

Anton looked at his old journalist source. He wanted the story out—to shake the bag in an investigation that had died before it had really got underway.

"For now, this is just between us. Is that a deal?"

"Roger. More?"

Anton shook his head. "No more."

Torp forgot his lukewarm filter coffee and hurried up to the *Daily News*, which was just a few minutes of illegal and somewhat difficult sidewalk cycling from there—it was still that time of day when vans and trucks took up more space more than pedestrians. There were yellow ribbons everywhere—on posts, bike racks, and bikes.

Simon was already sitting at Katrine's desk, which had been his all week. Like an eager child, he bounced in the chair when he saw Torp.

"I've been at it all morning, doing what you asked me to do."

Torp looked at him.

"Spang-Johansen, Brathenberg, and Henriksen."

He said the last name in a subdued voice due to the latter's son's position as editor-in-chief in the building. He directed Torp to his side of the desk and brought up a page on the screen, explaining as he did it.

"Brathenberg and Henriksen have been together all the way. Look at this."

He pointed to a review of department heads in the Ministry of Justice.

"Henriksen became head of department, a few months after Brathenberg became Minister of Justice. And then look at this."

He clicked on another tab: the Foreign Ministry a decade later.

"Then Brathenberg becomes Minister of Foreign Affairs and almost immediately brings Henriksen over to be the Ministry's administrative head. Those two have always been together."

"But this stuff is well known," objected Torp.

Simon's happy facial muscles fell, and Torp immediately tried to smooth things out.

"The widow said that Henriksen was Spang-Johansen's immediate superior in the Ministry of Justice, but that they had met at Kastellet."

"What happens at Kastellet?" asked Simon.

Torp was repeatedly amazed at the gaps that existed in Simon's large and curious mind.

"The Military Intelligence Service is located at Kastellet. It has been since its creation after World War II, Simon."

He could hear that he was again sounding patronising. Maybe it was meant that way, too. He omitted the lesson on the service originally being called the Military Intelligence Section, before changing its name in 1967 when it came under the Ministry of Defence, and thus, in principle at least, under more direct political control.

This time Simon ignored the tone, clicked the mouse a few times, and brought up an article from the *Frederiksborg News*, 5 January 1968.

"Then it all makes sense," he exclaimed smugly, almost to himself.

It was an article coming up to the general election later that month. Otto Brathenberg, the young parliamentary candidate for the Labour Party, was announced in the article as the new hope under the headline: *Local candidate on his way into Parliament.*

Otto Brathenberg currently works as an economist in the Labour Movement's Business Council but has a somewhat unusual background for the Labour Party, being a language officer who was for a short period associated with what is today called the Military Intelligence Service. "It was here I made some of my closest friendships in a common desire to defend Denmark," explains the young candidate.

"They met each other at Kastellet," mumbled Torp to himself. "They met each other at Kastellet—Henriksen and Spang-Johansen."

Simon had found several old articles. The *Daily News* the following year. A longer interview with "the new hope" in the Labour Party.

Otto Brathenberg makes no secret of the fact that he disagrees with many young people about the Danish defence forces. "I am a strong supporter of a strong defence force, and I honestly think that many people in my generation share that view. We just don't hear of them very much, but they are there. I also feel it among my closest friends," declares the young hope in the Labour Party, who has made a name for himself in his first year as a Member of Parliament.

Simon clicked on as he brought Torp up to date.

"Then came the exposing of the intelligence service's wiretapping centre in Kejsergade in October 1969, and then this article in the *Daily*

Worker in the early seventies." He swung his office chair away so Torp could get to see it, as if to announce a finale to his research. The article in the Sunday edition was an *at-home-with* article featuring the young MP. In the picture, Otto Brathenberg was sitting with Niels Henriksen and Johan Spang-Johansen. It was the same garden as in the picture from Martha Spang-Johansen's photo album.

Otto Brathenberg with his close friends, old soldier comrades, and political sparring partners: The defence of Denmark and the struggle for Western values is our generation's struggle.

"Ta-daaa!" Simon flung both arms wide. "So they know each other from the Military Intelligence Service. You can bet your bottom dollar, Woodward."

"Bet your bottom dollar? Do you have any other outmoded expressions?"

They laughed as a way of releasing the tension, both convinced that it was true. Spang-Johansen, Henriksen, and Brathenberg had met in the 1960s at Kastellet in the Military Intelligence Service, before first Henriksen and then Spang-Johansen as the baby of the flock came to the Ministry of Justice, Niels Henriksen presumably as office manager to Spang-Johansen. It might even have been he who had got him taken on as a civil servant. Some years later, after Spang-Johansen's death, Brathenberg had become Minister of Justice and had immediately made his friend head of department.

That was how the threads were tied between the three.

"Okay, you two." Neckhair was doing his leadership round. They looked up at their boss without saying anything. "Do you have anything for tomorrow?"

Simon and Torp both hesitated. Torp wanted to write the story of the pistol that connected the murder of Spang-Johansen in 1973 with the murder of Jeppe Mikkelsen, but he had decided that he first wanted to talk to Arne Lund about it. Simon sensed that the reportage manager shouldn't be told anything. The television was running in the background; Parliament's opening debate was in full swing. The meeting had begun with a formal election of the Speaker and an approval of the general election on the recommendation of the Committee for the Review of the Elections. Torp glanced sideways at the screen. The Labour Party's political spokesman—a former minister who should have known better—was criticising the Prime Minister and the government for spreading poverty and fear. Torp turned his head towards Neckhair, who was standing with his back to the debate.

"We should have some reportage on the contras and the yellow ribbons—they're spreading all over Copenhagen," Neckhair said.

He was looking at Simon.

"And you, Torp, you follow up on the stories about the sewers and the lack of maintenance—just write it up and we'll print it over the next few days after you've finished tomorrow, okay?"

Neckhair winked with one eye as if to mark that this wasn't just something between the two of them, but also a testimony to overview and leadership. Torp nodded without thinking about what he was nodding to. He needed to get hold of Arne Lund.

"Where's Emma?"

Neckhair looked around and at the clock. It was getting on for half past ten, and he made it clear that interns also had to show up on time. Yes, where was Emma? Simon and Torp looked at each other when the reportage boss had hurried off on his imaginary round.

"I'll get hold of her," exclaimed Simon, grabbing his phone.

Torp became nervous for a moment when he thought about the text message he had sent to Simon earlier that morning to find out if he and Emma were safe. Simon's naive why-shouldn't-we-be answer had clearly shown that it wasn't he who had smashed his living room window at night with a fist-size stone followed by a text message threatening him. Simon got in touch with Emma. They spoke briefly, and Torp could immediately hear that something was wrong.

"All her computers have been wrecked. Everything."

"How?"

"While she slept. Hacked. But she says it wasn't just anyone. They were super professionals with an advanced virus. She's never experienced anything like this, she says. Everything. Poof!" Simon spread his arms like a magician making the doves disappear.

"So what we found out yesterday . . . ?"

"She's getting her friends in Estonia to go into the Ministry's system again to check it." He whispered the last bit. Christian Crash was sitting a few metres away and was the only person who could hear what they were talking about.

Torp quietly brought his partner into the picture regarding this morning's talk with Anton from Police Headquarters and the breakthrough.

"Try and get hold of old Henriksen—get his reaction to the fact that his friend Spang-Johansen was killed with the same gun as Jeppe Mikkelsen. We'll write that story for tomorrow."

Simon's eyes lit up.

"And write a quick report on the contras and the fucking yellow ribbons, so you don't have to think about it anymore. Keep in touch with Emma. I'm just going to have a chat with Arne Lund. This is something we have to be a little careful about for many reasons."

Murder in Ørstedsparken connected to old murder case

By Simon Vestergaard
and Ulrik Torp

The murder of the young civil servant Jeppe Mikkelsen in Ørstedsparken about four weeks ago now turns out to be connected to a similar murder almost fifty years ago.

According to a source at Police Headquarters, the criminal police have by chance found out that the Neuhausen pistol used in the murder of Jeppe Mikkelsen is the same murder weapon that was used when another young civil servant, Johan Spang-Johansen, was murdered back in 1973.

At the end of the article, there was a section about Jeppe Mikkelsen working in the office in the Ministry of the Interior that was responsible for the general election, where there were rumours of "systematic irregularities" in connection with the counting of votes, especially for the Nationalists. The latter had given rise to a long—very long—negotiation with Arne Lund, who wouldn't guarantee that the passage would be included. In fact, he could almost guarantee the opposite. "Rumours" was too weak and "systematic" far too strong in his opinion. Torp agreed, but needed it in to be able to make a breakthrough with the story, he argued. Lund didn't care about that.

Torp wrote like he'd never written before. In agreement with Anton, he had contacted Police Headquarters through the official channels and received a "no comment." It was, therefore "a source at Police Headquarters." They had also negotiated a bit about that. Lund wanted "a source involved in the investigation" or just "close to the investigation," but Torp had promised Anton the wording "at Police Headquarters." They had finally agreed that that was enough. The experienced news editor immediately saw the potential in that part of the story, and also the problems. Not only was it a single-source story, it was an anonymous single-source story. But Arne Lund knew Torp, and he also knew that Anton had been a credible source over the years. The two things were enough for him and thus also enough for the *Daily News*.

The problem was the last bit about "rumours of systematic irregularity in the general election." Torp argued that the two stories were connected. That everything was connected. The last thing pleased Lund.

"Then it must be possible to document it," he remarked drily. "We'll just have to figure out how to extend your employment by a few weeks or more," he continued. "This story could well develop."

Torp felt the satisfaction bubbling in his stomach. This was the foot inside. Hardly a permanent job—it wasn't the time for that, and he could live with less. A maternity leave temporary contract, a permanent freelance agreement, a seasonal affiliation—there were many variants he could use as a stepping stone back to the world he had almost forgotten the existence, and the satisfaction, of.

This made a difference. It meant something. *He* made a difference and meant something. And if it could in addition ease his and Karen's agonising personal finances, then that was a welcome additional benefit. It would be the bare-bones journalist salary, far from the income he had had up until five years ago, but that meant less. Lund read his thoughts.

"It won't be big money, Torp, but you can give Karen a good dinner. She's deserved it, too," he remarked.

In his worn cardigan, Arne Lund looked not only like a relic from another time, but also the recent readership figures. The *Daily News* had declined 22 per cent compared to the previous six months, which themselves had been a sharp decline compared to the six months before that. Fewer people were reading the newspaper, fewer were buying it, and far too few were buying the cheap electronic subscription. Lund had for many years seen the inevitable development before him—the death of the newspaper—but he had always been firmly convinced that it would last for as long as he was employed there. He wasn't so sure about that anymore. It wasn't the young people who worried him. They had never read a bloody newspaper, not even thirty years ago. No, it was the older readers who had stopped. That was the new thing. They surfed the internet like their children and thought they could stay informed without paying, while without hesitation they spent thousands of kroner on streaming services that dumbed them down, red wines that made them unhealthy, and flights that polluted the atmosphere. This is what happened when you got a generation where no one had tried hoeing beets, was Arne Lund's serious opinion. He was a master at making his circle of acquaintances, especially the younger members, sick of hearing about his time as a beet hoer at home on the farm when he was a boy. The three times each summer when the beets had to be walked through with a hoe, beet after beet, weed after weed, row after row, hour after hour, day after day.

It required a very special psyche, he thought, to observe the day's work and then turn one's gaze to the huge field that lay ahead.

Taking care of a beet field was hard work. Few people thought about it, because today it was all done with pesticides.

No one hoed beets anymore.

Ah, well, the story of the murder in Ørstedsparken was a newspaper classic. Torp was a classic newspaperman and could also hoe beets, as long as he was given a hoe. Like himself.

"So far, it's the top story for tomorrow," announced Lund. "With or without the last paragraph on irregularities."

The top story!

Torp couldn't remember when that had last happened. Several years before he was fired.

Simon returned from his quick reportage on the contras and the yellow ribbons, as ordered by the reportage boss. There was a distribution taking place on Kultorvet, and Simon had been down there chatting with people; only half an hour—that was enough. An IT almost-billionaire who loved being in the media and participating in various reality shows was on the cover of today's *Express* about the phenomenon he was backing. *Don't believe what you read and what you see*, he stated to the tabloid newspaper's readers, of whom there were 17 per cent fewer than last year. Virtually all the media were left-wing, he believed, and again drew attention to Switzerland—the tax haven from where he usually fired off his excommunicatory bulls against Danish society. He was a strong supporter of the contras and proclaimed he would never in his life vote again for anything in Denmark. The almost-billionaire had jumped on the Hastings' bandwagon and stood for a few minutes on Kultorvet in honour of the photographers. Simon got a few quotes that could be used.

Neckhair was right. It was a good story.

Simon had tried to get a comment from old Henriksen, without success. The man had something as unusual as a landline telephone in his private home in Hellerup right down on the Sound. The first time, he picked up the phone himself and slammed it down as soon as Simon introduced himself. The second time, it was his wife.

"My husband never talks to journalists. You should know that. You know now in any case."

Simon tried laughingly to sound affected and old-fashioned as he reproduced the conversation. He failed miserably. They both laughed.

Torp wrote a new version of the article for Arne Lund with the addition of Henriksen.

Johan Spang-Johansen's immediate superior, the later long-term head of department Niels Henriksen, was, as a colleague and private friend of the victim, close to events back in 1973. However, when approached by the Daily News, *he declined to make any comment.*

Should that be included in the article? Torp was sincerely in doubt. It probably shouldn't be. They directed the angle straight at the Neuhausen pistol. On the other hand, the pistol came from the Military Intelligence Service, precisely when they had met each other in the 1960s. No, Henriksen didn't really fit in there. Then he sent it, so Lund would have to decide later.

"Is it completely fair that I'm on the by-line?" asked Simon. "I haven't really contributed to that story."

"You're forgetting that we are Woodstein."

Torp was being serious for once in their game with the Watergate heroes from the *Washington Post.* Christian Crash sniggered as he went past.

Simon didn't. Emma had called back. The Estonians had got into the special computer in Statistics Denmark, which they had hacked into the day before. The message was the same. Everything was gone. There was no evidence of anything at all. The visit on election night after the exit polls at 8:00 p.m. Gone. The altered algorithms. Gone.

The perpetrators had been very eager to clean up after themselves, albeit after a little delay, and they had made a thorough job of it.

CHAPTER 21

They were sitting in Simon's Polo on their way to Hellerup.

It was rush hour, and the route out of town on Østerbrogade was even worse than usual, as parts of the ancient sewer system had collapsed and half of the street—a stretch of several hundred metres—was being dug up for the second month.

The intern, who, like Torp, only had one day left on the *Daily News*'s reportage editorial team, forced the old car into first gear despite obvious protests from both clutch and gearbox. On Monday, the Christiansborg-loaned journalists would return to the editorial office, Torp's work activation would be ticked off on a form at the job centre, and Simon would be back on the culture section, unless, like Woodward and Bernstein, they could be allowed to continue their partnership for a few more weeks.

Torp had hinted at the possibility to Simon. It was up to Arne Lund, with whom he was going to have a chat the next day.

Simon manoeuvred the car up into second gear, while Torp thought of the meeting he had had a few hours earlier with Katrine at Café Victor.

Clash was perhaps a more appropriate appellation.

Torp had ordered a fizzy water. No thanks. He wasn't hungry.

"I know who you are. But I don't know what you are," he had begun.

She looked at him, smiled, and imperceptibly stroked her middle finger across the back of Torp's hand.

"What do you want to know?"

Why had she lied about her beans-on-toast background in South Zealand? All of that chat they had had about an ordinary, boring childhood and straitened circumstances, when in reality she came from something completely different. Why the story that her affiliation with the *Daily News* was completely coincidental, that it could have been a load of other newspapers, when the editor-in-chief's father, Niels Henriksen, was her godfather? Why not a word about her grandfather, Arne Taber, one of the founders of The Firm? Why had she lied about being sick all week? Why was she at Otto Brathenberg's house? Torp wanted an answer to all that and more.

She laid her hand on top of Torp's and let it lie there. Was she flirting? Definitely. Was it working? Equally definitely. Torp was nowhere near being unfaithful to Karen, had never been, but he could feel his member getting a bit worked up. That wasn't what he had intended. He withdrew his hand.

"I know who your grandfather was," he exclaimed. She parried effortlessly with a little laugh.

"But that's no secret. I even bear his name."

"So why all that stuff about your simple background in South Zealand?"

She shook her head, clearly surprised by the hostile undertone.

"Because it's true. Believe me, Ulrik, my background is nothing special." A hurt look came over her face. "Why am I being given the third degree?"

Torp ignored her. "And Niels Henriksen as your godfather. Maybe that's nothing special either?"

"Yes, it was something special for my grandfather. It was a great honour for him that Niels Henriksen would have me as his goddaughter."

"Why an honour, exactly?"

"Niels Henriksen is a role model for many people. He was for my grandfather. He is for me, too. He's like a brother to me," she added.

"Brother?"

"Okay, a father then. Grandfather, if it suits you better." She was becoming a little snappy.

"Why is he a role model?"

"Niels has made many important and difficult decisions in his life as a top civil servant. We're very grateful to him for that."

"We?"

"I am," she corrected herself.

"How did your grandfather and Niels Henriksen know each other?"

"They were friends in their youth. Old soldier comrades."

"No more than that?"

"For them, it probably meant everything." She smiled.

"So who are you, Katrine?"

She hesitated. At length.

"I am my grandfather's grandchild. That is who I am," she replied, stressing every syllable.

"And what does that mean?" asked Torp.

"That means . . ."

She stopped and considered her words.

"That means I'm worried about you, Ulrik."

"What do you have to do with all this?"

The waiter came with Torp's fizzy water and Katrine's café au lait. She thanked him and tasted it, leaving a spot of whitish brown coffee on her upper lip.

"Aren't you worried at all?" She looked at him curiously.

"About what?"

She spread her arms. "Everything. Denmark, politics, the EU, liberal democracy, our prosperity, human rights—everything that our parents and grandparents have built up. Aren't you the tiniest bit worried that it may all disappear?"

Torp came to think of Karen and her remark that everyone was just a single step from falling into the abyss. Marriage, jobs, health, children—a single incident can topple the load for a person. Did that also apply to a country, an entire society, a world order? Could a single or a couple of wrong decisions, unfortunate events, or people topple the load that generations had painstakingly built up, institution after institution, precedent after precedent, document after document, and agreement after agreement?

Was it all really that flimsy?

"I am," continued Katrine, when Torp didn't answer. "I'm genuinely worried."

"Like your grandfather?"

She nodded. "Yes, just like my grandfather."

Was it that simple? Did you become like your origins, no matter how much you fought against them? Torp had experienced it in relation to his own father; it was dawning on him more and more, in particular after his death, how much they resembled each other. It hadn't been an unambiguously nice thought earlier, but he had come to terms with it little by little, and since then more than that.

Proud wasn't the right word; nor was satisfied.

It was acceptance. An acceptance of one's origin, destiny, and situation—everything from the bowed back, the few grey hairs on the chest, the loss of hair on the head, the unruffled temperament, the at times rather square view of the world, and the way his mind worked in general. He could recognise it all from his father, and there was bugger all he could do, or wanted to do, about it.

Was it like that for most people? Also for Katrine?

"You could join." She tried to maintain eye contact.

"Join what?"

"Helping to keep everything together."

"And how do you do that?"

"By not taking everything for granted."

"Excuse me—what the hell are you all up to?"

For the first time in their conversation, she seemed indecisive. She had thought everything else through. Torp sensed that she was on the verge of telling him.

"What is Niels Henriksen's role in this?"

Now it was his turn to lay his hand on hers and let it lie there until she withdrew.

"You should be careful, Ulrik."

"Otherwise maybe more stones will come through my living room window?"

She blushed from her throat up and her eyes wandered for the first time. "I had nothing to do with that. Believe me, Ulrik."

Torp felt the disappointment spreading through his body. So she knew about that. Did she also know in advance? And who was behind it?

"Why should I be careful, Katrine? Why?"

"Because most things are bigger than you and me."

This time the answer came immediately, without the slightest hesitation.

"The system is more important than the person?"

"That's not what I said." She shook her head. Now it was her turn to put her hand on his. "Ulrik, promise me—drop this. You're already in far too deep."

"What were you doing out at Otto Brathenberg's?"

She pulled her hand back. "Who says I've been out at Otto Brathenberg's?"

"Yesterday, while you were on sick leave. You still are, aren't you? As far as I understand it. I saw your bike in the driveway."

"Otto is an old friend of my grandfather," said Katrine, and left it at that.

It was clear that she didn't want to continue the conversation, so she got up, put a hundred kroner on the table, and tried without much success to get elegantly out of the narrow space.

"Drop this, Ulrik. Drop it."

Her voice sounded as threatening as it was meant to. She turned and left.

Torp was in no doubt when he returned to the *Daily News*'s editorial office. He had to get hold of Simon and ignored Neckhair's question about when the articles about the sewers and the lack of maintenance would be ready—the reportage boss no doubt wanted to make sure there was something over the weekend and maybe even for a thin Monday.

"We're going to Hellerup. Up to Niels Henriksen. You have his address, right?"

Simon nodded.

"Get your car and pick me up at Kongens Nytorv."

"Why Henriksen?" asked Simon.

They had reached Svanemøllen, past the sewer repairs, but still in the middle of a nightmare of a rush hour.

"They all worship the ground Mr. Slotsholmen walks on. Spang-Johansen, Brathenberg, Arne Taber, Katrine. All of them," Torp explained. "'It was *an honour,*' she said. An honour, Simon. When was the last time he gave an interview?"

Torp knew the answer. It just needed to be emphasised.

"Never," replied Simon while keeping his focus straight out through the windscreen. They were driving behind a heavy truck.

Simon had surfed the internet comprehensively for any combination of Spang-Johansen, Brathenberg, and Henriksen. Spang-Johansen hardly existed. Brathenberg was everywhere, and Henriksen only as a shadow, the man in the background, never in front.

"Exactly. Never. It seems that he has never once said anything to a journalist. Most of his life in the central administration. More than twenty years as head of department. You can't find a single quote."

Simon protested mildly. It was strange, but they shouldn't make more of it than that. "Neither my father nor my mother is quoted for anything, and never will be. That doesn't necessarily mean that they're bad people with something to hide," he objected.

Torp ignored the protest. "Niels Henriksen is the boss, whatever it is, he is still the boss at the age of . . . how old did you say he is?"

"Eighty-seven. Eighty-fucking-seven. Be honest, Torp. Do you think it's totally fair to confront such an old man?" He turned his head away from the traffic towards his partner for a brief moment. "From a journal-istic ethics viewpoint, I mean."

"Excuse me, what are they teaching you in that university course?" It was a rhetorical question. "Just because you're old doesn't mean you can't be smart and evil. They aren't necessarily all happy grandparents with incipient dementia at that age, Simon."

They had got rid of the truck and were past Tuborg Harbour and up Strandvejen. Simon turned right at the avenue that led down to the Sound and concealed some of the largest and most expensive villas that Denmark's level, equal society could muster.

Niels Henriksen lived right down by the sea, in a large white box of a villa. Old trees and a wilderness of bushes made the driveway narrower than it originally was. The windows were in need of a coat of paint; the black roof tiles were old and filled with moss. Torp glanced up the avenue. Some of the villas had been thoroughly refurbished with black glazed tiles, granite pebble driveways, Audis, and the stench of new money. Not like Henriksen's and a number of others. In their own way, there was something classy about it, like an old leather sofa with lots of patina, where a little weed between the paving stones was a statement of you not having a gardener, not using Roundup, and not going in for that sort of thing. Here there was low-key prestige in wearing an old dressing gown and worn slippers when taking the obligatory hop into the Sound in the morning—also in the winter. In the villas with moss on the roof, books were read, the *New York Times* discussed, and even pipe tobacco smoked in one of the living rooms, he imagined. In moderation, mind you. Torp both despised and admired the seemingly carefree, casual approach to life, an approach that must have required generations of practice before it became established.

He had a strong sense of being an outsider while at the same time being both attracted and fascinated. It was the classy, respectable bourgeoisie, but they were living on borrowed time. The Audis and granite pebble driveways were in the process of exerting a slow but sure, first-class gentrification. It was only a matter of time before new money had taken over the entire area and demolished some of the villas in favour of architect-designed glass.

"What do we do now?" asked Simon. "We know he's never given an interview. He slammed the phone down on me a few hours ago. His wife was a little more polite, but the principle was the same. So, what do we do now?"

Simon turned the car and drove into the side of the road, diagonally opposite Henriksen's villa and with the rear facing the Sound.

"Now we wait," declared Torp. "Now we wait for him to come out. The man must surely go out for a walk at some point."

Simon sighed. "That could take hours, dammit."

"We wait."

Torp leaned back in his seat, opened the side window a little so it didn't mist up in the small car, and allowed a little drizzle to creep in.

"Now we just wait."

Through the windscreen, which was slowly becoming opaque from the drizzle, Torp could see that some of the large trees in front of the newly renovated villas had been draped with yellow ribbons. It fitted nicely with the election researchers' description of the contra movement. It wasn't only angry young people, misguided intellectuals, and homeless anarchists who backed Poul and Ulla Hasting's latest whim and had helped hammer election turnout down from around 90 per cent to just over 70. "If we were a party, we'd be one of the biggest," as Ulla Hasting had exulted to the *Express*, which with its usual sense for popular feeling had long ago lain in wait around the movement's potential for non-subscription sales and clicks.

The walk from the *Daily News* to Café Victor to meet Katrine gave support on its own to Neckhair's idea that Simon should write a report on the contras and the yellow ribbons. It was as if the ribbons were hanging everywhere; on bike racks, parked bikes, poles, posts—he couldn't walk ten metres inside the city without encountering yet another one. It was like an outbreak of measles, just replaced by yellow plastic. Some people were tearing them down, especially business owners who didn't want them hanging in front of their shops or on their café chairs.

"Fascist," a contra with her arms full of yellow ribbons had shouted when she saw an elderly man frantically trying to remove some of them from in front of his small shop selling designer lamps. The man had looked startled and hurried into the shelter of his shop.

Torp took another look up at the avenue's fleet of cars and the driveways full of paraphernalia. How it was possible for people who, if anyone, benefited from the current social order, to support thoughts and movements that could erode it all, was beyond his understanding. All in all, it was beyond his understanding that so many people—not just in Denmark—were so angry.

It wasn't the silent majority as some politicians and commentators called it.

It was the vociferous minority.

But it didn't have to carry on being like that.

"Someone's coming," Simon whispered.

They were parked forty to fifty metres from Henriksen's villa. There was no need to whisper. A metallic grey Jaguar stopped by the roadside right by the driveway. Otto Brathenberg got out on the driver's side and a man in his mid-thirties, whom Torp had never seen before, exited on the passenger side. Simon let the windshield wiper swish a few times when they had disappeared into the overgrown driveway. The October drizzle was close to stopping completely.

It was almost 5:00 p.m.

A bicycle came down towards them from up on Strandvejen. The cyclist was wearing a heavy waterproof cape, which also covered the cyclist's head, but it was easy for Torp to recognise the characteristic Biomega bike. He didn't need to see the small dent in the front mudguard to know who was, apparently out of habit, allowing the bike to freewheel the last bit into the driveway and all the way up to the villa. Another car parked behind Brathenberg's Jaguar a few minutes later. Two men and a woman, none of whom Torp recognised, got out and purposefully entered the villa.

"What the hell," muttered Simon.

"Precisely," said Torp. "What the hell!"

They waited a quarter of an hour.

"I'm going in," Torp stated suddenly, opening the car door.

Before Simon had time to comment on or problematise the plan, to the extent that there was a plan, Torp had gone diagonally across the empty avenue and was walking up the driveway. He had no plan other than to knock on the door and ask what the hell they were up to, a privilege reserved for all journalists in the Western world. The victims' privilege was then to slam the door, knowing that it could appear in the newspaper. Such were the rules of the game, which almost everyone complied with.

Was that also the case here? Torp began to have doubts. It was one thing with Johan Spang-Johansen and Jeppe Mikkelsen. That was in a way uncategorisable. But it was something else with the stone through his living room window. Katrine had actually acknowledged that they had been behind that—whoever "they" were, now assembling for what looked like a kind of crisis meeting in Henriksen's villa.

Torp went to the left, away from the main steps, towards the garden. The tall trees and shaggy shrubs made it easy to move unnoticed on the paved walkway.

They were sitting in a large garden room, practically a conservatory, with curved glass, that led directly out to a huge wooden terrace. It too desperately needed a coat of paint. By penetrating some shrubbery at the gable, Torp could get all the way to the corner, where the terrace began almost right by his head. He could hear there was a discussion going on, sometimes quite loudly, but the windows were closed. It was impossible to catch what they were talking about. Torp squatted indecisively. This was against all his instincts as a journalist. On the other hand, he knew that the discussion inside the conservatory contained a story that should be told. He was securely jammed between the high shrubbery and the gable, like a cave in the wilderness. They could walk past him on the paving just two metres away and no one would notice him. The voices in the garden room died out. Perhaps they had finished disagreeing. Torp stayed squatting where he was and could feel that his left leg had begun to go to sleep. He tried to move his weight.

Suddenly, he heard the front door at the driveway behind him being opened. Farewells were said, and Torp could see them leaving the villa between two trees. First to leave were the three in the last car, then Katrine, now without weatherproofing; the sun was slowly getting ready to set, but the weather had cleared up. Finally, Otto Brathenberg left with his friend.

"This has to be closed quietly," the voice that had to be Niels Henriksen's warned.

"It will be," replied Brathenberg.

It was clearly the former head of department who was sitting at the head of the table—also in relation to his former Minister.

"We must be able to say in Vienna on Saturday that there are no loose ends here. There are enough problems with Hungary," he warned.

"You can be totally relaxed about that," said Brathenberg.

They said their farewells, Torp heard the cars in the avenue drive away, and then there was silence. He waited two minutes, shuffled through the slightly wet bush, only now noticing that his shoes and designer trousers had become wet and covered in soil, slipped out of the grounds, and sat down heavy and wet beside Simon in the Polo.

"There wasn't much *meterman* about that," said Simon nervously and with a touch of reprimand.

Torp mumbled. His left leg was still asleep.

"Fuck, I was frightened when they came out and you were still in there."

"Everything's fine," Torp reassured him.

"What do you mean by everything's fine? Wasn't that Katrine who cycled out of there?"

Torp nodded.

"What does she have to do with this?"

"Now we wait."

"For what?"

"For Henriksen."

They sat like that for a quarter of an hour. It was getting on for 6:30 p.m. when a fairly new Volvo SUV carefully rolled out of the driveway. Henriksen's wife was behind the wheel, with the man himself in the passenger seat. They were nicely dressed.

"What now?"

"We follow them."

CHAPTER 22

It was a sudden impulse, not something Ulrik Torp had planned, let alone considered.

They followed the Henriksen couple's Volvo at a good distance up the avenue, onto Strandvejen and in towards the city. Henriksen's wife didn't drive fast and only reluctantly overtook, so it was easy for Simon and his Polo to keep up.

"I feel like a dog running after a truck. What are we going to do when we catch them?"

Simon drove through a late amber light just after Svanemøllen. There was a car between them that luckily chose to drive through an early amber.

"We have to talk to Niels Henriksen. He's the boss," stated Ulrik Torp.

"Of what?"

Third gear, overtaking on Østerbrogade. Now they were driving behind the Henriksens' car again.

"That's what we have to find out," replied Torp with a touch of irritation.

The Volvo braked abruptly as they approached the sewer roadworks. Simon avoided it by pulling the Polo out into an outer lane that didn't actually exist, and they were now beside the Volvo. There wasn't really enough space, so they were closer together than was natural in traffic. Torp turned his head and looked directly at Niels Henriksen's wife, who cast a reproachful glance from behind the wheel at the intrusive car. Simon wanted to brake but was being pressurised by a car behind. The roadworks a little further ahead meant the two cars had to get in the same lane. Simon sped up a little, while Henriksen slowed down correspondingly.

That was the moment Torp impulsively grabbed the steering wheel with his left hand and wrenched the Polo to the right, in front of the Volvo. They weren't travelling all that fast, but it was fast enough for a loud, metallic crunch to fill the cabin when Swedish safety and old German tin collided. The door on the Polo's passenger side was thrust inwards and pressed slightly against Torp's right side. The side window and the windscreen both shattered, while at the same time the Polo was pushed sideways six to seven metres forward and didn't stop until it met the concrete block that separated the sewer works and the road.

The Swedish safety technicians could never have anticipated the unexpected manoeuvre by the Polo, but despite that, the computer system ensured that 1.7 tonnes of Swedish high technology were automatically brought to a halt, just before the Volvo was about to collide again with what was left of Simon's car.

Torp succeeded in opening his smashed door after a struggle. He could feel his ribs on his right side were tender, as well as his right leg having taken a blow, but nothing serious. He looked at the Volvo less than a metre away. There was barely a scratch on the bumper to show that it had just crashed into an eighteen-year-old Polo. Henriksen's wife sat petrified with both hands clutching the steering wheel. It was her husband who got out. Torp looked back. Simon had managed to open the door on the driver's side and was about to crawl out of his car. He appeared to be totally unharmed.

"Excuse me, but what on earth do you think you're doing driving like that?"

Niels Henriksen was standing between the two cars, intimidatingly close to Torp. It was only now that Torp noticed he was wearing a dinner jacket.

"He did it on purpose. That man deliberately swung the car in front of us. He tugged on the steering wheel. I saw him." Henriksen's wife was shouting at her husband from the driver's seat. She was still clutching the steering wheel with both hands.

"Have you taken leave of your senses?" Niels Henriksen took a half step closer to Torp but seemed completely balanced in every way.

"Why did Spang-Johansen and Jeppe Mikkelsen have to die?" Henriksen took half a step backwards.

Simon had come up beside him. "Torp, for Christ's sake. My car!"

"Who on earth are you?" Niels Henriksen didn't respond to Torp's question. He was used to being in charge of conversations.

"Ulrik Torp, *Daily News*. What are you going to do in Vienna on Saturday?" Henriksen's expression faltered just long enough for Torp to see that he had touched a nerve.

"It's none of your business what I'm doing on Saturday."

"But you confirm that you're going to a meeting in Vienna?"

Henriksen took another half step towards Torp. He was impressively upright, taking his eighty-seven years into account.

"We would like your comment on Jeppe Mikkelsen and your old friend Spang-Johansen being killed with the same pistol. Isn't that a strange coincidence?"

"You're totally crazy. Who are you?"

Again Torp could see that a blow had got through. It was only his fifty years of hard decisions and even tougher tackles that enabled the old man to almost mask the effect on him.

"Ulrik Torp, *Daily News*." He handed out his business card from his inside pocket.

Several cars had started honking their horns. Some people shouted as they crept past. It was early evening and way past rush hour, but the traffic was vulnerable when road work coincided with a minor traffic accident. Some pedestrians crowded together, the odd one asking if they were okay, but it was clear now to everyone that the only casualty was a worn-out old car, so most people walked on. A few took pictures with their mobile phones.

Niels Henriksen took the business card and looked at it briefly.

"The address isn't correct," began Torp, but held back on any further explanation.

"Torp Communication . . . so you aren't from the *Daily News*," exclaimed Henriksen.

He put the business card in the pocket of his dinner jacket and looked from the Polo to the Volvo's bumper, which you would have thought was untouched if you hadn't known that it had just crunched the right side of a small car and thrown it five or six metres forward.

"My wife and I are on our way to the Theatre Royal, and we don't wish to involve the insurance company. This . . ." He gestured at the Polo. "This you will have to sort out yourselves."

Henriksen turned back towards his own car.

"We continue, Ingrid."

He got in the Volvo, which indicated, pulled out, and disappeared towards the city.

"Torp—for Christ's sake!" Simon was on the verge of tears.

The audience moved on and the traffic was rolling again as it should. They were right in front of the roadworks, where the road became narrower, so if they and the car wreck were disturbing the traffic at all, it was more down to a curiosity queue.

"My car," continued Simon.

Torp could now feel the blow to his right leg and the pressure on his ribs. There would be bruising and he would limp a little in the coming days, but otherwise nothing serious had happened as far as he could judge.

"Are you okay, Simon?"

"No, I'm bloody well not okay. My car is wrecked. You've fucking wrecked my car, Torp." Simon's Adam's apple was bobbing up and down, making it sound as if his voice was still breaking.

"It's an old car," replied Torp, trying to soften the blow.

Simon spread his arms, then pointed to what had been his vehicle until five minutes ago. "That's my car, Torp. It's not fully insured. I'd only just bought it."

"We'll work something out," said Torp as a consolation.

It was only now that he returned completely to the real world, from before he wrenched the steering wheel. He had no idea how they were going to work things out. How much did such an old car cost? Regardless of the price, he didn't have any money unless he was allowed to continue a few weeks or a month more at the *Daily News* for a proper wage.

Water had begun running from the car onto the road. It was steaming as it hit the damp asphalt. It had to be the radiator leaking.

"Sorry, Simon. I don't know exactly what got into me."

He held his side. His ribs were beginning to hurt.

Simon looked at Torp and his car, without saying anything. Then he started laughing. At first small ripples, like hiccups trying to get out of his mouth while he tried to suppress them. It was neither the time nor the place. So he gave up, relaxed in his stomach, and let the air out. Then the tears began pouring out of his eyes, running down his cheek; he wiped them away, managed to hold back a little again, but it was only a brief respite—like pressing down the lid on a pot that had started to boil and was already steaming vigorously. Then it all came out, the roar of laughter that made pedestrians turn their heads. There was a big boy, standing in front of a car wreck and some roadworks, laughing. Next to him stood an older man—his father?—observing the scene. Then Torp also started laughing, not forcefully and noisily, not with tears in his eyes, but happy and relieved.

What they were doing made sense, not exactly with the car, but everything else.

Torp looked around.

"Why don't we just leave the car and find a place to get a beer?"

Torp insisted on paying for the beer he at that moment had thought would be the only one. "As compensation for the car." Simon wasn't fully aware of how big a story they were close to. Even Torp was having difficulty fully understanding it. Election fraud in Denmark was historic, whether it was Russians controlled by the Kremlin or locals who were behind it. All indications were that the purpose of the swindle was to push the New Radicals and the Nationalists below the threshold. The connection between Spang-Johansen and Jeppe Mikkelsen was irrefutable. Tomorrow's front-page article in the *Daily News* about the murder weapon being the same, with a gap of almost fifty years, might "shake the bag," as Anton at Police Headquarters had put it. Hopefully, the section on "systematic irregularities" in the general election would be in it at the end. That article could be a breakthrough, both for the criminal police and for their upcoming articles. In the afternoon, Arne Lund had assured them that the story would still be on the front page but may not be at the top. The opening debate in Parliament could bring something in. It was still unclear, he explained.

Top of the page or lower down didn't matter. The most important thing was that the story was there and that it was high priority. The next article could be about Spang-Johansen, Brathenberg, and Henriksen's common past in the Military Intelligence Service in the 1960s, during the years when the private intelligence service The Firm was exposed and wound up without the public knowing anything. It was a good story, but in itself not a big exposé, as Torp knew.

"There's something I don't understand." Simon took a big gulp of his beer and looked at Torp, who was trying without success to formulate a remark in his head along the lines of . . . the older Simon got, the less he would understand. "Why was Spang-Johansen murdered?"

Torp, on the other hand, was in no doubt about that part, even though they couldn't prove it yet.

"He wanted to expose The Firm. Imagine the consequences for Brathenberg and Henriksen if their names had been linked to an illegal and privatised intelligence service at the very moment they were about to launch their careers. Farewell to ministerial posts and department head appointments."

"Is it that simple?"

"That part in particular is simple, yes."

"But what about Katrine? What was she doing out at Henriksen's, her godfather?"

Torp shook his head. He had no answer for that. He was having such a hard time accepting the betrayal on her part. And what were Brathenberg and Henriksen going to be doing in Vienna on Saturday? Vienna had been discussed at the meeting, and Brathenberg had promised Henriksen that the problems would have been dealt with before Saturday. Was it him and the *Daily News* that had to be dealt with? And what were the problems with Hungary that they had been talking about? Torp could feel that he had hit a bull's-eye when he confronted Henriksen with Vienna.

Simon thought they had plenty for a series of articles. Torp knew that in truth they had very little, especially after Emma's computers had been wrecked and the computer in Statistics Denmark had been wiped clean of clues.

They had circumstantial evidence, lots of theories, and a few specific things, but very little that could get past Lund's critical gaze. Tomorrow's article with the link between the two murders, no comment from Henriksen, and a cautious hint of election fraud with the term "systematic irregularities" was at the edge of the news editor's limits.

Journalism was facts, evidence, documents, times, names, contexts; in an emergency, confirmed by two independent sources. They were the building blocks of investigative journalism that Torp was lecturing his intern on.

"Like Woodward and Bernstein."

"But they had Deep Throat," objected Simon.

"And Deep Throat's assertions still had to be confirmed by one more source before they printed the articles. We don't even have an underground car park," said Torp, referring to the place where Bob Woodward had had meetings at night with his source, FBI Deputy Director Mark Felt, who only emerged as the main source thirty years later. "We don't have a damn thing, Bernstein."

By the third beer at the pub, Torp was starting to get a conscience over the death of the Polo. Simon brushed his concerns aside.

"I can't afford a car anyway, and I didn't really need it either. Forget it, Torp." And then they started laughing about it again. "I just hadn't twigged that you wanted to copy Christian Crash."

"You didn't have a very firm grip on the steering wheel. It was piss easy."

"You're just so far out, Torp," exclaimed Simon appreciatively when they had finished laughing once more. He ordered a fourth round of beers under mild protest from his partner. "And here was I thinking you were just a worn-out, old journalist."

Torp looked down, turning the half-full beer glass in his hands.

"You were a big shot once. Some of the old-timers at the *Daily News* say that, too."

"Argh." Torp took a gulp of his beer. He had had nothing to eat except a little lunch about ten hours earlier and was feeling the alcohol. It was nice.

"You should have had the Cavling Prize, they say."

"Argh," he repeated, this time with an attempt to make it sound like a yes, he should have. His stories about financial support to political parties just came at a time when in-depth exposés weren't a high priority in journalistic circles. In those years, it was the well-written features, the personal stories that won the awards—the Cavling statuettes, too.

"What happened, actually?"

"Some others got the prize." He shrugged.

"With you, I mean."

"What happens when you just take it all for granted."

"And what's that?"

"Then everything slides," said Torp. "Then everything slides, Simon."

"What did you take for granted?"

Torp hesitated and thought back, which he hadn't done for many years.

"That it was completely natural that I, as a prominent journalist at one of the largest newspapers, had direct access to everyone from the Prime Minister down. That it was only natural that the *Daily News*—and all the other newspapers—made loads of money without making an effort. That my handsome salary slipped into my bank account every month." Torp spread his arms. "That that was how the world was organised. It couldn't be any other way. We thought." He corrected himself. "I thought."

"Then what happened?"

"I became comfortable. Not lazy. Comfortable." Torp had never before reflected on his downfall. It was the first time he had put it into words.

"I couldn't imagine any other reality, and then . . . poof," he said, clicking his fingers on his right hand. "Then it was gone."

"You were expelled and fired from the *Daily News*, they say."

"They say so much, Simon. They say so much."

Torp couldn't be bothered to repeat that old story. He had crossed the line between being a journalist and a player, so the firing had been reasonable enough. But he didn't regret it. It wasn't there that the downfall, the comfort, set in.

"It was so many years ago, Simon. Just remember not to take anything for granted. Not even My or your car."

They laughed a bit and warmed themselves with the intimacy.

"And what about you, Simon?"

The boy shrugged and ordered a fifth round, this time without protest from Torp.

"What about me?" He gave it some thought. "I'm tired of hearing that everything was better in the old days."

"You shouldn't believe it either."

"I don't take anything for granted. Except My."

They drank up and said goodbye in front of the pub. Simon insisted on a hug and Torp in his intoxicated condition didn't have time to protest. They agreed that Friday would in one way or another be a big day.

Torp hobbled along by the lakes on the Nørrebro side. His right leg hurt, and what was worse, his almost new designer trousers, bought for way too much money, had been torn in the crash. He held his side. The bent ribs hurt but were no real problem. For the first time that day, he felt the lump at the bottom of his mouth with his tongue. It hadn't grown in recent weeks. He was sure of that. Tomorrow he was going to Rigshospitalet with Karen to get the result. He had decided to walk as far as Gammel Kongevej and take the bus from there. It would do him good to sweat some of the alcohol out of his body.

Torp had come past Rosenørns Allé and was further down Vodroffsvej. He should have taken a taxi, but now he would soon be at Gammel Kongevej and the bus, several hundred kroner less poor.

It was close to midnight, and Torp hadn't noticed the person who was following him at a distance along the more crowded walking and cycling path beside the lakes to the practically empty and semi-dark streets at the entrance to Frederiksberg. The first blow, therefore, came without warning, obliquely from behind on the left side of his head. It hit his nose, which split open. Torp fell over on the pavement, not because the blow itself was strong, but more because he was completely unprepared. He got two kicks in the side that made him roll from the pavement down off the kerb. One kick hit his damaged ribs and caused him to howl with pain. He curled up instinctively, preparing for more kicks. An elbow pressed Torp's face all the way down into the gutter and held him firmly so he couldn't see anything.

A mouth came very close to one ear; Torp could sense the man's breath, which was surprisingly normal.

"There are some people who really, really want the best for you, Ulrik Torp. You have to stop now. Final warning."

Torp remained there with his head in the gutter and his legs curled up to his chest. He felt the blood rushing out of his nose. Then he looked up carefully. The man was gone. It had probably taken less than a minute. He sat up with difficulty; there was no one to be seen. The man must have turned down Danasvej; he had vanished.

The first two taxis he hailed on Gammel Kongevej wouldn't take him. He found a few half-used serviettes in a rubbish bin and stopped the nosebleed, so the third taxi driver took pity on him.

One hundred twenty-three kroner later, he was home.

CHAPTER 23

Like last time, Poul Hasting sat reclining with his legs crossed in his designer chair. He read the article on Ulrik Torp's smartphone without expression. It was completely quiet in the house. Although it wasn't yet nine on Friday morning, Ulla Hasting and some of their young disciples had long since left in a small van with boxes of yellow ribbons. They were on their way to Jutland. The contra movement needed to spread outside the capital. *"Who knows? Maybe also outside Denmark,"* she had said to the television cameras before they left.

Torp sat opposite him, less familiar with the uncomfortable design. He could feel the lump with his tongue. Oh, how he longed for a soft sofa and a blanket.

He and Karen had been woken by the glazier two hours earlier. With a comment that it wouldn't take too long and whistling all the while, he set about removing the wooden board and putting a new glass pane in the window in the living room.

Ulrik had only slept a little, and badly at that. Karen had been shocked when she saw her husband standing in the doorway around midnight, tipsy, with a black eye, pieces of rolled-up serviette in his nostrils, blood on his face and clothes and his trousers torn. She had bound some bandages tightly around his chest to support his ribs and found a bag of frozen peas to lessen the swelling around the eye.

There was nothing more that could be done. She comforted herself more than the victim by saying it looked really nasty but was in fact fairly superficial.

Ulrik was tired and had a thumping headache. The eye, nose, ribs, and right leg all hurt. He swallowed two painkillers for the third time since returning home. The glazier's work in the living room meant they were confined to the flat's overfilled bedroom and narrow kitchen. He sat on the bed and tried to get his clothes on without unnecessary pain.

"If you don't call the police, then I'll have to," said Karen adamantly. She was standing in the doorway with her hands on her hips, the posture she always adopted when there wasn't much up for discussion.

"I'll call," promised Ulrik.

"Someone's after you," she argued.

Ulrik didn't answer. He sat with his mobile phone checking today's electronic edition of the *Daily News*. They weren't on the front page. Prime Minister Palle Enevoldsen and the opposition's Pernille Hjort had been given top billing with their fight over immigrants in connection with the opening debate, which, as usual, hadn't ended until late evening.

She was spineless, thought the Prime Minister. He was avoiding the issue, thought the leader of the opposition.

No. Yes. No. Yes.

Lower down, there was an article about a power struggle in Hungary after the Prime Minister's death last weekend and the possible consequences for agreement in the EU. So far, it was secure, but maybe it was on borrowed time, thought an expert.

"Who's after you?" Karen was still standing with her hands on her hips.

"That's up to the police to find out, surely" argued Torp, with most of his attention on the mobile's screen. He skimmed through the other pages of the first section of the newspaper.

Nothing.

There was no article on the same murder weapon used in two unexplained murders of civil servants in the central administration almost fifty years apart. No article about the investigation into the murder of young Jeppe Mikkelsen now intensifying after having been hampered by a total lack of motive and suspects. Nothing about a breakthrough or speculation about former department head Niels Henriksen's role in the affair or reports of systematic irregularities in connection with the vote count in the general election—especially for the Nationalists.

It was a fantastic story. It just wasn't in the newspaper.

"The article's not there," he exclaimed and looked up. "It should have been on the front page. It's not anywhere."

Karen looked at her husband, not understanding what he was on about. As he sat there on the bed with a black eye, bandages around his chest, wearing only underpants, and with his hand clutching his mobile hanging limply down by his side, he was more abject than she ever wished to see him.

"Get some clothes on, Ulrik. I'll make some coffee."

He needed to get that story in the newspaper, not just to be able to stay at the *Daily News* for a few weeks or a month more and earn some real money so he could pay Simon back for the car—what would it cost? Five thousand? Not just to use the story as a stepping stone either, back to the profession, away from the relative poverty he and Karen were experiencing. No, the story was supposed to be the domino that got the other dominoes to fall. Brathenberg, Henriksen, the algorithm in the election computer, Katrine, Spang-Johansen, Jeppe Mikkelsen, Vienna, the Military Intelligence Service, and The Firm. It all hung together; it just needed a kick in the right direction. That is what the article was to be used for. Why on earth wasn't it in? Arne Lund hadn't been in any doubt, not when Torp presented the article and handed it in nor when he checked it later in the day. It might have crept down the page due to weak documentation and the opening debate in Parliament, but that was the only reservation. And from a journalistic point of view, there was no doubt. The story was current, the newspaper had the scoop, and it was important. But it wasn't in at all.

Lund wasn't answering his phone. That in itself was highly unusual.

Torp made a quick decision on the way to the Metro and the *Daily News*.

He hailed a taxi on Finsensvej.

Poul Hasting handed the smartphone back to his guest. He hadn't commented on either the unannounced visit or Torp's swollen black eye.

"I can actually remember the murder of Spang-Johansen. There was a lot written about it." He drummed his fingers on the armrest.

Torp had told Hasting the whole story. About the algorithm that pushed the Nationalists and the New Radicals below the threshold. About Emma's computer being hacked so that all the evidence disappeared. About Spang-Johansen's widow, the pictures in her photo album, the visit to Henriksen, and the assault and the threats. He had allowed Hasting to read their unpublished article on his phone.

Now Hasting essentially knew the same as Torp, as far as the main points were concerned.

"I've never really liked Henriksen," Hasting continued. "He came to this house a lot when I was young. He's always been a sort of commissar type."

Torp pulled a face that that made his swollen eye hurt. Hasting smiled.

"Yes, just think that that should come from me. That commissar label isn't meant in a positive way, as I well know."

He had a thought, got up with remarkable agility considering his age, went to the huge bookshelf in the living room, and pulled out a few photo albums. He leafed through them energetically. At the third album, he stopped and pulled out a photo.

"Here."

He walked back to his guest with the yellowing colour photo in his hand, as if it were a trophy.

"From my father's funeral, which I boycotted, as already mentioned, to my mother's great sorrow. Although Father had been a Member of Parliament, she chose a quiet and private funeral. Only the closest family and friends."

He handed the picture to Torp. It had been taken outside the church. Six men carrying the coffin the last bit of the way. Torp immediately recognised Henriksen and Brathenberg.

"The old man in the middle is Arne Taber. At the back are my father's two younger brothers. I don't know who the last one is. The Firm, Torp." Hasting's voice was dipped in triumph. "The Firm. It never bloody well closed. They carried on. Right up until today."

"But it can't be the Russians they have in their sights any longer, surely?"

"Look around," exclaimed Hasting, spreading his arms, not in powerlessness, but as a demonstration. "Look around you, Torp."

"What are you trying to say?"

"Politicians and the media spend ninety per cent of their time on problems that have always existed, trivial matters, or pure nonsense. You only see the hair, never the soup. But if you're of the same opinion as Brathenberg and Henriksen, then this society works. The institutions and conventions still function as they created them. No borders, global agreements. And the people get flat TV screens and Audis in return."

"What does that have to do with The Firm?"

"Uncertainty reduction."

Torp put his hand up to his painful eye. He could feel the pressure on his side by the ribs.

"It all makes sense," continued Hasting. "Why did the New Radicals and the Nationalists have to be below the threshold?" He answered himself: "Do you think the real powers-that-be actually want a referendum on Denmark's membership of the EU? The people in other EU countries are just waiting to have someone to follow. Then it will end up overturning everything."

Hasting looked like someone for whom the whole world suddenly made sense. His eyes were shining with excitement.

"Goddammit, Torp. When we write this, it will all fall apart."

"When *we* write it?"

"This is the deep state. What I've always been writing about, even before realnews.dk. Finally, we can prove it."

"We?"

Poul Hasting was in another world, far away from Ulrik Torp. Decades of activism, shaming, and conspiracy suspicions could now be vindicated. He had to get hold of Ulla to share the triumph with her.

"It sounds completely crazy," protested Torp.

"Does it?" Hasting smiled. "Do you remember Pope John Paul I, who died in 1978? After only thirty-three days as pope?"

Torp nodded. He remembered that. The new and only sixty-five-year-old pope had been found dead in his bed one morning.

"He had wanted to root out corruption in the Vatican City State, the collaboration with the Mafia, and the fraud in their bank. Do you really think his death was accidental?"

Torp shook his head. The rumours that the pope had been poisoned by his political opponents were massive from the start. But it had never been proved.

"It was the deep state in the Vatican that struck. They were aware that they were the bad guys. Henriksen and Brathenberg, on the other hand . . ." Hasting looked like someone who had got vinegar in his mouth. "They think they're the good guys, self-righteous as they are. It's unbearable."

"What happens if this comes out?"

"When, Torp—when it comes out." Hasting stood up enthusiastically and made fencing movements with his arms and the photo from his father's funeral. "Let me tell you. A new election will be called; the Nationalists and the New Radicals will storm into Parliament. We'll have a referendum on the EU, maybe Denmark will leave, and it will get the chance to spread to more countries in Europe. Exactly what those hypocritical bandits were ready to kill to avoid."

Torp began to have his doubts about whether it had been a good idea to go out to Hasting. It had seemed so obvious two hours ago.

"This is my story. It can't be printed until I want it."

Hasting held back, looked at his guest, and sat down again. He hesitated.

"Of course. Understood. But you're a professional journalist, Torp. The truth must come out, right?"

Torp held back from replying. He had to get away.

"Ten minutes, Torp. Ten minutes after you send the article to me, it will be on realnews.dk."

His head was hammering; he was tired; he should go into the *Daily News*. Maybe there was a straightforward explanation for why the article wasn't in the newspaper today. Maybe it would all fall into place.

CHAPTER 24

Ulrik Torp limped the last stretch from Nørreport to the *Daily News* via Kultorvet. The drizzle and the dark clouds from the day before were gone. The sun was beginning to make its presence felt, and a few late-summer students were enjoying coffee to go and a touch of sun on the bench at the place where the Nationalist Annegrethe Hulsig had been attacked by the self-proclaimed anti-fascists a few weeks earlier. Now there were yellow ribbons hanging everywhere instead.

The pills weren't helping a great deal. His leg, ribs, nose, and head were hurting like hell.

"You look like shit," was the comfort Karen had offered him when he and the annoyingly cheerful glazier left the flat in the morning after he had promised to call the police and meet her in front of Rigshospitalet at five to one.

He still looked like shit.

Torp shuffled up the stairs, entered the *Daily News*'s terror-proof sluice, got out his ID and access card as the glass door behind him slid to, punched in his code, 1-2-3-4, and waited for the armoured glass in front of him to slide sideways.

Nothing happened.

He swiped the magnetic strip on the card through once more. Entered the code. Nothing. He tapped on the glass. Charlotte at the front desk looked up and let him in the last bit.

"My access card should be valid up until and including today. There must have been a mistake," he began.

"Just a minute, Torp," said Charlotte. She dialled a couple of times and spoke into the headset. "He's arrived."

She nodded to some journalists walking past them into the lift. Torp recognised them from the business editorial office but had no idea what their names were.

"I'm just doing what I've been told to do," she apologised.

"Told to do what?"

"Someone will come and fetch you in a moment, Torp. I'm sorry."

"Sorry about what?"

Torp stared uncomprehendingly at Charlotte, who was having such a hard time looking him in the eye. He heard footsteps on the stairs leading up to the editorial office.

"Charlotte, what's going on?"

"I don't know what you've done, Torp." She looked away.

Two pathetic short-haired guards wearing walkie-talkies and plain blue shirts with logos approached him.

"Ulrik Torp?"

He nodded.

"You've been dismissed from the *Daily News*. We've been asked to take you up to the editorial office, where you'll have the opportunity to open your locker and remove any personal belongings in it. After that, we will escort you out."

The guard who spoke sounded like a dilettante version of a Supreme Court Justice. It was clear, thought Torp, that he had been practising the sentences.

The second guard took over.

"But first we must ask you to hand over your ID and access card as well as your mobile phone." Same rote learning.

"What's happened? What have I done?"

"We're just doing what we've been told to do," said the first guard.

There was no apology, regret, or triumph in his voice. It was completely neutral. He held out his hand to receive the card and telephone. Then they went up the stairs to the editorial office, Torp in the middle, with particular pain every time the right leg had to be lifted. The guards could see he was having difficulties and accepted the slow pace without a word.

Everyone's face turned towards Torp as they came up on the editorial floor. It was clear that they knew more than he did. Torp stopped outside Arne Lund's office. The chief news editor was in the process of filling a couple of moving boxes.

"Torp," Arne Lund contented himself with saying. He stood there with a stack of books in his hand.

"What are you doing?"

"I've been given a severance package. A good one," said Lund.

"When were you given that?"

"Yesterday evening."

Lund put the books in the box and reached for the Cavling statuette that stood on his desk.

"Do you know why I've been dismissed?"

"Oh, Torp. It's not exactly career-promoting to drive into the editor-in-chief's parents' car on purpose and accuse them of murder." Lund pulled a face. "But just so you know, I would have had your article in the newspaper today. The whole article."

"Is that why you're packing up your office?"

"Torp. It's time for some fresh faces. Let's allow the young people to take over. We've done what we can."

He put the Cavling statuette in the moving box and reached out for a new pile of books.

One of the guards pushed Torp on. They went down to the end of the floor, towards the reportage group's desks and cupboards. Christian Crash and Grandma-Bente were standing next to each other.

"What happened to your face?" Grandma-Bente, her eyes glistening, almost whispered her question as he went past. Torp was so focused on his pain that he had forgotten what he looked like.

"This is the second time he's been dismissed from the *Daily News*," he heard an old employee inform a young one. Torp felt like a murderer on his way to the gallows, gawped at by old women knitting.

"Is this your locker?" asked the first guard, pointing to a door.

Torp nodded. He took out a key and opened it. The only thing in the locker besides the laptop was the biography of the thirty-third President of the United States, Harry Truman, which he had borrowed from Otto Brathenberg; with a personal dedication from the author.

"The key," said the guard, putting out his hand. Torp gave it to him and took out the book.

On the way back, he saw Emma and Simon. Simon's eyes were red; he had been crying. Emma seemed stable. He nodded discreetly to both of them. Emma nodded back, with an attempt at a little smile. Simon looked down. Further back in the room he saw Asbjørn Henriksen.

The editor-in-chief didn't seem either triumphant or uneasy at the situation. He was standing there as if to make sure that his orders were executed correctly and precisely. Next to him stood an expressionless Katrine Taber-Nielsen.

Torp wasn't thrown down the stairs like in a bad movie, but firmly and attentively led all the way out by the two stiff guards.

"Have a nice day," said one of them on the other side of the glass sluice. It sounded like an awkward attempt to be friendly—you had to say something. Torp forgave him immediately.

"You too."

They nodded to each other.

And so Ulrik Torp was left standing on the narrow street with Truman under his arm. A car honked, and he jumped onto the pavement outside the entrance to the *Daily News* without being able to decide which direction to take.

He took out his phone. Should he send the article to Poul Hasting and ask him to post it on realnews.dk? Ten minutes—then it's online.

"Hello, Ulrik Torp."

The voice came from behind him and sounded familiar. He turned around. Opposite him stood a mildly smiling Otto Brathenberg. There was a board meeting about the new savings round at 1:00 p.m.

"Last day at the *Daily News*?"

Torp nodded. "I'm assuming you've been of some help."

"You're crediting me with far too much influence, Torp. You did this very well all by yourself."

"I know everything."

"What do you actually know, Torp?"

"The Firm still exists."

"There is no Firm."

"What's it called, then?"

"We're just a group of former officials with some young helpers trying to keep society in the middle."

"It sounds like the deep state."

Otto Brathenberg smiled patronisingly.

"Dear Torp. If the deep state really existed, then Niels Henriksen and I could enjoy life as the pensioners we should be. We are the proof that it doesn't exist. Unfortunately."

"And that's why you intervene?"

"As best we can." He nodded.

"What about if the people want something else," objected Torp.

"Argh," exclaimed Brathenberg. "You know better than that. *The people*. What do *the people* know about anything? Society is changed from above."

"What became of those fine words in your book about true democracy?"

"Sometimes you have to change your position to get it right."

"Is it that easy?"

"No, Torp. It's that difficult. We haven't spent most of our lives building things up to then see a bunch of calculating populists topple it all with some posts on Facebook and Twitter."

"Who are *we*?"

Brathenberg looked up. It was clearly a slip of the tongue. Torp recalled the front page of today's *Daily News*. At the top, the opening debate in Parliament. Under that, the political crisis in Hungary after the death of their Prime Minister over the weekend.

"The Firm. It isn't just Denmark and old politicians. *We* is the whole of Europe," said Torp, replying to his own question.

Brathenberg let his gaze rest on Torp but said nothing.

"Hungary now. The Italian Prime Minister before the summer holidays. The car bomb against the journalist in Malta. Was that you, too?" continued Torp. He took a step towards Otto Brathenberg. "And Vienna tomorrow. Are there more murders and assassinations you need to plan? Now that you've made yourselves lords over life and death?"

"It must be easy to sit at your keyboard, Torp, and just type! I have . . ." said Brathenberg, pointing to himself. "I have spent more than half of my life making decisions about life and death. Believe me, I would have preferred not to have been involved, but that's how the cards were dealt to me."

"This is going to come out. As you well know."

Otto Brathenberg looked up at the façade of the *Daily News*. Torp understood the allusion.

"There are other newspapers. Other media."

"How can you be so sure they will print it?"

"I'll find a way."

"Are you sure this is what you really want?" Brathenberg held out his hand. "You must take care of yourself, Torp. There are several of us who would like to help you. I see you have my book on Truman with you. Fascinating, isn't it?"

Torp gave it to him.

"Thanks for the loan."

"You're welcome." He took a rhetorical pause. "You could join us, Torp. Katrine has mentioned it. We agree, after all."

Torp glanced at his watch; it was half past twelve. He could just make it in time.

"I'm a little busy right now, Brathenberg."

Ulrik Torp turned around and set off, hobbling slightly, in the direction of Rigshospitalet. He looked up. The sun was burning through the clouds.

It was a beautiful day.

ABOUT THE AUTHOR

Niels Krause-Kjær (b. 1963) is a Danish journalist and former press chief for the Conservative People's Party of the Danish Parliament. His political thriller *Solitaire* became the award-winning film *King's Game*, directed by Nikolaj Arcel. *Darklands*, the second volume in the series featuring journalist Ulrik Torp, is also being adapted for film.

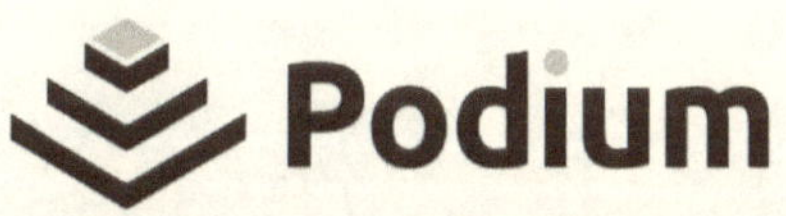